KNIGHT OF CHAOS

THE KNIGHTS OF THE ANARCHY
(BOOK 2)

SHERRY EWING

ARE YOU SIGNED UP FOR DRAGONBLADE'S BLOG?

You'll get the latest news and information on exclusive giveaways, exclusive excerpts, coming releases, sales, free books, cover reveals and more.

Check out our complete list of authors, too!

No spam, no junk. That's a promise!

Sign Up Here

www.dragonbladepublishing.com

Dearest Reader;

Thank you for your support of a small press. At Dragonblade Publishing, we strive to bring you the highest quality Historical Romance from some of the best authors in the business. Without your support, there is no 'us', so we sincerely hope you adore these stories and find some new favorite authors along the way.

Happy Reading!

CEO, Dragonblade Publishing

ADDITIONAL DRAGONBLADE BOOKS BY AUTHOR SHERRY EWING

The Knights of the Anarchy Series
Knight of Darkness (Book 1)
Knight of Chaos (Book 2)

The Lyon's Den Series
To Claim a Lyon's Heart

Knight of Chaos:
The Knights of the Anarchy (Book Two)
By Sherry Ewing

In the chaos of war, can one knight defy the odds to find peace with the woman warrior he loves?

Sir Theobald Norwood finds himself embroiled in a mission of loyalty and love as he stands by Empress Matilda in her pursuit of the throne. As he and her army head to Winchester, he stumbles upon a mysterious woman named Mistress Ingrid Seymour, hiding in the woods with her own quest in mind. What starts as a test of her worthiness quickly transforms into a profound connection.

As they join forces on the battlefield, Theobald and Ingrid face not only the challenges of war but also the enemies lurking in the shadows. Ingrid's identity is called into question, shaking the very foundation of her existence, while Theobald grapples with his own emotions. Amidst confusion, they must find a way to let love blossom and unite their hearts.

But with forces working against them, will Theobald and Ingrid be torn apart by the unpredictable tides of fate? Can they overcome their differences and trust one another, or will the mounting chaos consume their chances at happiness? Join them on a captivating journey as their destinies intertwine, promises are tested, and a love that could defy the odds hangs in the balance.

DEDICATION

For my nephew Josh…

You've become an amazing young man that any aunt would be proud of.
I love you very much!

PROLOGUE

I N THE TIME known today as The Anarchy, England was torn between two enemies, each claiming a right to the throne. Some of England's nobles pledged their allegiance to Stephen and declared him king whilst others cast their fate with Empress Matilda, the daughter of Henry I. Such unrest placed most of the country into a state of civil war lasting for almost a score of years. Many knights bore the burden of fighting for either side, each determined to win the land for whomever they served.

Amongst such knights were three brothers in search of fame and fortune. They pledged their loyalty to the Empress Matilda, vowing to fight for her rightful claim to England's crown. The Norwood brothers were close in age. Wymar was the eldest and jumped at the chance to swear his oath of fealty to the Empress, especially after their parents were killed when Stephen laid siege to their home, Brockenhurst Castle. Ousted from the only home they had known six years ago, Wymar plunged his brothers into the middle of war all in the hopes of having the Empress crowned queen. He prayed, in return for their service, she would return to him his lands and title, and name him her champion knight.

Theobald was next and the peacekeeper amongst them. He was used to following his eldest brother no matter that he would prefer to sit in front of a fire to rest his weary feet with a mug of ale in his hand. Reynard, the youngest, was always attempting to prove his worth even when the odds were stacked against him. He was more like his eldest brother than he would ever admit, even to himself.

All three swore to remain together as a family as they had no one else besides themselves. At that time, the land beneath their feet was home. Until they could reclaim their birthright and take ownership once more of Brockenhurst, the brothers had no plans to marry. They had no time to cater to some woman nor was having a wife as a camp follower an ideal situation. They had sworn their allegiance to the Empress Matilda and until she released them, they were committed to her cause to see her placed on the throne.

But sometimes the fate of man is fickle, especially when your life gets turned upside down from unforeseen circumstances outside of your control.

Every tale has a beginning, a middle and an end for the knights of the Anarchy. This is Theobald's story…

CHAPTER ONE

Outside of Oxford, England
July 1141

THEOBALD NORWOOD KEPT his eyes alert whilst gripping the leather reins of his horse firmly in his hands. The tension was high in the company in which he rode. After her victory the previous month at the Battle of Lincoln, including capturing her enemy, Empress Matilda had ridden into London, confident that she would quickly be crowned Queen of England. Alas, her hopes had been dashed. Theobald ran his gloved hand over the back of his neck. It seemed like 'twas just yester eve that he had sat with his empress to enjoy the evening meal before the bells began to ring out in alarm.

Panic ensued as the city revolted against her. The Empress, and the men sworn to protect her, fled London and traveled to Oxford. Theobald was one of those men, along with his younger brother, Reynard. But then the Empress was informed that a man who had once pledged his loyalty to her had defected. Henry of Blois, Bishop of Winchester and King Stephen's younger brother, had taken a force and had laid siege to the royal castle held by the Empress's Angevins. So now the Empress had a new goal to achieve. She was determined to strike back against the traitor in Winchester.

Time passed swiftly and yet Theobald could only wonder how his eldest brother, Wymar, fared. It seemed like a lifetime ago that they quickly met up in a London tavern before Theobald and Reynard fled the city with the Empress. If the last words spoken with Wymar were true, he would wed soon. Theobald pondered who the Empress would have chosen for his brother's bride. All he knew for certain was that Wymar would not be pleased with his soon-to-be wife. Not when he had already given his heart to the Lady of Norwich.

While Theobald worried over his brother's fate, most of his attention was focused on the situation at hand—which meant keeping his head firmly attached to his neck whilst waiting to be ambushed with every turn in the dirt road before him. Thus far, all had been quiet. He did not expect such a state to remain for long.

A horse riding towards the back line of knights caught Theobald's attention, and he quickly realized 'twas Reynard. He did not look pleased.

"What ails you, brother?" Theobald asked, when Reynard reined in his horse, turned it around to continue forward, keeping pace with Theobald's steed.

"I am to be sent home," Reynard complained, a frown forming between his brows. "At least for now."

"I would think the Empress would wish for the extra strength of your sword for whatever awaits us in Winchester," Theobald stated. "Did you anger her?"

A low growl left his brother. "Who knows?" he all but shouted before turning his angry grey eyes toward Theobald. "I was not privy to any sort of explanation for her decision. Some lackey informed me of her wishes that I make my way home to witness Wymar's nuptials... as though I am needed there more than strength is required for her army. I know I am but one of many but still... I asked to speak with her directly and was turned down. Honestly, I do not feel as though my efforts in the past fortnights have been appreciated."

"You would not be riding with her if she did not see and value you, Reynard," Theobald said trying to calm his brother's rising anger. Sometimes his younger brother let his anger rule his head when he should be thinking clearer.

Reynard pushed a lock of his dark brown hair from his forehead before rubbing his neck. Undoubtedly, he was beyond frustrated. "And yet she sends me home like some young stripling lad who cannot help defend her. From my perspective, the Empress does not appreciate her knights—nay, nor even her ordinary citizens. After the Empress acted as though she was superior to her subjects in London and then began taxing them, I am not surprised they revolted against her. I mayhap wonder if we should not be supporting Stephen."

"Quiet, you fool," Theobald warned before pulling hard on the reins whilst his horse reared its front hooves. Gaining control of his steed, he watched as the other knights began to go around him even as they cast curious gazes upon the brothers who moved to the side of the road and out of the way.

Reynard appeared as though he'd finally realized that voicing his thoughts aloud could cost him. "Theobald, I—"

"Not yet," Theobald counseled whilst the Empress's army continued to move forward. When they had a semblance of privacy, he lashed out at his brother. "What kind of imbecile have you become that you would dare to discuss such a sensitive subject on the open road? Do you not wish to keep your head or are you too stupid to realize you speak treason? 'Tis a punishable offense and could lead to your execution if any but me were to overhear you."

"I did not think—" Reynard began but Theobald cut off any further protests.

"Nay! You did not," Theobald fumed before raking his hand through his wavy dark brown hair. "I swear, you will be the death of me, brother. Your carelessness with your words may very well be your downfall one day."

"I shall endeavor to be more careful in the future," Reynard replied, looking downcast. He appeared as though his brief bit of anger had stolen all his energy.

"See that you do! *God's Blood!*" Theobald swore, more upset with the situation than with the young man before him. At only three and a score years of age, Reynard tended to be hot tempered and needed to keep control of his feelings. "I told Wymar this campaign would become a mess. We vowed to stay together and yet now we will be scattered across the breadth of England. At least the two of you will be reunited."

A snort left Reynard. "Sent home like a child."

"At least you will remain alive to fight another day. Mayhap our Empress has other plans for you that she will reveal at a later time. When do you leave?"

"Immediately, or so I was told. It should not take me long to reach Brockenhurst and then I am to wait there for further instructions if I am needed," Reynard replied whilst a small contingent of knights began riding in their direction. "As you can see, I do not ride alone."

"'Twill ease my mind that you have others to watch your back. You will relay my best wishes to our brother," Theobald stated.

"Aye, I will," Reynard said before reaching out his hand to clasp his brother's forearm.

Theobald nodded before a smirk turned up the corners of his mouth. "Try to look on the bright side of things... at least it seems that you will be able to stay out of trouble by returning to our ancestral home."

"Mayhap Wymar's new bride will have a lady attending her that will catch my eye," Reynard declared chuckling.

"Then you best be prepared to wed her, brother, lest you wish to encounter the lady's wrath." Theobald stared at his brother wondering when their paths might cross again. "Seriously, Reynard... behave and Godspeed on your travels home."

"Stay alive, Theo," he replied, "and make your way to Brockenhurst when you are able."

Theobald watched his brother turn his horse and canter down the lane they had previously traveled. Stay alive... Aye, he planned to do just that. He had no desire to meet his maker anytime soon. But the choice might not be his to make. While he had every intention to be careful, Theobald sensed that there were dangerous times ahead and he was not looking forward to whatever the future held for him in Winchester.

CHAPTER TWO

A small farm outside of London

MISTRESS INGRID SEYMOUR took one last look around the tiny farmhouse that she had called home for the score and two years of her life. The single-story house with a thatched roof had kept her safe and yet there was nothing left but memories to keep her here, or so she reasoned with herself. Her mother, Jonet, had been long gone from this world, having perished giving birth to Ingrid. Her father, Harold, had done his best to raise his only child by himself. The neighboring tenants had warned him when Ingrid was young that 'twas foolish to teach her sword play but her father had insisted the lessons might come in handy one day. They had laughed at him, jesting that he treated the young girl as though she were a boy, and that he would one day regret his decision.

More days than not, Ingrid could be found in tunic, hose, and boots and rarely would be seen in a gown. And as she grew into a young lady, she saw no reason to give in to what the villagers thought was proper. If her father did not mind what she wore, then neither would she. Besides, 'twas difficult to heft a sword in a gown, and her usual attire also made it easier to handle the chores in the fields.

In between tending the land, Ingrid's father had taught her all he knew on the art of defending herself. She never questioned how a mere farmer had become so skilled in the art of self-defense and hefting a sword. Ingrid felt that the lessons had given her strength both in body and mind and had helped form her into the strong woman she was today—but that was not how everyone saw it. The villagers complained constantly about how improper she was. At times Ingrid felt like an outsider. And yet, she had always raised her head in defiance. What did they know anyway?

When her father became sick and Ingrid had to realize he would not recover, she swore she would do him proud one day. His dying words had been of how much he loved her. They still echoed daily in her mind. Now, he rested in the ground not far from this very house in the village cemetery next to the mother she never knew. This house and land were all she had left of him but 'twas just an empty space without her beloved father keeping her company. Life, as she had known it, had become so unfair.

She had not felt as though she had the ability to tend the land by herself for very long. Most of the inhabitants of the village were too busy tending their own fields and could hardly take on the extra work to tend Ingrid's. When word reached the village that Empress Matilda was marching south, Ingrid came to the decision to join her company. She was certain the Empress would appreciate another woman who could hold her own against the world.

Ingrid heaved a sigh when she closed the door for the very last time, the palm of her hand resting momentarily upon the hard wooden portal. Her horse stood nearby, already saddled to begin their journey. She went to the steed and rubbed her hands along his mahogany-colored coat. She began checking the cinches one last time, along with the leather straps keeping her gear and provisions attached to the saddle.

Satisfied all was ready and she had left nothing important behind, she turned to face the one person who had supported her for most of her life. Sadness reflected in his amber eyes. Ingrid pondered if the man had feelings for her that went way beyond the friendship between them. They had been friends for more years than she could remember. His hushed words confirmed her worst fears.

"Are you certain you wish to leave, Ingrid?" Charles asked, reaching for her hand. "I am certain my parents will look out for you if I explain that I wish to marry—"

Ingrid's eyes went wide and she held up her hand causing Charles to go silent. His lips snapped shut and his features appeared mutinous. Charles had been her friend when she had no others, and yet she could in no way think of him as a possible husband. He was more like a brother she never had. He had stood by her side since their youth, and they had formed a bond of friendship that she had cherished to this very day. But that was part of the reason why she knew that marriage would be a mistake between them. Ingrid had always been something of an outcast. Charles deserved a wife who would be accepted amongst those that lived in the village.

She watched a range of emotions race across his handsome face. Hope. Love. Fear, most likely for her safety. His blond hair became untamed in the morning breeze and she reached over to push the locks from his forehead. He took her fingertips in his and raised them to his lips. She shook her head before squeezing his hand, and he let her go with a look of anguish flashing in his amber eyes.

"Charles… I am sorry but you know my answer. We have discussed this before." A timid smile was all she could offer him and 'twas as if the fight to keep her by his side left him.

"You cannot blame a man for trying one last time," he confessed before crossing his arms over his chest. "I worry for you, Ingrid. You cannot travel alone. Mayhap I should join you."

Fear caused her heart to race. Not for herself but for her friend. He had none of the training with a sword that she had gotten. An image of him fighting with a pitchfork and nothing else to help keep himself alive made her shake her head once more. He would never live a day in a battle against seasoned knights. She only prayed she was trained well enough to do better.

"You know you cannot leave here, Charles. Your family needs you, and I am more than capable of taking care of myself." She lifted her chin waiting for the next round of arguments that were sure to fall from his lips. He didn't disappoint her.

He cursed, anger now replacing the love that recently showed in his visage. "Your father was a fool to teach you the use of a sword. He did you a disservice not imparting upon you your place in a world ruled by men!"

"Do not dare defame my father and the decisions he made on how to raise me," she fumed, certain her hazel eyes showed him her displeasure.

"You are only a woman, Ingrid. Look at you! As soon as anyone gets a good look at you—which everyone will do when that dark red hair of yours catches their eye—they will instantly see that you are a woman in a man's clothes."

His words were as though he tapped directly into her own doubts about her ability to conceal herself. Her lips momentarily quivered before she once more composed herself. Tears would in no way help her on what lay ahead on her journey. Charles could very well be correct but this would not sway her from her course to follow the Empress.

"I believe you have said enough, Charles," she said quietly knowing the friendship that they had shared all their lives was at an end.

A low growl left him. "I am only trying to make you see the reality of your situation if you are to leave the safety of this farm. What makes you think you are capable of actually killing another in the fight to stay alive?"

"My father trained me well," she argued lifting her chin defiantly.

"If that is so, then you should be fighting for King Stephen who is the rightful ruler of England," he thundered in return.

She gave a brief laugh at his comment. "'Tis just like you to think that a woman has no right to rule, let alone make up her own mind on how she must live her life. When did you all of a sudden become a supporter of Stephen? What happened to the carefree man of our youth? You have become just like the rest of the people who live here, Charles. Single minded with no thought of what your words do to another."

"At least I know my place in this world. I do not aspire to be more than I am. Whereas you..." His words trailed off and lingered between them.

There was nothing left to say, and yet she still delayed her departure in order to stay near the young man who was really only concerned with her safety... or so she supposed. He had not changed her mind as he had hoped, and she could see for herself that regret filled his heart.

She reached up to cup his cheek, his hand briefly resting over her own. She stood on the tips of her toes to place a chaste kiss on his other cheek and heard his heavy sigh. Looking into his eyes, she smiled. "Farewell, Charles," she murmured before turning to her horse and leading it to a mounting block.

"Godspeed, Ingrid. I shall look over your land until your return." He said his final reply and she gave him a brief nod of thanks.

"Let us be on our way, Valor," she said to her horse. Hoisting herself into the saddle, she put on leather gloves and took up the reins. With one last look at her friend and her home, she flicked the reins to put her steed in motion. Whatever awaited her in the future, she would meet the situation head on. Her new life was just beginning, and she looked forward to the challenge.

CHAPTER THREE

ANOTHER DAY IN the saddle after another night sleeping on the cold ground. Theobald should be used to the conditions of camp life and yet still he wished for a roof over his head and a bed to rest his weary body. He didn't foresee such a happening in his near future until they reached Winchester and he could have his tent set up.

Word had traveled throughout the ranks of the current situation into which they would shortly be thrust. The Empress hoped to surprise Bishop Henry with an attack whilst he laid siege at the royal castle garrisoned by Angevins on the southwest side of the city. Now only a day away from Winchester, Theobald could only ponder if the Empress had enough forces to defeat the bishop.

Bringing up the rear of their company, Theobald had few words for any of the knights that rode beside him. Having the dust of the road in your face whilst following behind the army ahead of him made Theobald crave a hot bath to wash the dirt from his body. His mood was irritable and he began to wonder if Reynard's words had left more of an impact on him than he had thought. But, nay! He was still committed to the Empress's cause—still believed that she was the rightful ruler of England.

Laughter broke out from several knights riding next to him. Blake Kennarde, Oswin Woodwarde, and Kingsley Goodee had been faithful to the Empress's cause since Theobald met them at the Battle of Lincoln. They were as good as companions as any, but today their laughter made him miss his brothers. Their goal to stay together had fallen apart and Theobald could only wonder when their paths would cross again.

Blake leaned over in his saddle and gave Theobald a slap on his arm. "You were far away, my friend," he said before continuing. "Is aught amiss?"

Theobald considered his words before he responded. "Nay, unless I wish to complain about the amount of dust we are wearing riding in the back of the army."

Oswin chuckled. "Mayhap the leader of the Empress's troops feels we are better suited to guarding her rear."

"Bah!" Kingsley complained. "You would think we were not seasoned knights fit to ride with those more *worthy* in the lead. Did we not prove our worth when we rode with the earl and he and his men captured King Stephen?"

"There are worse things in the world to worry about then where we ride in the Empress's forces—including the possibility of an ambush at any moment," Theobald replied, leery at every turn in the road. He hated the feeling of always looking over his shoulder for trouble. He supposed the feelings came from his youth when he and his brothers had fled their home after the siege.

Blake nodded. "You seem more on edge than normal, Theobald. What ails you?"

Theobald shrugged. "Call it a premonition but something tells me to stay alert."

"You worry over nothing," Oswin remarked with a smirk. "No one would dare an attack on the Empress's knights."

A flash of red behind a nearby tree caused Theobald to pull on the reins of his black warhorse. 'Twas as though Oswin's words had prompted some cruel fate to prove them untrue. The knights slowed their mounts, but Theobald waved at them to proceed forward. "Ride on, men, but stay close in case I need aid. I shall catch up."

Kingsley laughed and made a lewd comment about using the

forest for a privy but Theobald did not reply as he brought his steed to a halt. The men rode on at a slow pace.

Eyes peering into the shadows of the woods, he barely made out the form of someone cautiously watching the army as it passed by. It might be nothing ominous. But still… Theobald would be wary of anyone hiding in the forest who may be a spy for Stephen or the bishop. Even if it weren't one of their enemies' soldiers, it might still be a thief looking to rob someone.

He quickly dismounted, flicking the reins over the horse's head to lead it to a nearby tree opposite of where he'd glimpsed the man. His horse neighed and shook its head in defiance and Theobald scowled at the steed.

"You best behave, you damn ornery beast, lest I have you butchered and made into a meal for the men," he warned watching as the horse flapped its lips to appear as though he was smiling. 'Twas as if the animal knew Theobald's threat was empty. After all, if he no longer had a steed, how would he ride into battle?

The army moved on whilst Theobald looped the reins on a thick tree branch. He told his steed to behave again after it neighed once more, then Theobald took his sword from the scabbard at his side, pointing the blade forward. Crossing the road, he made his way into the woods. The rustling of a nearby bush caught his attention, causing Theobald to again be wary of what or who he might meet. He quietly made his way to where he could once more make out a hint of red through the leaves. Before the man could get away, Theobald reached into the bush to grab the forearm of the stranger, pulling the body forward to stand before him.

A voice rang out in outrage—a very feminine voice—causing Theobald's eyes to widen at who he held. A woman dressed as a man was always an unusual sight to behold. This woman briefly brought to mind Lady Ceridwen Ward of Norwich, the maiden who had fallen in love with his brother Wymar. A tale of lost love, Theobald was certain, that would never come to fruition given that their responsibilities had forced them to part. Still… he was caught off guard whilst hazel eyes narrowed before she swiftly reacted. He stepped back just in time when the woman's own blade came forward to connect with Theobald's. There was a blinding flash from the sunlight as the two swords met, causing them both to blink.

'Twas enough for Theobald to once more step back, holding up his hands to show he meant the woman no harm. She continued to hold her blade out in front of her and he could not blame her. He took in her appearance, noticing how her hose pleasingly hugged her long well-shaped legs. Her tunic stretched across firm, full breasts. If this lady was attempting to conceal her figure to make those she encountered believe that she was anything else but a woman, she was failing miserably. Men's garments would in no way hide the fact that the person beneath the fabric was a young, lovely woman. Her dark auburn hair was tied with a leather strap and left uncovered. But this had been her mistake in the first place for the color was like a beacon for all to see. It would be wiser to conceal it with a hood or scarf if she truly wished to avoid notice. Hazel eyes were set in a lovely round face that was tanned from the sun, causing Theobald to assume this woman had spent a fair about of time out of doors.

He sheathed his sword and waited for her to relax her guard. Considering she still held herself poised for a fight, he did not think this would be happening any time soon until she was assured she would be safe in his presence. He would silently applaud such a decision to not trust a stranger were he not the one in danger of being stabbed should she lash out in haste.

"Are you mayhap lost, my lady?" Theobald asked politely, hoping to put her at ease.

She watched him suspiciously, still keeping her blade firmly gripped in her gloved hands. "To whom do you swear your alliance?"

Her question surprised him. 'Twas not what he had been expecting. "Does it matter?"

"Aye, it does," she answered with a tilt of her head whilst she continued to peruse him. "There are many rumors surrounding London of who should be crowned England's ruler."

He folded his arms across his chest, feet spread apart. "I go to fight on behalf of Empress Matilda in Winchester. Does this perchance answer your question, or do you have more?"

A smile lit her face brightening her entire countenance. "'Tis her army that just passed?" she inquired, whilst slightly lowering her blade.

"Aye, my lady," he answered when she finally placed her sword in the scabbard at her side. A huge sigh of apparent relief left her and the woman at last relaxed her stance. If Theobald thought her beautiful before she began to speak, she was more so now.

"I am no lady," she said lifting her chin.

"Well, you are a woman, are you not? You cannot expect the clothing you are currently attired in would hide such a fact," he stated pointing to her garments.

She shuffled her feet. "I suppose not, although I had hoped to pass for a man whilst journeying along the road."

"Why?" he demanded, wondering what this woman's purpose was.

She appeared puzzled at his question. "'Tis not obvious?"

"Mayhap you can inform me. I am a simple man with simple needs and cannot fathom why on earth you would wish to pass for a man," he replied, curious as to this woman's motives.

"I am dressed thusly in order to ride with the Empress and fight for her so she might win the crown," she answered with a confidence that would be impressive from anyone but even more so from a woman.

Her words took a moment to sink into his head before he roared with laughter. This lady could hardly be more than a score of years and should be married and seeing to babes at her lovely breasts, not traipsing across the countryside in search of glory.

He was bent over chuckling and therefore did not see her

approach. She kicked him in his side harder than he expected and momentarily lost his footing. He recovered quickly and held out his hands once more when she appeared ready for a fight. Whether with her fists or sword, Theobald was not sure, but he would not be so overly confident again in her presence.

"You will not make fun of me, sir," she warned. "My purpose is honest. Trust me when I inform you that I am perfectly capable of defending myself with a sword."

Theobald composed himself whilst attempting to keep the smirk of laughter from his lips. "I will bow down to your inner knowledge of the competence of your blade, my lady."

"I told you, I am no lady." Her head lifted higher once more with her words.

"Then what am I to call you, oh beautiful wanderer of the woods?" he teased.

For a moment her eyes twinkled in delight at his jest. "My name is Ingrid. Ingrid Seymour."

"And I am Sir Theobald Norwood. I am pleased to make your acquaintance, Mistress Ingrid." He bowed as though he was in court and a short laugh escaped her which she quickly hid with her hand.

"A pleasure."

She bobbed an awkward curtsy, giving Theobald the impression she was not used to performing such a gesture. Now he was indeed curious about this woman. What in the world was he going to do with her? He certainly could not leave her on the open road to continue her travels to join the Empress's army without someone to watch her back.

⸺ · ⸺ ❧ ⸺ · ⸺

CHAPTER FOUR

INGRID GAZED AT the handsome knight before her, still filled with a fair amount of skepticism toward the idea that she was safe in his company. Still, whether he was honorable or not, there was no denying he was a comely man. Wavy dark brown hair fell to broad shoulders and the green of his eyes could rival the forest around them. His nose was slightly crooked, giving her the impression that it had been broken a time or two. A small scar along his left cheek made her ponder what other battle lines might be on his muscular body. Heat flared to her cheeks at such a thought and she briefly tore her gaze from his to peer through the woods toward the open road, hoping to refocus her thoughts.

She nodded in that direction. "So, the Empress is on her way to Winchester."

"Aye, she is to set up a base there," he answered before he took his hand to his chin. "I cannot in good conscience leave you here to your own devices nor do I have the time to return you from whence you came."

One of her brows arched at his words. "Oh, I am not going home. I'm joining her army."

A snort left him. "Surely you jest. You can hardly be prepared for what we will encounter, especially since you have in no way made an attempt to conceal the fact you are a woman."

"Since you do not know me, then how can you claim I am unprepared to fight for the Empress?" she asked impatiently, tapping her foot upon the ground.

Amusement lit his face. "I will give you that. But until you prove your ability with a sword, I fear for your safety if you continue to travel alone. Enemies can and will hide everywhere whilst traveling upon the open roads."

"I *can* take care of myself," she reaffirmed before continuing, "and you will not persuade me to give up my vow to defend the Empress's right to the crown."

Theobald nodded. "I can appreciate your enthusiasm for a cause I, too, believe in," he responded, and her heart leaped at the idea that she had so easily won her argument. She was about to respond when the knight held up his hand. "However, such a vow does not mean you are capable of killing to stay alive, if the need arises, or that you have the strength to take on a warrior knight bent on ending your life. You must needs prove such to me."

She gulped at the thought of actually pushing her sword into another human being. But this was what her father had trained her to do. She knew she was proficient from his teachings and could accomplish the deed if necessary. Her life may depend on it.

"Why I must needs prove anything to you is beyond me," she murmured before continuing. "What do you propose?"

He clasped his hands behind his back. "You shall come with me. There is a market town called Basingstoke nearby. We will be making camp for the night, but I may be able to procure you a room at the local inn if one is available. Mayhap a hot meal can also be procured if we are lucky." The fact that he seemed to be taking charge of where she would go and what she would do should have made her feel uneasy, but instead of being leery of this stranger, she felt relatively calm in his presence. She had no idea why since he was a completely unfamiliar to her.

"And then…?"

"Come the morn, you prove your worth to me with a small demonstration of your ability with your blade. If, as you say, you can handle your weapon to my satisfaction, you may ride with us."

She lifted her chin. "And who made you my keeper to have a say on if I go to fight for the Empress or not?"

A chuckle left him. "You did when you did not conceal yourself properly from my eyes. If I can spot you so easily in the forest, then so can others. Most men would take advantage of a mere woman alone on her travels."

Her guard came up again. "And you are not one of these men?"

"If I were, I would have already proven this to you by now. Instead of having this witty conversation, I would be silencing you with my kisses... among other things." His smile was completely wicked, and her heart flipped in amazement as she began wondering how it would feel to have this man's lips pressed against her own. *Good heavens! Where had such a thought come from?*

Still... she must needs be careful. "And do I have your word you shall remain a gentleman whilst I am in your care?"

"Aye, Mistress Ingrid. I shall remain on my best behavior."

"A knights vow?"

"Aye," he answered quickly. For whatever reason, she believed him.

She nodded hoping he would keep his word. "Then let us be on our way."

His penetrating gaze swept the forest with a frown. "Dare I hope you have a horse tethered nearby?"

Her eyes widened. "Oh dear. I almost forgot about Valor. Aye! He is nearby." She turned from him and began making her way deeper into the forest until they came to her steed tied to a tree.

Theobald came up to the horse, running his hands down his flanks and studying the animal as though also assessing its worth to carry her into battle. "He will do," he finally said before cupping his hand to assist her in mounting the steed.

She came up to him, hesitating with the thoughts of actually placing her hands on his broad shoulders. "I can mount Valor myself."

"Aye, I am certain you are most able, but a knight will always assist a lady when she is in his presence," he stated as a matter of fact.

Since she had never encountered a knight before living in her little farming village, she could only assume this was a common courtesy among those of the nobility. Placing one hand on his shoulder, she placed her left foot into his cupped hands and she was easily lifted to swing her right leg over the saddle. Once seated, she held out her hands for the reins but an amused chuckle escaped him as he began leading Valor toward the road.

Once they reached the edge of the tree line, he swore. "My damn horse got loose and took off," he fumed before bringing his fingers to his mouth and giving a shrill whistle. Tossing her the reins of her horse, he stepped into the middle of the dirt road looking both ways to see which direction his steed would return. The only thing he saw was dust left from his friends' horses whilst they continued their journey. Their laughter echoed in the air as if they knew Theobald was horseless.

He continued watching both directions of the road. Finally, the black beast high stepped down the lane towards its master, sauntering along as though he had an agenda of his own making. Apparently, this was to rejoin the army since the steed came from the direction the men had been heading. He came to halt in front of Theobald before neighing and then proceeded to give him a gentle nudge that became more demanding when he did not receive what he wanted.

"You think to get a treat when you return after running off and rather than staying put where I left you, Buttercup?" Theobald demanded when he took hold of the reins dangling from the bridle. "You will be lucky if I feed you this eve, you ungrateful beast!"

Ingrid burst out laughing whilst Theobald tossed the reins over the horse's head and vaulted into the saddle. "Buttercup?"

"Aye. I gave him a ridiculous name and certainly one not

suited to him based on appearances alone. But rest assured, he deserves the indignity of it in recompense for his contrary spirit. This horse has the beauty of an angel and the soul of the very devil."

"I sense a story here. Your horse is, indeed, very beautiful," she said waiting for his reply.

"And he knows it," Theobald snorted. He studied her for a moment before he began to speak. "Not that I wish to share all my secrets, but I have been unseated in both life and love too many times. I decided to name this cursed horse Buttercup as an act of revenge against life's injustices. He is a reminder to myself to not take anything too seriously. If I do, I am certain to lose it."

Such a confession was not what she expected and Ingrid was momentarily at a loss for words. Before she could form any sort of comment, Theobald pushed his heels into the side of Buttercup and both man and beast began to trot down the road. Ingrid clucked her tongue and Valor easily caught up to the pair. She could only wonder what revelations the remainder of the day would bring.

CHAPTER FIVE

THEOBALD ANGRILY CURSED his own stupidity after his failed attempt to barter for a room at the Old Crow's Nest, the only available inn in the tiny market town of Basingstoke. Considering the tavern was full of the very men with whom he had been traveling, he should not have been surprised to learn any vacant rooms had already been rented for the night. Most of the knights traveling for the Empress had already set up camp in the surrounding area of the town. Sometimes it did not pay to be late but what else could he have done once he encountered Ingrid traveling on her own?

He left the dimly lit inn emitting the delicious smell of roasted venison. His mouth watered in hunger even as he made his way toward where Ingrid stood, holding the reins of both horses and appearing as if she were cooing to them both. Buttercup, for once, seemed to be behaving for the lady despite having the male steed vying for her attention. A knight, who was clearly into his cups, passed her by whilst slurring an inappropriate invitation that caused Theobald to reach for his blade. But in the end, Theobald chuckled when he heard Ingrid tell the man to *piss off!* Mayhap she could take care of herself after all.

"By the frown upon your brow, you appear as though you do not bear good news." She gave him a slight smile as if to appear confident but he could see for himself that she was weary to the bone.

Theobald came and took Buttercup's reins. "Unfortunately,

we are too late to have a bed in the inn this eve. We were lucky they have room in the stable so I've paid for the horses along with coins to see them fed. The innkeeper said we were free to sleep in the loft above."

"Together?" Her chin trembled with her words.

"As I mentioned before... you are safe with me, Mistress Ingrid," he reassured her... or at least attempted to. He was too tired to worry overmuch about her apprehension. She either trusted him or she did not. He gave a heavy sigh knowing in his heart that he might not be so easy to trust a stranger if he were in her situation. She did not know that had no intention to dally with a woman. He had given up on falling in love as his brother had done. The betrayal of one woman from his youth still haunted him after all these years.

He began leading his horse in the direction of the barn and Ingrid followed quietly behind him. Inside, the stable was dimly lit with only a few torches set in sconces upon the walls but there was enough light to find the last two empty stalls side by side. The bridles and saddles were taken off their horses. Ingrid worked silently but efficiently, even going so far as to find a brush and comb to groom her mount. He had no idea how long or far she had been traveling this day, not that it mattered. Once the horses were taken care of and fed, he would see that they found a place in the tavern and order them a hot meal.

Wooden stairs were located at the back of the barn and Theobald took it upon himself to take his satchel along with Ingrid's up to the loft. 'Twas clear they were not the first who had slept in the barn before as several blankets were neatly folded on a small, worn wooden table. Their makeshift *bedchamber* would have to do for the night. At least they would not be sleeping on the ground. And thankfully, the worn mattresses on the floor appeared free of vermin. Hoping their belongings would be safe, he went back down the steps to find Ingrid had ensured both horses had a pail of oats.

"Hungry?" he asked.

"Starved," she replied with another small smile.

"Then let us find ourselves a table and sup. The tavern is busy but I believe I saw a vacant table."

"Will I be safe with so many inside?" she asked whilst concern flashed briefly in her eyes.

"As out of harm's way as I can keep you, but mayhap you should have asked yourself such a question prior to embarking on this foolish journey," he muttered seeing for himself that Ingrid was uneasy to be around a large group of men. There was certainly no guarantee that she would be treated with respect. Still… He knew nothing about her but he also did not want to underestimate her given his past association with the woman his brother had come to love. Ceridwen could yield a sword as well as any man of his acquaintance and Theobald could only pray Ingrid could do the same if there came a need to defend herself in the tavern.

"I *will* hold my own, Sir Theobald," she stated firmly with a stubborn tilt of her head.

"We shall see." He waved his hand for Ingrid to proceed him and they left the stable together. When they got to the tavern door, raucous laughter could be heard within giving the impression that most had already indulged in their fair share of several cups of drink. Ingrid went to open the door but Theobald reached out his hand to stop her. They shared a brief moment gazing into one another's eyes before he cleared his throat. "Best be careful. Stay behind me."

He expected another argument about how she was more than capable of taking care of herself but this time she remained silent. Making his way into the tavern, he espied a small booth near the rear of the taproom. He nodded toward Blake, Oswin, and Kingsley who sat at a table with other knights. Blake's brow rose when he witnessed Theobald escorting a woman. He scowled when he heard Blake's laughter reach him over the crowd. He was certain he would hear more from his riding companions once they learned Ingrid was under his protection.

Reaching the booth, he made Ingrid scoot herself along the bench making her position difficult for anyone who had ideas to reach her. He took his place next to her and for all intents and purposes, they appeared as though they were a couple, which he hoped would halt any man who might think of getting to the woman. He planned on keeping his word that she would be safe within his presence.

A serving wench with a welcoming "come hither" look came to the table. She briefly glanced at Ingrid before she licked her lips, bending forward until she was all but spilling her breasts from her garment as she ran a hand down Theobald's arm.

"What can I get ye, govn'r?" she asked in what Theobald supposed was an invitation. It seemed odd that she would behave so blatantly when he was, to all appearances, already committed to another woman, but mayhap she was of the sort who enjoyed competing with those of her sex. Perhaps she thought she would achieve some triumph in "stealing" him away from Ingrid.

"Ale," he replied shortly before casting an eye to Ingrid. "Or would you prefer wine, my dear?" His endearment caused Ingrid's lips to twitch in suppressed amusement. Theobald gave her a warning look.

"Ale would be fine… *darling*," Ingrid replied with an enchanting smile.

He nodded and returned his attention to the barmaid. "Bring ale for the both of us. I also saw venison being served. If there is any left, bring that along with meat pies and whatever else you might recommend."

"Is there anythin' else I can be gettin' ye, govn'r?" she asked in one last attempt for him to accept her unspoken proposition.

He scowled and the maid finally backed off. "Just the ale and food." He waved her off and soon two tankards were set before them along with a thick crusty bread and freshly made butter. He took a sip of his ale and sighed in pleasure.

"Has it been that long since you've had a cool drink of ale to parch your thirst, Sir Theobald?" Ingrid asked before reaching for a piece of bread at the same time Theobald did. A gasp escaped her when their fingertips touched and she yanked her hand away from the food before them.

"'Tis been a while." He hid a smirk and moved the plate of bread closer to her reach. Taking up his tankard again, he nodded in her direction. "A good ale, a fair meal, and the company of a lovely young woman. What more could a knight ask for?"

She took a bite of her bread before washing it down with her drink. "You answered the serving maid as though we were together."

"Together?" he teased, giving her a wink.

She leaned forward. "Aye! Together... you know... in *that* way," she hissed.

A chuckle finally escaped him. "Best to keep up appearances so your situation looks as though you are spoken for," he replied. "Keeps the rabble away."

Before she could answer the maid came back with a heavily laden tray. Dishes were put before them: roasted venison, meat pies, root vegetables, and even fried fish. Their tankards were topped off and they were then left alone to consume the feast in front of them.

"Is there someone else who is joining us? There is enough food here to satisfy the whole of the Empress's army."

He reached over to stab a piece of venison before placing it on the trencher in front of him. "You best eat your fill. This may be the last decent meal we have for a while."

She attacked the meal as though it would indeed be her last meal for some time and he did the same. The food filled their bellies, the ale quenched their thirst, and before long Theobald sat back on the bench satisfied. Those in the tavern began to disperse, giving testament that the hour was growing late. Knowing they must rise with the dawning of the new day, Theobald left coins on the table, stood, and held his hand for Ingrid to take whilst he assisted her from her place at the table.

Her fingertips gliding into the palm of his hand caused a

reaction he did not expect. Tingling sensations ran up his arm but he dismissed such a sign as his body reacting to a woman since he had not been with one in some time. He tucked her hand the crook of his elbow and escorted her from the inn to return to the stable.

He checked on the horses whilst allowing her a few minutes of privacy. When he heard her softly spoken words that he could come up, his boots echoed on the wooden stairs. The stable was now dark and only one nub of a candle was lit on the table. She had taken the time to place one of the blankets on the mattress where he was to sleep whilst she was already tucked into her own.

Thoughtful but he would not rest until he was assured that no one had plans to follow them. He hoped no one would be so aggressive, especially since there were plenty of willing maids offering their services in the tavern for the taking, but he still would be careful. He took a seat on the last step, resting his back on the wooden railing.

"Surely you do not plan to stay there all night long," she asked quietly sitting up and clutching the blanket to her chest. "You must get your rest, Sir Knight, lest you be useless come the morn."

"Go to sleep, Mistress Ingrid, and know this knight protects you during your dreams."

She sputtered a reply before finally laying back down. An hour or two passed before Theobald felt 'twas safe to find his own rest. Silently, he moved to his mattress, took up a corner of it, and pulled it closer to the stairs before laying down. His sword was placed in reach in the event he needed its use.

CHAPTER SIX

I NGRID AWOKE TO a stream of sunlight shining in her face from a crack in one of the planks in the roof above her. Birds chirped outside giving testament to the lateness of the morn. A soft snore gave her a moment of alarm before the realization of where she was and with whom registered in her tired brain. She raised herself up on one elbow to see the knight who slept nearby. She was pleasantly surprised to see he was protecting her whilst she slept by moving his pallet to the entrance of the stairs.

Theobald had been true to his word, and it had not taken her long last eve to be thankful for his presence and the ruse he conjured to make their situation appear as though they were a couple. She had already confronted one scoundrel who offered her a lewd suggestion of spending the night with him. From the jeering looks she received when she had entered the dimly lit tavern, had it not been for Theobald, she was certain there would have been more. Ingrid had not been sure she would have made it out of the inn on her own without being compromised.

His words, and that of Charles, were a constant reminder that she, in truth, had not thought out her plans well enough. Aye, she could handle a sword with skill but she would in no way be able to hold off multiple men if they were bent on harming her. She shuddered at the thought of losing her virginity in such a manner.

She began folding the blanket that had covered her for she had slept in her garments last eve. She trusted the man still asleep nearby but only to a point. There was no sense in tempting

Theobald to whatever gentlemanly limits he may or may not have. After all, they had only just met.

With thoughts of repaying his kindness, she took up her boots and scabbard from where she had placed them near her satchel, carefully climbed over the dozing man, and tip toed down the stairs. Sitting upon the last step, she put on her boots, stood, and then belted the scabbard around her waist. She would go to the inn and get them something to break their fast before they began their journey again. Since the new day had dawned, surely everyone would now be sober and would be more intent on preparing for their departure rather than seeking companionship, thereby allowing Ingrid to go about her business without confrontation in the early morn hours.

Leaving the stable, she noted that there were several people who idly milled around the yard between the barn and inn, but not nearly the number she had expected. She began to wonder exactly how late the day had become, for it appeared as though the majority of the Empress's army had already begun their journey to Winchester. She began to hurry. She entered the inn, quickly procuring her and Theobald a light meal with the few coins she owned, although the smell of hot porridge tempted her. But there was no time to take their ease with breaking their fast. Her stomach growled in protest whilst the innkeeper's wife wrapped their meal in a linen and handed it to Ingrid.

She had just rounded the corner of the inn, her bundle held closely to her chest, when the same knight from last eve who had slurred his snide comment, stepped into her path.

"Where are going in such a hurry, my pretty?" he asked with a grin that more than spoke his intentions.

Ingrid went to go around him, but he continued to side-step into her path, blocking her way back to the barn. "Let me pass," she warned before putting her meal on the ground at her feet. If this was to turn into a fight, she'd need her hands free.

"You must have time for a bit of fun," the knave continued. "We can have some sport together before you head back to your husband."

"I think not." She pulled her sword from the scabbard at her side holding it menacingly before her.

The man laughed before pulling his own blade and swinging the weapon to meet her own. "Your husband is not here to protect you, foolish woman. You actually think you can defend yourself from me?" he jeered. "I shall teach you your place in life and then take what I want!"

Ingrid observed the crowd that had begun to gather before she laughed, causing her adversary's scowl to deepen. "You can try but you will not win," she taunted before striking her blade against the sword the man held in front of him.

The man was momentarily taken aback, giving Ingrid a moment's advantage that she seized eagerly, swinging her blade again and again. The people gathering in the yard began to exchange bets on who might become the winner in the contest before them. When their blades met again, the man gave Ingrid a mighty push causing her to stumble and a groan rose up from those few who had bet their monies on a woman. But she recovered quickly and noticed her opponent had turned his back to her, assuming the fight was over. A mistake no one with any common sense would make—but it was apparent her opponent had none. With arms raised above his head, he pumped his fists with his sword raised high causing the crowd to cheer.

With his attention averted, Ingrid made her move and took her blade and slapped the flat side onto his arse. The noise of the crowd rose along with the rude comments made to the knight who was being mocked by a woman. He turned with murder flashing in his eyes and Ingrid realized that her attempts to humiliate the man may have gone too far.

Their swords met again and again but Ingrid was still able to hold her own even though she could feel her arm tiring. She caught a brief glimpse of Theobald who had come to the sidelines to watch her performance. Was that respect she saw flickering in his green eyes? She had no time to ponder the matter whilst she fought for her life. Thankful for the hours of training her father had given her, she continued to swing her blade until she saw an opening in her opponent's defense. Quickly, she took the advantage, and her sword went to the man's throat.

"Yield," she warned, "and you will live to see another day."

The man's eyes widened whilst he gulped, his Adam's apple moving closer to the blade. He frowned as if still weighing his options and Ingrid brought her blade even closer, nicking his neck until a small trickle of blood spilled down.

"Do you yield?" she asked again, and the knight carefully nodded.

Some of the crowd cheered, others who had chosen poorly groaned. Ingrid at last stepped away from her opponent and heckled the man who had lost to her. "Next time I would be careful with your words."

Ingrid began making her way toward Theobald when he yelled out her name.

"Ingrid! Watch out."

She quickly turned back and raised her blade in time to deflect a dagger the cur had hurled at her back. She fumed, weighing her options before speaking to the crowd. "This man has no honor and I leave him for you to decide his fate. I have important fighting to do on behalf of Empress Matilda, so I have no more time to waste with such low-life scum."

She walked backwards in the event the man wished to continue to once more take things further. But apparently his last cowardly act had been enough. When he disappeared into the crowd that continued to yell embarrassing comments toward him, Ingrid realized that the match was now indeed finished.

She went back to where her meal had been left for she had not forgotten her original purpose for leaving the stable in the first place. She went to Theobald and gazed up into those green orbs that took note of her from head to toe, apparently looking for injuries.

"Have you met him before?" he asked whilst continuing to

keep an eye on the dispersing crowd.

"Nay. Our paths have never crossed before last eve when he hurled his nasty remarks."

"He looks familiar, but I cannot recall where I might have seen him," Theobald remarked. He continued to gaze upon her with an amused expression.

"Well? Have I proved my worth in your eyes? Not that your opinion of my skill matters to me, of course." She grinned sheepishly.

A chuckle rumbled in his chest. "Aye, more than proved it."

"Good! Then I have a small repast that we can eat whilst we travel. I have a feeling we are running late… again."

They entered the stable, saddling their horses in no time, and resumed their journey to Winchester.

⟵━━━•━━━❧❧━━━•━━━➤

CHAPTER SEVEN

THEOBALD MUNCHED ON the bread and cheese Ingrid had provided to break their fast, watching her from the corner of his eyes whilst he rode next to her. She continued to give him a satisfied grin whenever she caught him looking. If she could ride her horse whilst in battle as well as she had protected herself with her sword this morn, Theobald knew she could indeed hold her own against any foe… at least for as long as the strength of her arm held out. One bout of sword fighting could in no way compare to a full-on battle that could last far longer than this morn's event.

But she was just as talented as Wymar's lady. Ingrid reminded him of Ceridwen in many ways, at least with her talents with a sword. He still did not know much about the confident woman who rode beside him, but there was plenty of time to learn more of her past. Or so he hoped.

There were but a few straggling knights who rode with them giving testament to the lateness of the hour. Theobald could not remember a time where he had not awoken prior to the rising of the sun. He did not wish for the Empress to learn he was no longer riding with the full strength of her army. He had no wish to become out of favor with the woman. She had a temper, and he did not desire to be on the receiving end when she hurled out her words in anger.

Riders coming up from the rear drew his attention and he reined in his mount whilst putting his hand on the hilt of his sword. He immediately recognized the standard of Robert Fitzroy, the Earl of Gloucester. The earl was the Empress's half-brother and had been her chief military supporter for many years. The illegitimate son of King Henry I of England, Gloucester was acknowledged at birth and had been raised at his father's court. He had the reputation of being an educated man.

"Hold!" a knight in the front line called out, causing Ingrid to also turn her horse in their direction bringing Valor alongside Buttercup.

She leaned over in her saddle. "Who is that?" she questioned.

"Later…" Theobald answered before Gloucester himself rode forward. Theobald did his best to bow considering his current position on his horse. "My lord…"

Gloucester narrowed his gaze whilst he took in the pair of them before he returned his attention to Theobald. "You look familiar. Have we met?"

Theobald nodded. "Briefly, my lord, at the battle of Lincoln when you captured the usurper Stephen."

"Aye… Norwood, is it not?"

"Theobald Norwood at your service, my lord."

"You and your brothers have been staunch supporters of my sister. I suppose this is why she returned Wymar's lands and title to him, along with allowing him and Lady Ceridwen to wed."

Theobald's eyes widened at his words. "My brothers and I are all grateful to have had our lands restored, my lord. However, while I knew the Empress had selected a bride for him, I had no knowledge Wymar and that particular lady were to wed, although I know my brother is probably most grateful. He has long favored the lady of Norwich."

"If they are not already married, they will be soon, or so I was told," Gloucester murmured before his gaze returned to Ingrid. "Will you not introduce me to your own wife?" he asked, obviously assuming he and Ingrid were wed.

"Oh, we are not—" Ingrid began.

"—husband and wife, my lord," Theobald interjected with a

warning glare toward the lady. "My apologies for my lack of manners. May I present my cousin, Ingrid Seymour. Ingrid, this gentleman is Robert, Earl of Gloucester."

Ingrid had the decency to not negate Theobald's words. "My lord," she murmured with a nod of her head.

Gloucester moved his horse forward so he could take Ingrid's hand. He raised her gloved fingertips to his lips. "A pleasure, my lady," he replied before moving his horse back into line with his knights. He pointed to the sword at Ingrid's side before he chuckled in mirth. "Another woman who fights for the Empress. How is it you Norwoods raise or find such brave women?"

"Sheer luck, my lord," Theobald said whilst his lips twitched in suppressed laughter.

"Lucky, indeed, and if she fights half as well as Lady Ceridwen then the Empress has gained another woman worthy to be a part of her army," Gloucester said whilst watching them closely.

Before the earl could question them further, Theobald spoke up. "My cousin was impulsive and wanted to lend her arm to the Empress's cause. With no other family, she sought me out. I was lucky to find her on the open road."

The earl finally nodded as though he still doubted such a story. "Since you appear to be lagging behind, join our company for now. When we arrive in the city, you may once more join the Empress's ranks. Fall in."

Gloucester gave them no further time to reply. He waved his arm forward and his knights began to follow. Theobald and Ingrid joined their ranks but it was several minutes before Ingrid at last voiced her displeasure.

"*By Saint Michael's Wings!* You must needs tell me when you plan to change our story. One moment you imply we are a couple. The next I am now some cousin. Why did you not correct his assumption, Theobald?" she fumed louder than she apparently intended since several nearby knights looked their way.

Theobald's laughter rang out. "My cousin is miffed with me," he jested for their benefit whilst several men laughed at his situation. When the men returned their attention to their horses and the road, he gave her a gentle smile to placate her hoping his ruse would work. "Forgive me, Ingrid," he whispered using her name with a familiarity as though they were in truth related—a necessary intimacy in the event anyone was still paying attention to their conversation.

"'Tis not right to lie to the man, you fool!"

"Mayhap 'twas not the best choice but such a charade will continue to keep you safe and within reach in case you have need of me. Telling the earl you were my wife seemed as if 'twould stretch the lie further than I should since he might ask questions as to why you are not at Brockenhurst where a wife should be kept. But a cousin…" He hesitated briefly before he continued. "A cousin with no other family is something he could possibly understand, especially a woman who is… impulsive."

"And who made you my hero," she pointed out, her voice full of indignation.

He chuckled thinking back to their conversation when they first met. "You did when you decided to trust me. Do not lose faith in me so readily. I have your best interest in mind with any decision I make on your behalf."

"You assume much, Norwood," she hissed between clenched teeth.

"Mayhap so, but at least you will not become some plaything for an army of men," he returned whist watching her carefully and preparing himself for some form of outburst.

Another curse left her lips, but luckily for him, she did not voice any further objections. Whilst he had a feeling that she was still displeased, he also had some hope that Ingrid could agree his remarks and logic made sense. But he had no idea what was going on inside that beautiful head. Instead of continuing to voice her complaints, Ingrid remained silent. They continued to ride this way for the remainder of the day. He was uncertain which he liked better: a quiet Ingrid who was anything but subservient or the woman with the fiery hazel eyes whom he enjoyed verbally sparing with.

CHAPTER EIGHT

Siege of Wolvesey Castle
31 July, 1141

INGRID ENTERED THE relatively large tent she shared with Theobald and barely made it to her bedroll laid out upon the ground. Exhausted, her arm felt heavy from lifting her sword over and over again to strike down the enemy and protect her life now that they had entered Winchester and its battle. She stared at her pallet in agony. The floor felt as though 'twas miles away. If she laid down now, she would never be able to rise on her own accord whilst still wearing her chainmail. She was that drained.

Her body felt as though she had been bound and dragged behind a cart for days. There was not one inch on her that did not rebel from some sort of pain. She unbuckled the belt holding her scabbard, the release of the heavy weight a welcome relief. She placed the blade nearby with care, for it had served her well this day. Her decision made, she crossed the tent to her pallet. Falling back onto the softness of the blanket, she cared not when the chinks of her chainmail dug into her back despite the layer of padding to protect her abused skin.

She stared up at the fabric of the ceiling whilst memories assailed her mind. Their arrival in Winchester had completely surprised Bishop Henry, who quickly fled the city. His soldiers retreated to Wolvesey Castle, which belonged to the church and was situated in the corner of the city walls. Now, the Angevin host had Wolvesey Castle under siege, putting strong pressure on its defenses. Ingrid could now rest… or so she prayed. For the moment, there was nothing more that she could do and she was thankful for the respite from war.

When Theobald had showed her to the large tent that had been erected for them, she had been momentarily surprised since this was a luxury she had been unprepared for. She had resigned herself to taking a bedroll and sleeping upon the ground… another part of her plan she had not given enough thought to. She continued to gaze at the fabric of the tent above her. Theobald had mentioned his older brother Wymar and how everything that was before her had once belonged to him. Apparently, his brother was now lord of their estate after having his title and lands restored to him by the Empress. When Ingrid had asked when Theobald had last been home, he evaded the question. She assumed it had been some time.

Ingrid closed her eyes as her mind continued to wander with all she had learned after they arrived in the city. Empress Matilda had set up her headquarters in the royal castle previously occupied by Bishop Henry. Robert of Gloucester had established his command post near Saint Swithun's Cathedral. Ingrid now only awaited further word from Theobald who would be able to tell her more on their current situation.

As though he had been summoned by her thoughts of him, the tent entryway flapped open and the man himself filled the space before once more closing out the world behind him. He appeared just as weary as she had been when she had entered the tent. Ingrid had spent long hours whilst riding with this knight to observe him, noting both how handsome he appeared and how determined he was to keep his word in regard to seeing to her safety. He had been a gentleman to the core. Ingrid continued to be thankful that she had met Sir Theobald Norwood instead of someone else who would have taken advantage of her person.

"Do you have news? Have you spoken with the Empress? Will we leave Winchester anytime soon?" she asked full of concern. With a fair amount of difficulty, Ingrid managed to sit up before crossing her legs beneath her.

"A moment, if you would be so kind, Ingrid," he said quietly and she swore beneath her breath realizing she was overwhelming the man with questions when all he probably needed was a few minutes of quiet and rest.

"I am most sorry, Theo," she said shortening his name for the first time. Her mouth opened in an *O* of surprise causing Theobald to raise a brow. A wicked grin then slipped across his mouth. "I—I m-mean Th-Theobald."

Laughter rumbled inside that muscular chest. 'Twas such a comforting sound, considering all she heard this day were the moans of the dying. "'Tis fine to shorten my name, Ingrid. I shall take it as a compliment you are at last comfortable enough to do so in my presence."

She nodded her head, grunting in agony when she slowly rose before turning her back to him. She strolled over to where a small table held a pitcher of wine and two chalices that Theobald had laid out earlier to have ready for them when they returned from the battlefield. She poured him a cup. The simple task gave her the time she needed to attempt to calm her racing heart. She took a deep breath and turned once more with cup in hand.

He gave her a grateful smile and came forward reaching for her offering. She held back a gasp when their fingers touched. All she could do was look up into his visage pondering his thoughts. Had he felt those tingling sensations too? He gave no hint of any emotions other than gratitude.

"My thanks, Ingrid," he murmured before drinking his fill as though he was consuming water.

"You have a mighty thirst, Theo," she murmured quietly before going back and picking up the pitcher to refill his cup.

"Aye," he replied before inspecting her for possible signs of injuries. "Have you been injured?"

"A few cuts and bruises. Nothing serious," she said quietly.

"You held your own well today... more so than I expected, although I must admit I thought you would have found your slumber by the time I entered."

She went and filled her own chalice before turning back to face him. "I only just arrived here but a few minutes before you did. As you can see, I did not even have enough strength to remove the chainmail you found for me... unless I will need it again this night."

"Nay! You have done enough fighting today for our Empress. But let us remedy the situation for you cannot sleep with chain links digging into your back."

"But I should be prepared for—"

"—sleeping," he finished her sentence even though that was far from what she had been preparing to say. "You shall do nothing more than rest and mayhap take in some sustenance so your empty stomach does not rumble all eve long."

"Will we dine at an inn?" she asked in hopeful anticipation. A hot meal would do wonders for her body and mood. She hesitated briefly when he silently waved a finger toward her attire. Hesitating, she finally gave in to her short-lived embarrassment of undressing before him and took off her tabard with the Empress's emblem. This, too, he had found for her use from heaven only knew where.

He came to her. "Bend forward," he ordered whilst he assisted with the removal of the chainmail covering her upper body. It felt as though an unfathomable weight had been lifted from her torso as she exhaled a sigh of relief. "Better?"

Gratitude filled her eyes when she lifted her face to stare upon him. "Aye," she answered before wrapping her arms around her chest. The garment of padding used to protect her skin was soaked in sweat and she could only imagine the horror of what she smelled like. She took a few steps back. "And the meal at an inn?"

His green eyes seemingly reached into her soul and Ingrid was not entirely sure if she was dreaming this whole encounter with this handsome man. Her tired head must be imagining the brief look of what she thought was desire before he masked his visage once more. "Not this night," he at last answered. "'Tis too dangerous. I will retrieve a meal for us myself whilst you see to changing into something more comfortable to sleep in. I am sorry I cannot have a tub brought over for your comfort but this is life at camp and such luxuries are not often available. The best I can offer you is a basin of water to wash yourself."

"I understand," she said quietly. Before she could say anything further, her embarrassment reached new heights when the flap of their tent opened and began to fill with men. A startled gasp left her whilst she reached for the tabard and quickly flung it over her head.

"Look who we found—" the knight who opened the flap of the tent said before his words ground to a halt.

"It appears as though we are interrupting," another replied.

"God's Bones, Theobald! Where do you find the time or the energy?" another said to add to Ingrid's humiliation whilst the men's laughter echoed in the air around them.

Theobald came to stand in front of Ingrid and she nervously peeked around from behind his back at the men who seemed to fill every corner of their tent, making it feel smaller than it truly was. "Who are they?" she whispered reaching out to take his hand. Although she had ridden with these men and had fought beside them for many days, she had not actually been introduced to these knights. And one man with them was completely unfamiliar to her—she was certain he had not been with the Empress's army prior to now.

Theobald gave her fingers a small squeeze and she supposed that meant all these knights were his friends.

A chuckle left Theobald before he crossed the space and began to give one of the younger men a fierce hug. "Thank God you are safe, brother," Theobald said before searching the man's face. "And what of Wymar? Wed?"

The man nodded. "Aye, to Lady Ceridwen. They seem most content."

"'Tis the best news I have heard. I am most pleased to know

they found one another again. Obviously the Empress chose well for our brother," Theobald replied before casting his gaze to the other men. "I suppose formal introductions are long overdue. Mistress Ingrid Seymour may I first present my younger brother, Reynard Norwood. Also present are Blake Kennarde, Oswin Woodwarde, and Kingsley Goodee. All good men who I have been riding with and fighting alongside. You may or may not have encountered the latter three knights whilst fighting this day. They have certainly been well aware of you, although I did not confide details of the reason why you are here."

The men all bowed whilst she gave a clumsy curtsy. "Gentlemen," she answered shyly.

"As you are aware, I encountered Mistress Ingrid upon the road to Winchester and offered her my protection, although I have told a falsehood that she is a distant cousin of mine in order to keep her as safe as possible," Theobald replied before he gazed sternly at the men before him. "I can trust you to keep such information confidential, can I not?"

The men began murmuring *of course* before the one called Blake stepped forward.

"She has been amongst the fighting?" he asked, his eyes went wide in curiosity.

"Aye," Theobald answered before returning to her side. Ingrid held onto his arm as if he was the last person in the world who could stop her world from spinning.

"A woman fighting in a man's war..." Oswin remarked in disbelief whilst the men began to erupt in laughter.

Ingrid's own mirth finally broke free and the men all became silent. "A *man's* war?" She smirked at the audacity of these knights. "You fight for the Empress Matilda... a woman! If anything, this is a woman's war."

Theobald patted her hand. "Enough. There is no sense in having heated words spark more discontent. Aye, Ingrid is fighting for our Empress much like Lady Ceridwen did. You all know how well that particular lady held her own at the Battle of Lincoln. Ingrid is just as well-trained. I can assure you she is worthy to be fighting for our just cause. Otherwise, I would not allow her on the battlefield."

"Thank you," she said quietly although she felt slightly miffed that Theobald seemed to believe he could control her life. The men began to mumble between them.

"You are most welcome. Now, the gentlemen and I shall give you time to yourself, Ingrid, whilst I go procure us that meal. I shall not be gone long and will ask Reynard to stand guard outside until my return."

Ingrid was not given any time to reply whilst the men all left. She could see Theobald whispering to Reynard, who stood at the entrance of the tent, before the flapped dropped back down into place.

The space seemed empty without Theobald's presence but she assumed since his brother was the one to guard the tent, she was safe enough to continue to clean herself as best as possible. A pitcher of water sat on a small table along with an iron bowl and she made use of the small cloth and soap found next to it. After she finished, Ingrid had a moment to wonder when Theobald had found the time to have this set up in the tent for her use. She was thankful to at least have the grime from the battle removed from her skin.

The thought of once more donning the smelly garments she pulled from her drenched body was abhorrent but she would have no other choice come the next day of fighting. For now, she was as clean as she could be, and she redressed in another spare pair of hose and a tunic.

With nothing more to do, she laid down upon her pallet to await Theobald's return. She would close her eyes for only a moment to rest—or so she thought. Instead, she fell into a deep sleep and dreamed of a man with eyes the color of the forest and dark wavy brown hair who kissed her until she was happy for the first time in her entire life.

And upon awakening, her dreams proved to herself that somehow and someway, Theobald Norwood had crept into her heart. She could only ponder if perchance he might stay there…

❦

CHAPTER NINE

Theobald led the way to the nearest inn, found a vacant table, and called for ale. Blake, Oswin, and Kingsley took their places and when filled tankards were placed before them, they all sighed in pleasure as the cool brew slipped down their parched throats. Theobald ordered food to take back to Ingrid whilst the men all silently stared at him obviously waiting for further information on the woman who was now waiting in his tent.

"Remember when I held back on our way here to Winchester?" he asked while the men all nodded. "I caught a glimpse of her hair through the forest. She was hell bent on joining the Empress's army. What else was I do to but offer the woman my protection?"

"She's lovely," Kingsley commented. "You are a lucky man to have such a treasure near at hand."

Theobald groaned beneath his breath. "'Tis not like that, you fool. I but offered to help keep her safe and when she proved more than capable to handle a sword, what was I going to do? Just toss her away to find herself surrounded by knights who may not be as honorable?"

Oswin chuckled. "Nay, of course not, but do you not see this woman for the beauty she is? *God's Blood*, that red hair alone would drive any man insane with desire."

"Do not speak so lightly of her," Theobald warned.

Oswin held up his hands. "You protest overly much for a

woman whom you say means little to you."

"I am treating her like the cousin I told the earl she was, nothing more," Theobald replied, although the lie was bitter on his tongue. If things and times were different, perchance…

Blake leaned forward. "Mayhap you will not mind if I also offer her my *protection*." His smile was wicked and it took all of Theobald's willpower to keep from pulling out the dirk hidden in his boot.

Theobald watched Blake warily. "Be careful you do not test my patience more than you already have, my friend."

The men's bellow of laughter caused the heads of those seated nearby to twist around to find the humor of the situation. They quickly turned back to mind their own business.

Kingsley slapped the wooden table. "Enough, men. Leave Theobald alone to deal with the lady as he sees fit. If he cannot appreciate the woman, one of us can be nearby to pick up the pieces of her shattered heart."

Blake chuckled and slapped Theobald's back. "For a moment I thought that mayhap you were finally going to let your guard down and allow your heart to become ensnared by a pretty face. Considering what you told me of your past, I was surprised. Now I see you have no notion to pursue the fair lady. I am relieved."

Theobald cursed and for once his frown of displeasure only heightened the amusement of the men seated with him instead of causing them to keep their opinions to themselves. A fleeting vision of a woman raced across his mind before he let the memory fade once more. He refused to even think her name and would in no way relive memories of their brief time together. When the servant placed a wicker basket before him, he gave her several coins to pay for the meal, promised to return the hamper on the morrow, and bid his friends a restful good night.

The streets were eerily quiet and dark but the moon above shone bright enough for Theobald to find his way back to his tent. He was thankful for the small comforts he would find within but knew this might not always be available for his use. 'Twould all depend on which direction this war would go next… not that this particular siege was over. As he drew closer to his temporary dwelling, he nodded to Reynard who continued to stand guard despite the fact he, too, must be exhausted.

"'Tis quiet inside?" Theobald asked his brother whilst resting his hand upon his shoulder.

"Aye, nary a sound," Reynard replied nodding towards the entrance. "You have taken on a lot having to see to a woman's safety along with fighting for our Empress."

"I can handle the situation, Reynard."

"Can you?" his brother teased.

"Let the matter rest, young scamp," Theobald warned whilst listening to Reynard sputter obviously put out about the reference to his age. "You have a place to rest this eve?"

"Aye. I have already made arrangements for a place to put my pallet for the night with Blake."

"Then I will bid you a good night so you may take your ease, brother," Theobald said.

"Until the morrow, Theo," Reynard replied before taking his leave.

Theobald pulled open the flap of the tent before letting the canvas fall back into place. Despite the darkness of the night, he could still make out where everything was located since Ingrid had left several candles lit so he could see upon his return. Setting down the basket, he made his way over to a nearby chair and sat. He pulled his tabard from his body, leaned forward, and began to pull the metal chainmail from his frame. He took off the rest of the garments from his chest before standing and making his way over to the pitcher that contained the water from Ingrid's *bath*. 'Twould not be the first time he reused water and he was thankful to at least have the chance to become somewhat clean.

He hurried, knowing the food grew colder the longer he took. Pulling out a clean tunic from his belongings, he strode the few steps to kneel next to a slumbering Ingrid. He looked down upon her… *really* looked upon her in a way he hadn't since their first encounter in the forest. In the time since, he had been so focused on protecting her that he had managed to put all other thoughts to the side. But now that he was looking again, he could in no way discount what his friends had immediately witnessed where Ingrid was concerned. She was a true beauty. Her flaming red hair would be any man's downfall, that was for certain. Her skin was tanned to a golden hue from her time spent in the sun making her appear even more surreal. What happenings could have shaped this woman's life that she now fought in a war she should be far away from?

"Theobald…"

His name left her lips in a breathy whisper and he bent forward and saw she yet slumbered. Odd that… The sound of his name reminded him on how a lover would call to him. Something in him stirred and whilst he hesitated to touch her skin, he took a lock of her hair, rubbed it between his fingers before tucking it behind her ear.

"Ingrid." He murmured her name, placing his hand gently upon her shoulder to give her a gentle shake. She must be having one hell of a dream for her lips formed into an enchanting smile that would entice even an angel to do unspeakable things to the unsuspecting woman who continued to slumber.

"Kiss me," she whispered before reaching out her arms to take hold of his tunic, pulling with a strength he was surprised she still possessed after hefting her sword all day. His mouth was but inches from her own before common sense swept over him. Nay! He would not take advantage of what she offered when she slept, tempting though it might be.

He took her hands from his garment and sat back on his heels, still reeling from how close he had come to kissing those perfect lips. "Ingrid," he said more firmly. He gave her another shake. This time more forceful than the one previously uttered.

A frown formed upon her brow before her eyes began to flicker open. "Theobald, is something amiss?" Her voice was laced with confusion most likely from the fact his tone when he said her name sounded gruff and full of censorship even to his own ears.

"I have food. Come eat before it gets any colder and becomes inedible." He stood and held out his hand to assist her from her pallet. Her fingers easily slid into his palm as if they belonged there. His breath caught in his throat. Shockingly, tiny burning sensations raced from his fingers and straight up his arm, making him even more aware of the woman before him. Never had such a thing happened to him and he began to wonder what kind of spell this lady would hold over his heart in his future.

He let go of her hand as though branded by fire, ignoring the fleeting look of confusion flashing across her features. But she was quick to recover—much faster than his own racing heart. He turned away from her, picked up one of the candles so they might see their meal better, and went to the small table where he had placed the basket. He pulled a stool out and motioned for her to take a seat whilst he began to unpack their small repast.

"'Tis not much but 'twill have to sustain us until we are able to procure another meal," he said. The smell of meat pies had already filled the tent and he watched Ingrid lick her lips in anticipation of what he had provided. Bread and cheese were also laid out and before he also took a seat, he went to where wine awaited him, poured two cups, and brought them back to their table.

"'Tis a feast fit for a king and queen," she purred not knowing what her words did to him…especially the phrasing that made it sound as though they were somehow a couple. He handed her one of the chalices and they both took a sip.

Silence filled the tent as they began to eat their fill. "Delicious," Ingrid at last murmured. "I do not know when I have tasted anything better."

"'Tis simple fare. We had better at the other inn," Theobald commented dryly. The candlelight from their table cast soft glows upon the woman seated across from him making her red hair appear to dance before his eyes as if her tresses had a life of their own.

"But not as satisfying as after fighting all day," she replied before pushing the rest of her pie before him. "You might as well finish this."

"Are you certain?" he asked still feeling as if he could eat his horse.

"Aye. I am stuffed and could not eat another bite."

"Then I am obliged," he replied and with her nod began to finish the rest of what their banquet still held. She leaned her elbows upon the table and studied him intently. She appeared as though she had many questions but instead of giving her time to ask whatever she had on her mind, he spoke up. "Tell me of yourself, Ingrid."

Startled, she hesitated before she answered him. "There is not much to tell. I lived a simple life in a village outside of London where my father and I farmed the land."

"And your mother?"

Her eyes closed briefly before opening again. Her fingers gripped the stem of the chalice as if her memories caused her pain. Her next words confirmed his thoughts. "Died upon my birth," she said softly. "There have been many times over the years when I wished I had known her."

"I am sorry for your loss. I, too, have known how the death of loved ones affects your life and causes much suffering. My brothers are all the family I have left in the world." A silent look passed between them as they shared a common memory that still remained fresh in their hearts.

"And what of your father? How is it that he gave you permission to join the Empress's army?" Theobald asked as he finished the last of his meal and took a sip of his wine.

"He has gone to join my mother in the heavens. He would have never allowed me to leave the village if he still walked the earth." She gave a heavy sigh before reaching for her cup as though the wine would sustain her from all she had lost.

"No other family or friends to take you in?" he inquired almost knowing what her answer would be.

"Nay. We had only each other. We were not well accepted in our village. The others felt my father did me an injustice by teaching me swordplay at an early age."

"What do these people know? You have done your father proud this day with your fighting skills."

"Your words bring me joy, Theobald. Thank you."

"There is no reason to thank me. 'Tis your father you must needs thank," he said with an honest heart.

She watched him intently before voicing her thoughts. "And what of you, Theobald. Is there no fair lady to share your life?"

A snort of disdain escaped his lips. "The strength of my arm to heft my sword, along with my horse to see me through battle, is all I need in life."

Ingrid took another sip of her wine before her brow arched upward. "Seems like an awful lonely existence, Theobald Norwood."

His lip curled upwards whilst he stared at her across the table. "Your situation appears as if you are in the same predicament, my dear," he teased, whilst tossing her a roguish grin.

She shrugged off his comment. "Perchance…" Her words lingered between them but she did not offer anything more.

"From your response, I take it there is not someone whom you might fancy waiting for your return?"

A faraway looked briefly crossed her visage. "Nay. None other than one I consider more like a brother and friend. You can see the problem with such a situation," she said softly before she turned those mesmerizing hazel eyes toward him. He swore he could see straight into her soul and see for himself her desire to find someone to love.

He cleared his throat and, to distract himself, began clearing the table and placing the dishes back into the basket. "Aye, I certainly can. I suppose when this war is all over, you will have more than one knight who will be begging for your favor. Mayhap even one of those whom you met this very eve might suit you. They thought you might favor one of them." He had no idea why those words tumbled from his mouth.

Her mouth opened in an *O* of surprise before she snapped her lips shut. She stood and pushed in her stool before turning her back on him and striding to sit on her pallet. "Because I need a man to take care of me?" she sneered. 'Twas apparent his words angered her. That had not been his intent.

"They are good men. I assumed you would want a husband one day so you could build a family and not be alone. Any of them would be a good husband for you," he replied, even though his heart was not sure he could stand to see any of his friends as Ingrid's husband.

This conversation had gotten out of hand, and he wished he had never brought the other men to her attention. 'Twas foolish of him to speak such thoughts, especially when he was beginning to see what a treasure this woman could have been in his life if he'd wished to settle down. But such a thing was not to be. Even though he could admit he desired her as a lover, it would be a stain on his honor to push for such intimacy when he could not make her his wife. His future was unknown and he did not have a home to call his own. He was by no means fit to be anyone's husband.

"You could so easily allow me to spend time in their company, letting them get to know me?" Her voice was so quiet he almost missed her words.

"You are your own woman, Ingrid, and I am not your jailor. I have but offered my protection. Nothing more." The moment his words left his mouth he knew them to be a falsehood. Could he honestly allow Blake, Owen, Kingsley—or, heaven forbid, Reynard—to spend time with the beautiful Ingrid? He was a fool to have made such a suggestion but could in no way retract his words. He had a duty to his Empress and had no time for a dalliance with a woman. But what if such a liaison could lead to something more? Although he continued to tell himself that he had no right to marry when he had so little to offer, he would be lying to himself if he said he had not thought of having a wife some day in his future. Was he not hoping that he would be handsomely rewarded by the Empress, just like Wymar, and that perchance this would allow him to take a wife?

Silence. 'Twas deafening until she at last found her voice. "Very well. At least I know where you and I stand," she muttered but he swore he heard a catch in her tone or mayhap a small sob. God help him if he had hurt her feelings!

He pulled his pallet near the entryway of the tent and laid down. "Good night, Ingrid."

"Good night, Theobald."

Far into the night did Theobald regret his words to the woman who shared his tent. He had a feeling that come the morn, guilt would consume him once he saw her in the light of the new day.

CHAPTER TEN

INGRID SWUNG HER blade repeatedly in an offensive move until she did so without thought. The enemy was fearless in their pursuit to win the day nor were there any signs they were about to retreat any time soon. The ground beneath her boots was a river of blood and mud from the dead or dying. The stench was overpowering but she had no choice but to fight on. The other alternative was not an option.

Ingrid had pledged herself to the Empress's cause and had proven her ability to defend herself. She would deal with the overwhelming regret of the lives she had taken another day. God must forgive her of such a sin. She pressed ever onward to gain even an inch of ground beneath her feet. She swore for every step forward, she was forced two steps back, mayhap more.

With a slicing motion of her blade, she dispatched another foe and took a deep breath. Although she was tiring, she refused to give in to the exhaustion that wracked her body. When the body before her fell to the ground, she gave a heavy sigh. Bringing her blade forward, she held the hilt with two hands. Another enemy stepped forward to take his comrade's place. There was always another ready to do battle.

She was briefly stunned to witness the startled gaze of another woman. Hazel eyes met green whilst they stood staring upon one another, each seeming to feel the same reluctance to raise their blade against the other. Ingrid could only nod her head at the other woman in respect for her right to fight for the cause of the usurper Stephen. With their gazes still locked together, this unknown woman also gave Ingrid the briefest nod before she quickly turned to throw herself back into the battle with a different adversary.

Chest heaving, Ingrid pulled herself from her dazed state, wondering what had possessed her to allow the woman who would be considered her enemy to turn to fight another of her comrades. But she did not have long to ponder the matter when an unknown man came up to her taking hold of her arm.

"Who was she?" he yelled over the mayhem surrounding them.

"Does it matter?" she bellowed back whilst swinging her sword as another enemy came forward.

The knight became distracted with the next enemy who attempted to claim his life. He thrust his sword forward vanquishing the knight before he quickly glanced at Ingrid. "You let her go. Why?"

"Does it matter? If you are so concerned for her, be my guest to go and try to find her in all this chaos."

She barely saw when the knight ran off in the direction of the woman. Ingrid had no time to worry over what he planned to do with the lady if he found her. Once again, Ingrid needed to be on the defensive whilst she hacked away at one more knight who thought to end her life. But she lost her footing, slipping on the wet ground. Pitching forward, she was unprepared for her enemy to head butt her. She staggered backward crying out in dismay when her helmet went flying off her head. A curse left the knight's lips whilst he grabbed her heavy braid and yanked her forward into his chest.

"*Bloody Hell!* 'Tis you," the man bellowed. He began to wind her hair around his fist. "You and I have unfinished business to take care of for the humiliation you caused me when last we met. I can think of a better way to spend this day than keeping up the pretense of fighting to keep this land for a damned woman."

"Get your hands of me," Ingrid shouted, pushing against his

chest to regain her freedom but 'twas to no avail. Of all the knights to meet upon the battlefield, 'twas the same knight she had bested at the inn. His words penetrated her tired brain. This man may have been fighting for Empress Matilda but 'twas apparent he was a traitor in their midst. His true alliance was to the usurper Stephen!

Alarm caused her heartbeat to increase whilst her chest heaved to gain more air. 'Twas one thing to fight amongst an army of men with your identity concealed. 'Twas another matter entirely when all those near enough to care about anything other than staying alive began to realize there was a woman in their midst.

"Look what I have caught, men," the man jeered before he placed a disgusting, wet kiss upon her lips. "Anyone else up for a bit of sport?"

Ingrid tried not to gag. The knight's hold on her hair tightened as he gave the heavy braid a jerk. His breath was foul. His sweaty blond hair hung in wet strands giving testament to how hard he had been fighting. She swore, causing him to laugh whist his steel-blue eyes appeared as cold as ice.

No one appeared to be ready for anything other than keeping their heads upon their shoulders. The frenzied fighting around her continued. Ingrid thought she heard a growl of outrage coming from somewhere on the field. She had no time to ponder the matter, for she was struggling to keep her footing. Her sword was yanked from her hand. The man holding her captive obviously was on a mission that had nothing to do with furthering his cause for King Stephen or Bishop Henry.

"I have plans for you, wench," the man murmured whilst dragging her along. "The bishop will not care if I take a few moments in order to see to my needs."

He continued pushing her forward despite her best efforts to be free of his grasp. With her back up against his chest, he had captured her arms leaving her defenseless. The fact she had been apprehended in the first place was a testament to how truly tired she had become. If she could only reach the dirk she kept hidden in her boot, she knew that with little effort she could slip the slim blade at the very least into his thigh to give her enough time to flee this cur.

"I think not," she yelled out but no matter how hard she struggled to reach down to grasp the hilt of the blade, she couldn't get a handle on it. Before she knew what was happening, she was roughly turned around and pushed up against one of the stone walls of Wolvesey Castle. There was no fighting in her current whereabouts, and she highly doubted anyone was near enough to hear her cry for help. Besides... who would come aid her instead of wishing to take this man's place once he was finished?

His mouth descended upon hers again, but she clamped her lips tight against his onslaught. She heard more than saw when he unbelted the leather holding his sword in place. It hit the ground giving Ingrid the smallest bit of hope knowing the scum manhandling her was now unarmed. She felt him fumbling with his clothing knowing he was attempting to release his manhood. God help her! She was running out of time and needed to save herself. She squirmed in his arms and called out for aid. His hand came towards her mouth to silence her. Left with no option, she bit down hard and was momentarily satisfied to hear his cry of outrage. 'Twas short lived when she felt his palm slap her check making her head snap back against the stone wall.

"You damn bitch," he swore. "I shall show you who is your master."

"'Tis certainly not you."

Just as Ingrid was about to lose hope, a voice resounded as though the angels had sent a guardian down from the heavens to protect her.

"Get your hands off this woman unless you wish to lose them at the wrists," a knight proclaimed. Her assailant was wretched backwards, and Ingrid stared up at the helmet of her rescuer. His voice sounded familiar, but 'twas only when she looked closely that she recognized Theobald's friend Oswin. He was a sight to behold. She had never been happier in her life to see a friendly face.

The cur who had attempted to do his worst to her, grabbed his belt before sneering in her direction. "Make no mistake… we shall meet again. You shall rue the day you ever crossed paths with Roger de Payne! I am not yet done with you and the score that must needs be settled between us."

Oswin stepped forward, his blade pointing at the knight's chest. "Aye, you are finished with the lady, de Payne, if you wish to live to see another day."

Ingrid frowned wondering why Oswin did not run the man through rather than allowing him to escape. Yet in all good conscience, she cared little for his reasoning and was thankful she was for the most part unharmed. The realization she had almost been raped finally penetrated her mind causing her knees to buckle. Oswin caught her before she could fall to the ground.

"I have you now, Mistress Ingrid," Oswin stated placing his hand around her waist to steady her. "Let me escort you to your tent."

She shook her head before placing her hand on her forehead and feeling a bump that was growing. "I must needs return to the fighting and find my sword."

Oswin began helping her walk away from the battlefield. "Given the bruise upon your brow, your fighting is over for the day, mayhap several more. We can find you another sword."

"But my father gave it to me," she cried out knowing she could not lose the last connection she had to her sire.

"Then I will look for your blade when the fighting is over for the day. Until then, 'tis my duty to see you to safety. Theobald would expect no less of me," Oswin declared as they continued walking in the direction of her tent.

A gruff tone left her remembering Theobald's words of the night before. The low hum caused Oswin to stare at her in confusion. Or was it interest? 'Twas hard to tell at the moment, especially when her vision blurred.

"Theobald is not my keeper and has no say in anything relating to my life," she snapped. Her head was beginning to pound, and she could only pray she did not pass out from whatever injury her head had sustained.

"I suppose that remains to be seen, Mistress Ingrid." A deep amused chuckle left his lips causing Ingrid to raise her head to peer upon this man who had saved her.

Whisps of his blond hair could be seen underneath the edges of his helmet. She could barely make out blue eyes from the slits in the heavy metal protecting his face. He appeared about the same height as Theobald with even the same muscular build. *God's Blood!* Why she was even comparing the two men was beyond her ken. Her injury must be addling her wits!

"He is not my keeper," she repeated.

"If you say so, then it must be true," he teased with a chuckle, but she could not for the life of her find the amusement in this situation.

A sigh of relief left her when she espied her tent. Oswin opened the flap for her and made her sit on a stool at the table before demanding she lean forward so he could assist with the removal of her tabard and chainmail. He took off his helmet and waited. She was too tired to complain and finally did as she was told. He began tsk tsking upon viewing the various cuts and bruises on her body. He began to scowl.

"You have sustained a deep wound underneath your chainmail padding," he mentioned before walking across the room. He began inspecting the tent for various objects. Finding water and thread, he returned. "Carefully take it off so I might access how much blood you have lost." He placed the items on the table and awaited her compliance to his orders.

"Excuse me?" Her hands shook at the thought of undressing in front of a man who was very nearly a stranger.

"Do you wish to bleed out?" he asked with a raised brow.

"Nay." 'Twas the only response she could give him. Any

further words would betray how uncomfortable the situation had become for her.

"Then let me inspect how deep the wound is, and if needed, I shall sew up the skin." His voice was flat as if this was a common conversation being held in a dining hall.

"I can see to it myself," Ingrid announced lifting her chin. She had not gone from one dangerous situation only to find herself compromised in another. The man before her may be friend or foe but by damn she would not strip naked for him or any other man.

"Stubborn, woman. Theobald will not approve..." His voice trailed off whilst he continued to assess her for further injuries.

Her head cocked to one side. "I believe Theobald would not care to find me undressing for you inside *his* tent," she chimed in until Oswin burst out in laughter. She stood and made her way to her pallet.

"You may have that aright, my dear. Do not fall asleep, Ingrid," Oswin warned. There was a sense of comfort when she heard the formality of her name passing his lips. "I will see if I can find a surgeon or Theobald to see to your injuries since you will not let me attend you. Will you be able to fend for yourself until my return?"

"Aye, of course. Thank you for coming to my aid, Sir Oswin," she muttered watching him carefully. He went to the table to retrieve his helmet.

He turned back to stare upon her before a wicked smile spread across his handsome face. "Mayhap you will do me the honor of calling me Oswin, given all we have been through together?" he asked waiting for her reply.

"We shall see," she answered not wishing to give him an indication she might be interested in him after the battle was over. She may have been saved from one ruffian this day, but she truly did not know the man standing before her enough to completely trust him.

"Stay awake," he reminded her before he left her to her solitude.

She had every intention of obeying Oswin's command. Truly she did. But when her body started to sway, her pallet seemingly called to her to rest for only a moment or two. Laying down, she quickly fell asleep where Theobald once more filled her dreams.

CHAPTER ELEVEN

THEOBALD DUCKED, NARROWLY missing the sword aiming for his neck. The battle this day had been as brutal as the one the day before with no end in sight. He had lost sight of Ingrid hours ago and prayed she was still safe and unharmed. Reynard fought close by and was, of course, holding his own. Theobald would expect no less from his brother. Whilst the battle had continued, he was unsure if the Empress's army was making any advancement to gain control of the city or to overtake the castle where the bishop's men were held up. There seemed to be no end in sight.

A familiar face briefly came into his vision. Theobald was surprised to see none other than Lord Richard Grancourt fighting near at hand. Grancourt shared a deep friendship with his older brother, Wymar, but in truth, Richard was akin to another brother. They were all that close and they had all fought together for the empress's cause at Battle of Lincoln.

"Grancourt," Theobald shouted in an attempt to gain the man's attention. He watched Richard continue to fight until his enemy's helm went flying off his head.

Richard's fist swung forward and landed in his adversary's uncovered face. He turned then smiled broadly at Theobald. "Norwood! A good day for a fight, is it not?"

Theobald laughed. "Aye, as long as we win the day," he called out. Swinging his blade, he felled the knight before him. Another, as always, quickly took his place. Theobald fought onward.

"I have no doubt 'twill be so," Richard at last answered. "I will seek you out when the day is over."

Theobald had no time to reply. His concentration needed to be at the task at hand… to stay alive to see yet another day. Before long, a white flag appeared upon the battlement wall. A call to cease for the day to collect the dead and injured. Theobald was thankful for the reprieve. As he began to leave the field, he espied the hilt of a familiar looking sword half buried in the muck beneath his feet. *Good Lord! This belongs to Ingrid.*

The hilt of her sword was familiar to him. The actual blade, not so much since Ingrid kept the weapon close to her at all times, carefully sheathed in her scabbard. He wiped off the dirt and blood that had covered the steel. The engravings etched in the metal came into focus and he frowned. Upon closer inspection, Theobald realized this sword was costly and did not appear as though it should have been in the hands of a mere farmer. But this was of no consequence for now. He would ask the lady about it later.

Frantically, Theobald's gaze traveled to those lying upon the ground. Ingrid was not to be seen so where the devil was she? His name being called out caused him to level his eyes upon Kingsley who was running in his direction.

"Hurry," he ordered when he reached Theobald's side.

"What has happened?" he asked afraid of the answer considering his friend's worried frown.

Kingsley whipped his hand over his eyes. "Oswin sent me to fetch you. 'Tis Ingrid. She has been injured."

"How bad is it?" he asked picking up his pace to reach his tent.

"I have no idea." Kingsley met him step for step. "I only met Oswin on his way to find a surgeon."

By Saint Michael's Wings! 'Twas so bad that she required a surgeon, he thought. He began running in the direction of the tent he shared with Ingrid. Upon his approach, her screams rang out leaving a gut-wrenching hole in his heart.

Flinging open the flap at the entrance to his dwelling, his steps faltered at what he was witnessing. A surgeon was kneeling on one side of her pallet, busy in his task of apparently stitching up her flesh. On her other side was another familiar friend. She had a death grip upon Oswin's hand, if her white knuckles were any indication of the tightness of her grip and the pain she was going through.

"Please do not leave me, Oswin," she murmured between clenched teeth. Theobald's heart lurched to hear another man's name pass her lips, but 'twas even more unsettling to witness Oswin stroke her hair.

"Be at ease, Ingrid. I shall not leave you," Oswin vowed.

Kingsley elbowed Theobald. "Bad luck, that," he muttered. "I thought mayhap I might have a chance with the fair lady, but it looks like Oswin beat both of us to earn her favor."

Theobald gave Kingsley a glare that would silence most men. "Do not be so sure," he advised, although he was uncertain where he stood with the lady given their conversation of last eve. Oswin may very well win over the lady's heart. Did this matter to him? The sour mood suddenly enveloping Theobald proved to him that such a happening most certainly did.

His friend had no claim as yet on Ingrid, as far as Theobald knew, leaving him the opportunity to pursue the matter if he was so inclined. Apparently given this situation, Theobald realized he best make up his mind, and quickly.

He placed Ingrid's sword on the table where they took their meals before he marched forward, determined to see for himself how bad the lady was injured. When he approached, her eyes were squeezed shut, a grimace etched upon her face whilst the surgeon continued his work to sew up her injured flesh.

"How bad is she?" Theobald inquired. Three sets of eyes met his. Oswin appeared to be on the defensive. Ingrid's look relief held, or so he hoped—but 'twas visible only briefly before she masked her face with disinterest toward his presence.

The surgeon went back to his work. "'Tis not as bad as it

appears. She's a bleeder this one is," he remarked, inspected his work, and then began wiping his hands on a rag.

Theobald nodded whilst continuing his inspection of Ingrid. "And what of the bump on her forehead? Should we be concerned?"

The surgeon packed up his belongings and stood. "Nay. She should be fine with a couple days' rest. I do not, however, recommend her picking up her sword any time soon. Thrusting herself back into battle will only open the wound, not that she belongs anywhere near a battlefield in the first place," he muttered.

Theobald watched the man depart and Oswin at last stood. His fists clenched at his sides. He moved quickly, grabbing Theobald's tabard giving him a shake.

"Where the devil were you that you could not protect her?" Oswin bellowed.

Theobald gave his friend a push. "You saw what was going on out there. 'Twas every man for himself as is the case with any fight we are thrust into. Ingrid can take care of herself."

"Nay, she could not. *God's Blood*," Oswin cursed. "You have no idea what was happening to her when I found her, do you?"

Accusing eyes momentarily caused Theobald to pause in his response before anger got the better of him. "Well? Spit it out. 'Tis clear you came to her rescue."

Oswin stepped forward "The alternative was not an option! She was about to be raped!"

With that last word, the tent began to fill with Reynard, Richard, and Blake. Theobald's breath left him whilst his gaze flew to the woman who cheeks flamed red in embarrassment. Everyone started talking at once as each man's voice grew louder to talk over the other.

"Enough!" Ingrid ordered, causing the knights to halt their conversation. "All of you get out so I can rest. You can bicker over my situation come the morn."

Theobald stepped forward but not before Oswin went and

knelt back down by her side. He took her hand and held it to his chest. "I am not leaving you," he swore.

Turning her head in his direction, she gave him a weak smile. "Aye, you are. I appreciate your help this day but there is nothing more you can do for me this night. Go take your ease so you may meet the next battle fully rested. Thank you again for your aid."

Ingrid let go of Oswin's hand and he reluctantly stood before taking his leave. The rest of the knights followed in his wake leaving Theobald and Ingrid alone.

"Ingrid…" He came to stand over her and she turned her head away from him.

"Not now, Theobald. Please… just let me rest."

He gave a brief nod and turned away from her, noticing her sword still laying on the table. He went and took up the blade and returned to Ingrid's side placing the weapon on the floor within easy reach. "I found this upon the battlefield," he stated whilst watching her carefully.

Hazel eyes filled with tears as she reached over to touch the sword her father had given her. "How did you manage to find this with all the chaos that was happening today?" she asked, searching his face for answers.

Theobald gave a brief shrug. "Luckily for me the hilt was visible in the mud. 'Twas only right I return the weapon to its owner."

She closed her eyes and when she opened them again, there was gratitude shining within their depths. "I will be eternally gratefully to you, Theobald, for its return. Thank you," she managed to whisper.

"You are most welcome, Ingrid. Now, I will let you rest so you might heal," he replied before once more turning from the lady.

He went to remove his tabard and chainmail. Rinsing himself off and putting on a clean tunic, he saw her discarded chainmail. His inspection proved that several links were in need of repair. 'Twas obvious a blade had been able to penetrate what should have protected her. He gave a heavy sigh knowing he would repair it himself. Pouring a cup of wine, he went to sit on a stool he placed near her pallet. Whilst she slept, Theobald hovered over a woman who was slowing chipping away at the ice surrounding his heart.

❦

CHAPTER TWELVE

*S*HIVERING, HER BODY *betrayed her whilst she lay between the sensations of hot and cold. One moment her feverish body was overwhelmed in heat until the next she sensed cool night air caressing her skin. She was troubled and confused as to her whereabouts until a deep baritone voice calmed her whilst she relived the horror of the day. The outcome could have been so much worse!*

"Open your eyes for me, my sweet." That seductive tone could lure any woman with only a fair amount of common sense to sin. His voice pulled at her heart strings, even whilst she fought off the urge to comply.

"Nay... I wish to dream the night away," she whispered.

"Dream another night, my dear. Open your eyes so I may look upon your beauty," he urged.

Her eyes flickered open to see a hazy glow around the man who sat next to her. His image distorted she could only ponder her fate. "Am I dead?" she asked.

He chuckled leaning forward. "Most certainly not, mistress."

She reached out her hand. Grabbing a lock of his brown hair, she rubbed its length between her fingers. "I think I am, for surely you are my own personal guardian angel to watch over me from heaven."

"Angel?" he uttered in disbelief. "I am far from an angel, Ingrid."

"Theobald?" Green eyes twinkled in delight and a smile began to form on her lips. But 'twas short lived.

He grabbed her wrist none too gently. As her eyes began to focus, his image that was once comforting began to transform. Horror filled her soul when she realized who now held her captive. 'Twas the knight who had tried to do his worst to her. Somehow, he had found her again.

"I told you we had unfinished business, my sweet," he snarled. "You will never get away from me again! Never!"

He pulled her into his arms and a scream left her. Flames erupted around them as if they were in the depths of hell. And as the fire began to creep ever closer to engulf her, she cried out the name of the one person she knew could save her. "Theobald!"

INGRID AWOKE WITH a start. The sound of Theobald's name being called out from her dream still lingered on her lips. 'Twas as though she had in truth spoken it aloud. The sound of dripping water reached her ears until a cloth was laid upon her forehead.

"Hush now, Ingrid," Theobald murmured softly. "You have nothing to fear. I am here—and you are safe."

"Theobald?" Her eyes adjust to the darkness of the tent. With only one candle flickering on the nearby table, his image became clear, and she realized she dreamed no more.

"Aye. You became feverish so I have been putting cool clothes upon your brow to ease your suffering," he replied. The back of his hand touched her cheek. "I believe your fever has at last abated."

"How long have I been asleep?"

"Not long enough to satisfy my desire to see you fully rested." He took the cloth from her brow, placed it in the bowl he had been using, and stood to place the object on the table where they took their meals. He began to pull his pallet near the door.

"Theobald?" She bit her lip in indecision. She did not want to sleep alone and she craved the presence of this man who her heart told her she could trust.

"Aye, Ingrid?"

She hesitated in her uncertainty of what she wished to ask him. Once she voiced her question, there would be no going back, at least in her mind. Their easy friendship might never be the same.

"I know this may be an odd request, but would you lay beside me whilst I slumber?"

Silence met her ears. Mayhap she erred in making such a bold suggestion. She only knew she did not wish to dream again of that evil man who even now haunted her waking hours.

Theobald returned to her side and sat on the edge of the pallet. "Why?"

"I—I am s-scared. I—I d-do n-not wish to b-be alone," she stammered with an honest heart.

He seemingly pondered her words. "What of Oswin?"

Her eyes became wide at his words for this was not what she had thought he would ask. "What about him?"

Theobald took her hand, his thumb rubbing its back made her easily calm. "You asked him to stay earlier. I thought mayhap you favored him."

"If you recall, I had a damn surgeon sewing my skin back together. I would have asked the devil himself to stay if he could offer me a bit of support to see me through the ordeal."

"I can fetch Oswin, if you would prefer him to be at your side," Theobald suggested.

"He is not who I prefer, otherwise I would not ask you to lay beside me, you foolish man," she muttered. Even though she had to admit she hardly knew Theobald any better than she did Oswin, she trusted Theobald for he had more than proven himself to her in the short time of their acquaintance. Besides, she felt drawn to him in a way that she had felt for no other man.

"'Tis a highly unusual request considering we barely know one another," he murmured.

"I am aware of all I need to know about the person you are, Theobald Norwood," she answered. "I only wish to slumber knowing I will not again dream of what almost happened to me this day. Mayhap, with your arms around me, I shall sleep easier."

"We should talk about him and how he must pay for the insult to you."

"I do not wish to discuss him tonight. The morn is early

enough."

Theobald nodded. "If this is what you desire, Ingrid, I will not mention him further for now."

Relief flooded her entire being. Now if only he would agree to what she needed at this very moment. Arms to hold her ensuring she was safe. "Would you please hold me through the night, Theobald? I will not ask more of you than that."

"And what if I wish for more?"

Ingrid peered at him to access the truth of his words. "I am not entirely sure you are even certain what you wish for when it comes to me, Theobald. At least not yet."

A sound rumbled in his chest. "You must think me a saint if you believe I can lay down beside you and not wish to explore every beautiful inch of you, my dear," he confessed, and his words gave Ingrid hope that mayhap all was not lost. She cared for this man and now she knew he desired her, too. Mayhap when all the fighting was at last over, they could take their relationship further. Dare she hope, mayhap, that Theobald would ask her to be his wife? But such dreams were for the distant future. For now, for this night, her wishes were far simpler.

"I am trusting you to give me the comfort I stand in need of. Nothing more… at least for now. The rest we can figure out later, wherever life might take us." She pulled on his arm, and he carefully settled himself next to her.

"I do not wish to further injure you."

"I will not break, Theobald," she answered. She turned onto her uninjured side and took his arm whilst his hand carefully slid into a safe place around her. She gave a contented sigh.

"Better?" he asked.

"Oh, aye," she said with a soft smile. "You see… 'tis not so bad to just hold a woman through the night with no further intentions. 'Twill not hurt your manly pride."

"God give me strength," he groaned.

Her laughter filled the tent. Before long, a soft snore left

Theobald when he finally found his slumber. Knowing he would chase away her nightmares, Ingrid at last succumbed to her efforts to stay awake. And when she slept, 'twas without any dreams or monsters to cause her to cry out in alarm for Theobald had his arms around her keeping her safe.

$$\longleftarrow \!\!-\!\!-\!\!\cdot\!\!-\!\!\cdot\!\!-\!\!\textbf{ }\!\!-\!\!\cdot\!\!-\!\!\cdot\!\!-\!\!-\!\!\longrightarrow$$

CHAPTER THIRTEEN

THEOBALD LIFTED HIS arm from a slumbering Ingrid then rolled over onto his back. He might have dozed off upon first laying down next to the fair lady last eve, but he awoke shortly thereafter. His entire body had been on fire, and she was the one who had lit the flames. His attempt to move slightly away from her only gained him further agony when she pushed insistently back into his body. Every delicious inch of this woman was snuggled into him as though he had grown a second skin. In her sleep, Ingrid gave a moan of contentment that caused Theobald to inwardly curse knowing he could in no way take advantage of a woman who had trusted herself into his care.

The night with no sleep had revealed many things. 'Twas apparent he did indeed care for the woman. The more he thought about her over the night, the more he admired her for all she had overcome in her short life. She was a rare gem amongst the weeds. He had no plans to become involved with a woman whilst he was in the midst of a bloody campaign for his empress. Yet here he was… thinking throughout the night of what the future might hold with Ingrid after all the fighting was over.

Wymar had been rewarded for his service after the Battle of Lincoln and had his title and the family lands restored to him. Theobald was thankful for such an outcome. He could only pray that he, too, might be rewarded lands and monies from the Empress after the battle here at Winchester had been won. This would allow him the opportunity to further prove he had something more to offer a woman like Ingrid.

Dawn came sooner than he would have liked. He carefully left Ingrid's pallet, tucking the blanket around her. He stood there, hovering over her to gaze upon her like the angel she appeared. He would get nothing accomplished this day if he did not get his mind where it belonged. He dressed and was about to leave his tent when he heard his name being whispered from outside. Opening the flap, he espied Richard. Theobald held a finger to his lips to forestall any further conversation, so they did not wake Ingrid. Stepping outside, the two men took each other's forearms in greeting.

They began to stride from the tent and 'twas not until they were away from his dwelling that Theobald finally spoke. "You are the last person I expected to see here yesterday upon the battlefield. All is well?"

Richard gave a weak smile. "As well as can be expected."

A short chuckle left Theobald. "I have the notion you have a story there."

"'Twas my sister, Beatrice…" Richard rubbed at his eyes as though they pained him.

"And what trouble was the lady up to this time?" Theobald asked with another laugh.

Richard groaned. "You know her all too well."

"Of course I know her, the little minx. She *did* grow up with us and came to visit Brockenhurst enough times that we kept a room for her there for whenever she might stopover."

Richard sighed. "She seems to have become overly bold in her desires since I have been away. My parents do little to discourage her."

"Has there ever been a time that Beatrice has not gone out of her way to get whatever she thinks she desires? What did she want this time?"

"Your brother."

"Wymar?" he asked, aghast at the thought.

"Aye!"

"But she is like our little sister," Theobald bellowed. "That could not have gone over well with my brother. Especially when the Empress had already decided he was to marry the woman of his heart."

"I could have wrung her neck when I found out she had been passing herself off as the bride the Empress sent for Wymar. Luckily, your brother was immediately suspicious and was able to delay until Ceridwen arrived. Considering I was the one escorting Ceridwen to Brockenhurst for their marriage, the whole situation could have been disastrous."

Theobald thought of the blonde beauty he had fought beside during the battle of Lincoln. Another rare gem. Wymar was very blessed in his marriage. "How did Ceridwen handle such a reunion?"

Richard smirked. "With all the grace God gave her. I do not think Beatrice was ready for a woman who would not let another stand in the way of her wedding to the man she loved."

"Good for Ceridwen," Theobald said. "You know how much we care for your sister, but Beatrice tends to think she can wrap anyone she wishes around her finger."

"Aye. My parents were not pleased when I returned home with her and informed them of her ploy to ensnare Wymar in wedded bliss," Richard growled out reaching an area where a makeshift kitchen had been set up to feed the Empress's army. They each grabbed a bowl of porridge and began to eat whilst continuing to stand.

"I can only assume you made a hasty retreat to return to the campaign," Theobald replied between bites. He saw Reynard in the distance and waved him forward. His brother nodded to Richard as he, too, took up a bowl of food to break his fast. 'Twas not much but the porridge would fill their bellies.

"Aye and met the Earl once I arrived here at Winchester, so I joined his ranks. Still, I must admit I am tired of war," Richard answered with a heavy sigh. "'Twould be a pleasure to just sit and relax in front of my own fire for a change."

Reynard almost choked on his meal. "You would be bored within the week," he chuckled.

Theobald joined him. "We are destined to win another victory for our Empress, Richard. Think of the glory and fame once we have achieved our objective of having her crowned queen. She is sure to reward us greatly for our service to her cause, possibly even granting us lands belonging to her defeated enemies."

Richard scowled. "There are times when I wish I could foresee the day before us and have the matter done. I have the notion this war may go on for years."

Reynard wiped his mouth on his sleeve. "Surely you jest, Richard?" he said putting down his now finished meal. "Once we take this castle, all our troubles will be over. Do you not agree, brother?"

Theobald and Richard passed a look between them. "We shall see, Reynard," Theobald replied. "Now, I must needs take some porridge to Mistress Ingrid. Watch each other's back today and I shall see you upon the battlefield."

Theobald observed the two men leave, praying both would survive to fight another day. He had his bowl refilled and began striding towards his tent. He about fell over when he viewed Ingrid struggling to sit up.

Rushing forward, he placed the bowl on the table and then quickly made his way to Ingrid's side. *"Bloody Hell*, woman!" he cursed. "Are you trying to rip open your stiches? What the devil do you think you are doing?"

Her eyes held unshed tears as her cheeks pinkened in her embarrassment. "If you must know," she began whilst rolling her eyes, "I am in desperate need of taking care of my business."

"What business?" he roared. "There is nothing outside of this tent that needs your attention this day!"

"Must I hit you over the head or are you that unaware that I must needs see to…"

She could not seem to finish her sentence and then her situation dawned on him. He was a thick-skulled dullard! "Ah... I see," he said helping her to rise. "There is a chamber pot over yonder. Can you make it that far?"

"Aye, as long as you leave me a few moments of privacy," she scoffed. Slowly, she made her way across the tent on wobbly legs. She turned to look back over her shoulder. "Well? May I have a few moments to myself?"

"Aye... of course. I will be right outside if you have need of me," he murmured. He took his leave, but he did not go far. After several minutes of worrying, he finally heard his name being called. Entering, he found Ingrid sitting on the stool at the table with the porridge in front of her.

"My thanks for the meal," she said taking a spoonful. "I did not realize how hungry I was until I started eating."

"You should be back resting on your pallet," Theobald replied in concern. Her face that was flushed pink but moments ago was now white as though she had used up all her energy.

"And you should not be coddling me," she said sternly. "I am not some delicate flower that must be handled with care."

"Even a hardy flower needs nurturing on occasion, my dear," Theobald replied. She gave a small smile, and he was pleased she was well enough to offer him a brief glimpse of her inner beauty.

She finished her meal, pushing the bowl away. A sheepish look appeared on her features. Raising her eyes to stare upon him, she ducked her head in what he assumed was embarrassment. Her words were so soft he needed to lean forward to hear them. "About last night..." she began letting those three little words linger between them.

He took a stool and placed it next to her. Taking her hands in his, he gave them a gentle squeeze. "You do not need to explain. If I was able to offer you even a small measure of comfort or safety, then you do not need to embellish any further details of your request last eve."

"'Twas hardly a ladylike thing for a woman to request from a man she barely knows. What you must think of me." Her breath caught in her throat whilst her head turned away from him.

Theobald let go of one of her hands before he reached over to gently take her chin, turning her head to face him once more, not allowing her to avoid his eyes. "Ingrid, you must know I hold you in the highest esteem. Please do not dwell on the unpleasantries that caused you to make such a request in the first place. I shall deal with this traitor who dared to harm you."

"Oswin stopped him before he could do lasting damage," she whispered, tears welling in her eyes.

"And I am thankful for his service to you, and that you did not come to further harm," Theobald said watching a tear escape her eye. His hand once more reached out whilst his thumb brushed the wetness from her cheek.

"Since I begged him to stay with me, Oswin will think I—"

"—care for him," he finished. "We shall worry about Oswin and whatever he thinks he feels for you, and you for him, once you are healed and are back on your feet."

"I do not wish to give him hope..." Her words trailed off whilst she appeared uncertain of what she should do next.

"You are not to worry over anything or anyone at this time aside from yourself. For now, all I require of you is that you rest," Theobald answered. He took her elbow to help her rise and walked with her back to her pallet. Once she was settled, he tucked the covers around her.

"My father used to tuck me in like this when I was a child. He called it my princess tuck." A sob caught in her throat at the memory.

Theobald reached down to caress her hair. "Then I am glad I am able to give you a reminder of your sire, my lady."

"You are a good man, Theobald Norwood," she said with a sleepy yawn.

A chuckle rumbled inside his chest when his thoughts got the better of him, reminding him of what he would rather being doing with the lovely Ingrid if she were but healed. If she could see his thoughts, she would be more likely to slap his face than to call him good. Fortunately, his passionate thoughts remained hidden. "Aye," he laughed trying to keep the conversation between them light. "I am a saint amongst men."

She giggled merrily. "Oh… you are certainly no saint, Theo." His shortened name brought a wicked smile to his lips.

"Aye," he murmured as she closed her eyes. "And be sure you never forget it, my dear."

Her smile curved upwards, and Theobald was unsure if she heard his words or if she had already slipped away to dreamland.

"Ingrid?" He watched her carefully realizing she had indeed fallen asleep. He kneeled next to her pallet and placed a gentle kiss upon her cheek. His mouth hovered over her face until he felt her hand take hold of his arm. He carefully disengaged her grip and yet he could not stop himself from giving her just one more kiss. The remembrance of the softness of her skin, along with the racing of his heart from what he thought would be a simple act, stayed with him the entire day.

CHAPTER FOURTEEN

SOUNDS OF THE raging battle in the distance had become a constant companion to Ingrid over the past se'nnight whilst she recovered in the tent. Another morn in her recovery had dragged on at an unbearably slow pace until Ingrid thought she might go mad. Theobald had forbidden her to return to the fighting and made it clear she was to stay put. This left her with little to do.

She had never been one to remain idle even whilst living on her father's smallholding. After all, there had always been one chore or another that needed to be accomplished back then. However, she was now far from her home and from the life she had known. She had not thought she would miss it, but she had not imagined the monotony she would face as she waited for her body to heal. With no one to keep her company, she had become completely bored to the point where she contemplated disobeying Theobald's orders and finding something to occupy her mind outside this dwelling and amongst the living.

"Ingrid," a familiar voice called from outside, "are you decent?"

Overjoyed that someone was finally coming to rescue her from her low spirits, she went to the opening of the tent and saw Sir Blake Kennarde, one of Theobald's friends. His tabard was covered in blood, his face dripping with sweat as he held his helmet with one hand. 'Twas clear he but recently came from the battlefield and she could only ponder what he held behind his back.

"Welcome, Sir Blake. How goes our Empress's cause?" she asked, hopeful the siege would end soon, and the Empress would be victorious. Any news would be welcome, along with someone to have a conversation with even if it lasted but briefly. But admittedly, she was surprised he had not come early in the morn to visit her before he was covered with blood from the battle. Surely his presence might be missed at this hour of the day.

"'Tis the same as the day before, Mistress Ingrid. I did not, however, come to talk of gruesome things like the war that is practically on your doorstep. There has been a temporary truce to collect the dead allowing me time to briefly step away."

"Then what can I do for you?" she asked whilst he shuffled from one boot to the other.

"Here." He thrust a small leather book at her leaving her no option other than to take it. "I thought you might wish to read something to pass the time. 'Tis mine. Just a book of short stories but the tales might keep you entertained during your confinement."

Her hand caressed the worn leather. The pages, she noticed, had also been read many a time. "This is very considerate of you, but I cannot keep such a treasured gift. 'Tis obvious you have read this yourself on many an occasion."

Blake shrugged. "Then consider it a loan. You may return it once you have finished."

"'Tis very kind of you, Sir Blake. Thank you," she said quietly. She was unsure if she should ask him to keep her company.

"You are most welcome, Mistress Ingrid." He appeared as though he would say more yet he refrained. Instead, he bowed giving her a teasing wink and turned to leave. At the entrance he looked over his shoulder but gave her no opportunity to see if he would stay. "Good day to you."

"Be safe upon the battlefield, Sir Blake," she replied watching him depart.

Her brief respite from her own dreary company was now

gone, but at least now she had something to do. Blake's thoughtful gift, even if 'twas only a loan, cause Ingrid to smile in gratitude. Slowly, she made her way to the stool set at the table where she and Theobald took their meals. Laying down the leather book, she sat. Opening the cover, a faded inscription from father to son was etched on the very first page. This was indeed something Blake treasured as she had surmised. Ingrid was unsure how he could allow her to keep such a gift from his father for even a small measure of time. She would have to make sure to treat the volume with great care. She would feel horribly guilty if it took any damage whilst in her possession.

Determined to read the book throughout the day and return it to Blake as soon as she was able, she quickly began to absorb the stories. Some caused her to laugh. Others to cover her mouth in sadness. 'Twas a mixture of tales as though from someone's life and she began to ponder if mayhap 'twas more of a diary than a collection of fictional yarns to keep oneself amused. She was about halfway through the book when her name was called again. Another knight had come to call upon her. She was beginning to have a suspicious notion he would not be the last.

Rising from the stool was difficult from sitting too long. She held her side whilst she again made her way to the opening of the tent. Pulling back the flap, she saw Sir Kingsley Goodee holding what appeared a meal for her. It appeared that the few friends of Theobald's that she was acquainted with would all choose to make an appearance this day. Did they somehow know that her confinement and lack of anything to do had started getting the best of her? Whatever their reason, she was glad for the company.

"Sir Kingsley. What a pleasant surprise," she said watching his face brighten with her words. Stepping aside she waved him inside. "Please come inside.

"You are too kind, Mistress Ingrid," he replied placing his bounty on the table she had just vacated. He began spreading out the feast he had brought her as she made her way back to her seat. He held onto her elbow to steady her.

"Others must be joining us for you to have brought so much," she murmured. Her stomach growled giving testament she was famished. "Are the rest of Theobald's friends coming as well?"

Kingsley handed her a trencher and began serving her as though she were incapable of handling the task for herself. When he had given her the choicest of meats, he finally spoke. "This is all for you to enjoy, Mistress Ingrid. I would not wish to intrude long on your solitude or Theobald might take me to task."

"Did Theobald send the food, then?" she questioned with a raised brow. If this were so, then she would have wished he had delivered her meal himself.

"Nay. He does not know I am here. This is my own doing to see that you were well taken care of," Kingsley replied with a crooked grin. "Please enjoy the meal. I will have a servant come fetch the dishes later."

Holding onto a two-pronged fork, she pointed at the food she knew she could in no way finish by herself. "You must join me and eat your fill."

Kingsley bowed. Another knight making a hasty retreat from her presence. "Alas, I cannot… The battle resumes soon, and I am needed upon the field."

She nodded at his excuse for what else could she do? "My thanks for the meal, Sir Kingsley."

Without another word he left her, and she was once again plunged into solitude. She ate what she could but before long she was full. She wrapped up what was left of the meal so she could share it with Theobald, or partake of it later herself if she became hungry once more. She tried to engage her mind with reading again but after several pages and a full stomach, she had become sleepy. Perchance a short nap would help the day go by faster. Laying down upon her pallet, she fell into a restful sleep.

Restful… until she was jolted awake. Goosebumps shivered across her arms as if in warning that she was being watched. Her eyes skimmed the interior of the tent when she saw the shape of a man pouring himself a chalice of wine. Thinking 'twas the villain who had almost done her harm, she gasped.

At her sound, the man turned in her direction. Oswin's smile of happiness that she was awake caused her to give a sigh of relief. Or was this a release of the pent-up helplessness she experienced when she could not stop that man's actions? She had no more time to ponder the dread left over from her ordeal with de Payne. Oswin strode forward to lessen the distance between them and stood before her. His features were relaxed and appeared almost boyish despite he was in truth probably several years older than herself.

Ingrid took the blanket that covered her and pulled it up to her chest. She managed to sit up and was about to stand when Oswin took her hand.

"Do not rise on my account, Ingrid," he said. His voice was like a velvety purr in an attempt to ease any awkwardness between them.

"Why are you here?" she asked whilst her gaze went to the entrance in the hopes that Theobald might enter to save her from having this conversation alone. She would be most grateful for his company.

"'Tis not obvious?" Oswin teased. Leaning down, he brought her fingertips near his lips. Her attempt to pull away only occurred after his mouth made contact with her skin. He arched one brow. "You are not glad to see me?"

"Sir Oswin..."

"I thought we agreed to be on a first name basis, Ingrid. Have you forgotten?" he asked waiting for her answer.

After coming to her rescue, Ingrid suspected the knight before her had reached his own conclusions as to her feelings for him. Although she knew Oswin would most likely make a good husband, her feelings for Theobald were at the forefront of her mind. She wanted to see if something could develop between them. She did not wish to hurt Oswin, but she also did not want to encourage him that there was more between them. He should be spending his time concentrating on the battle outside this tent instead of making attempts to woo her. Ingrid was craving to be doing the same, if only her wound would heal faster.

She stood and moved around him so she was no longer at a disadvantage whilst sitting on her pallet. "I believe there has been a misunderstanding between us." Her reply was firm, causing a frown to develop on his handsome features.

A grumble of discontent rumbled in his chest. He slowly raised the cup he held to his mouth and took a sip. His eyes followed her about the tent whilst she put a fair amount of distance between them. "You have nothing to fear from me, Ingrid," he said. His words seemed to be honestly spoken but she was still on edge.

Her chin rose. "Did I say I feared you?"

"Nay, but if you get any farther away from me, you shall wander out into the battlefield."

"What do you want, Oswin? As you could see, I was trying to rest so I can once again fight for our Empress."

He stepped forward, holding out his chalice. "Will you drink with me?"

Shaking her head, she went and poured her own cup. Sharing a chalice with Oswin would be too intimate and would imply a lover's connection. "Why are you here?" she repeated, waiting for his answer.

He gave a heavy sigh before downing the remains of his cup and setting it aside. He made his way to her. She had to lift her head to look upon him for his height once more had her at a disadvantage. "I but came to check on you to see if you required anything." He watched her carefully. "I did not mean to disturb your slumber."

"Did you expect anything else when you failed to announce yourself before entering?"

The corners of his mouth lifted. "I had hoped to find you awake and in need of company."

"Surely your presence is required in the fighting, Sir Oswin. I can hardly believe you have the time to spare for a purely casual social call. It seems to me that you, along with the others who have suddenly come to visit me today, have deliberately chosen a time when Theobald is too busy and cannot interrupt our conversations." She took a step back to give her the space she needed. She did not feel threatened by this man, only put on her guard that he would enter Theobald's tent without first announcing his presence.

"As I said, I took a moment to see how you were doing. Do you need anything? How may I be of service to you?" he inquired. Stepping forward, he reached for her hand.

"Sir Oswin," she began but he surprised her when he dropped to one knee. Humbling himself before her was not about to change her mind where this handsome man was concerned.

"Mayhap you would favor me once this battle is over. We can see if we might suit," he began rubbing the back of her hand. Ingrid was at a loss for words.

Suddenly the flap of the tent was snapped opened and Theobald filled the space of the entryway, his brother and a knight she had briefly met on the battlefield directly behind him. The smile Theobald had on his face quickly left his visage whilst he thrust a bunch of wildflowers into Reynard's hands.

"Am I disturbing something?" he fumed, clearly upset with the situation he had interrupted.

Ingrid pulled her hand away whilst Oswin rose to his feet. The cocky grin the knight had upon his face was like a challenge. The two men came face to face and Ingrid could only ponder what would happen next.

CHAPTER FIFTEEN

T HEOBALD WOULD NOT back down, especially inside his own bloody tent! Oswin appeared far too smug for his own good. 'Twas as if he believed he had some claim upon the lady since he had rescued her. But Theobald was in no mood to spar with the man, nor would he allow Oswin to think he could get the better of him.

Theobald walked around Oswin, giving him no opportunity to voice whatever had been about to pass from his lips. Coming to stand before Ingrid, he took her chin between his fingers to gaze into her eyes. "You are unharmed?" he asked quietly in what he hoped was a concerned tone. *By St. Michael's Wings, how he wished to kiss those lips.*

Oswin stepped forward. "Of course she is unharmed. What kind of man do you take me for?"

Theobald looked over his shoulder, his brow raised. "I find you in my tent with the lady without the company of a chaperone and you do not think this would cause me concern? Or did you forget Ingrid is in my care?"

A short laugh erupted from Oswin. "Yet, where is this chaperone when you come to this very tent each night? She needs protection, not just for her virtue but for her very life! I told you to keep her safe but here I find her alone without a guard at the entrance," he fumed.

"A matter that I will rectify immediately," Theobald replied, turning to face the angry knight. Nodding to his brother, Reynard went to stand outside at the entrance of the tent.

Richard stepped forward staring at Ingrid with a frown. "I know you…"

Ingrid nodded. "But not formally."

Theobald looked between the two of them wondering where on earth they would have had the chance to meet. "Ingrid Seymour, may I present Lord Richard Grancourt. He is a family friend who is more like a brother to us."

Ingrid and Richard continued to stare upon one another from across the tent. "What am I missing?" Theobald asked.

A knowing look passed between Richard and Ingrid before she spoke up. "Did you find her?"

"Nay," Richard answered, "I did not. She should have never been allowed to go free in the first place."

"'Twas a courtesy… One woman fighting for a cause dear to her heart to another."

"She could be dangerous," Richard continued with a grim expression.

"Aye… I suppose she could be just as we are dangerous in our own right to pursue what we view as a just cause," Ingrid said whilst she made an attempt to appear steady on her feet.

Theobald shook his head. "I hate to interrupt this discussion that makes sense only to the two of you, but we have more pressing matters at hand," he said with a frown marring his brow. "Richard… if you do not mind… would you give us a few moments to settle what is between the three of us?"

"Of course," Richard replied before he gave a slight bow to Ingrid. "My lady…"

There was a moment of silence before the two remaining men began yelling over each other.

"What are you doing here?" Theobald began.

"What if de Payne had come back to do her harm again?" Oswin continued with clenched fists. "Do you think she is well enough to even lift her sword to protect herself?"

Ingrid came to stand between them. "Enough! Both of you.

By the Blessed Virgin Mary, I have had enough of the two of you squabbling over me like two roosters in a hen house." She swayed, and Theobald came to steady her.

His arm wound its way around her waist. "Ingrid, should I fetch the surgeon?"

"Nay. I am fine, Theo," she whispered, "just tired." They both turned to stare upon Oswin waiting for him to take the hint to leave.

"Obviously, I have outstayed my welcome," he grumbled. "Ingrid, please send someone to find me if you have need of my company."

"She will not," Theobald answered for her before she swatted him.

"Behave…" Ingrid said. Making her way to Oswin she gave him a small smile. "I thank you for your concern for my welfare but as you can see, I am mending perfectly well."

Oswin nodded, his gaze traveling to Theobald before he returned his attention to the lady. "And mayhap, your heart is not as yet spoken for…" His words trailed off as though he knew what her answer would be.

"I believe it may have already been claimed. I hope we can remain friends," she replied shyly.

"Friends? Aye, I suppose if there is no chance for me to win your favor, I must needs bow out. One can never have too many friends to watch your back, eh Theobald?" Oswin jested. "Mistress Ingrid… Norwood…"

Oswin gave a short bow and left leaving an awkward silence in his dwelling. 'Twas clear Oswin wished to claim the lady whereas Theobald had the same notion. But she told Oswin that her heart may have been claimed and this was a promising sign giving Theobald hope. When he gave Ingrid his full attention, he noticed her steadying herself whilst leaning on their table. A basket sat upon it and he lifted the linen covering over the wicker hamper. The remains of a meal were inside. He flicked the fabric closed and noticed a small book. Apparently, Oswin was not the only one who had visited Ingrid this day.

"You have had company," he complained bitterly.

"But not the company I desired. At least until now," she answered with a bright smile.

He went to Ingrid, placing his hand at her waist. She stepped closer, reaching up to wind her own hand around his neck. Her fingers massaged his neck. He pulled her closer.

"Who else besides Oswin has been visiting you this day?" he asked as morbid curiosity ran amuck inside his head.

"Must we talk about them? They are your friends and now mine, I suppose."

"Friends?"

"Aye. They have no hold over me beyond friendship. They only came to see to how I fared. Can I assume you were also concerned, and this is what took you away from the battlefield?" Her voice held a silky tone that went straight to his pounding heart. "Also... did I not see flowers being thrust into your brother's hands when you thought you were interrupting something that to me was of no import? I assume they were for me." Her hazel eyes twinkled mischievously.

The flowers! He had forgotten all about them when jealousy had overtaken him seeing Oswin on bended knee. Theobald tried to turn to fetch them, but she held firm. "I should retrieve them from my brother. I thought you might like them."

"I love them, but please wait to fetch them later..." Pressure from her hand had him bending forward until his lips were but inches from her own.

"Are you certain you wish for this, Ingrid?" God help him if she suddenly changed his mind.

"Aye. Now kiss me, Theobald, and give me what I have been missing my entire life."

'Twas as though the heavens shined down upon them at her words. He brushed his lips over hers giving her small kisses and allowing her the last chance to change her mind before things went any further. But far from pulling away, she pulled him closer until their chests rose as one. The breaths mingled together until Theobald could stand this sweet torture no longer.

His lips overtook hers in a hungry possession. His tongue swept into her mouth to dance with her own until he lost all common sense. His heart beat fiercely, consumed by the sensations of finally holding this woman against his body. A soft moan escaped her, and Theobald held back one of his own. As much as he wished to stay with Ingrid and finish what they started, he was still needed to fight for their cause.

"Theo…" She whispered his name as if her soul was reaching out to his own. It was almost enough to cause him to change his mind about returning to the battlefield. *Almost…*

Reluctantly, he pulled back from her. Desire sparkled in her eyes like the brightest star in the sky. "Ingrid, we cannot continue what we have started just now," he said, placing a quick kiss upon her forehead.

"But I thought…"

"'Tis not that I do not wish for this to continue but I am needed," he began and at her quizzical look he continued, "to return to the fighting, my dear."

"Oh… aye… of course, the battle. How silly of me to forget," she said turning her back to him.

He came and turned her around. He placed his forehead against her own whilst her hands wrapped around his waist. "I will also not dishonor you by taking what has begun between us too far without the blessings of a priest. We have time to continue to get to know one another to ensure we might wish to wed," he proclaimed, coming to the conclusion that she would take him for her husband when the time was right.

"Are you declaring your intentions, Sir Theobald?" she asked with what appeared like hope filling her eyes.

"When the time is right," he repeated. Placing a soft kiss upon her lips as though sealing his vow, he turned to leave. "Reynard will be outside if you have need of anything."

"Theobald," she called out after he opened the flap of the

tent.

He peered over his shoulder. "Aye?"

"Be safe," she said, giving him an encouraging smile.

He nodded and left. His brief reprieve from the battle over, he would thrust himself back into the fighting as though to finish this once and for all—with the hopes of gaining lands and monies in return for his valor. Only then could he court the fair Ingrid as she so deserved.

CHAPTER SIXTEEN

INGRID SNEEZED, RUBBED her nose then her irritated eyes. She was unsure what had disturbed her slumber. Something was definitely wrong, but her mind was still hazy whilst wishing to return to dreaming the morn away. She turned over, placing her hand beneath her cheek. Smiling, she began recalling her visions and more importantly her kiss with Theobald. 'Twas everything she had wished for and more. She cared for the man, that much was clear. If his response was any sort of an indication of what he felt for her, she could be nearly certain that he favored her, too. She stretched, still relishing the memory, until she realized what had caused her to awake in the first place. Smoke!

She dressed quickly, a sense of urgency overwhelming her as to the danger that surely must be nearby. She was just putting her sword in her scabbard when Theobald rushed into the tent. His eyes scanned the dark interior before starting to light several candles. He began to collect his things.

"What is happening, Theo?" she asked in concern.

"You must needs grab what you can," Theobald ordered whilst he continued rushing through their dwelling, tossing garments and whatever necessities that could fit into a satchel. He turned to her. "Do you need help?"

She shook her head finally coming out the daze that had held her in place. She was unsure what she needed to take with her that she did not already have on. She did not own many possessions. The speed with which Theobald was moving through the tent spurred her into motion. Her own satchel sat on the floor nearby and she grabbed it. "Will you tell me why we are in such a rush?"

He stopped mid-stride to stare upon her with a worried frown. "Can you not smell it?"

Clothes were rapidly stuffed into her bag with little thought of wrinkles. "Smoke but such is common during a siege."

"Aye, well, in most situations this might be true. But there has been a development. The bishop fled when the Empress laid siege to Wolvesey. The garrison, apparently acting on his orders before he left, decided that throwing burning material from the walls would be a good distraction. The fools! They have set fire to Winchester. Already, a section of the city is in ruins. If this continues, there will not be much left."

"Good heavens! Where are we going?"

"The Empress has requested I make my way to the royal castle. She wants me close by in the event she has need of me. You, my dear, are coming with me."

"Is that allowed?" she asked. A frown marred her brow as she wondered if she would be welcome in the castle. She had not been schooled in the art of courtly manners nor had she learned to adhere to the dictates the ladies of an empress's court must needs follow. She was a simple woman, with simple taste. She was quickly overwhelmed with thoughts of making a fool of herself.

"Allowed or not, your welfare matters to me. Hence, you must needs hurry. I am far from certain that this tent will survive the fire. We shall have to hope for the best that anything left behind shall survive."

"But shall we be safe at the castle?" she asked.

"As safe as any other place. We must protect the Empress. If she decides she must flee the city, then we will guarantee she has a strong contingent of guards to ensure her safety."

They worked in silence until they had packed what they could. She quickly grabbed the flowers Theobald had given her and shoved them into her satchel. If they survived, she would press them into a book. Theobald took a firm grip of her hand. Leaning down, he placed a quick kiss upon her lips before ushering her from the tent. She took one last look backwards until the flap at the opening fell into place. Reynard was outside, holding the reins of his horse along with Theobald's and Ingrid's. He was not alone. Nearby were Richard, Blake, Oswin, and Kingsley as they waited for Theobald and Ingrid to mount their steeds.

Theobald tossed his satchel to Reynard who began to attach it to Theobald's saddle. Ingrid stood near her horse while Theobald took her bag and began doing the same. He then cupped his hands together. She placed her foot in his palms and when he lifted her up, she swung her leg over her steed. She tried not to flinch from the pain when she settled into her saddle. No need to worry Theobald. He handed her the leather reins and then placed his hand upon her leg.

"Ride hard. Stay close," he ordered.

"I will," she declared offering him a slight smile of encouragement.

Theobald gave her a nod, went to his own horse, and took up the reins. "Help me keep Ingrid safe," he demanded of the men he rode with. He kicked his heels into Buttercup's side, putting the horse into motion and taking the lead. The other knights quickly placed their mounts in a circle around Ingrid. 'Twas as if she was in a cocoon-like barrier, safe from the turmoil that she was about to encounter. Surrounded with knights who would die on her behalf, they swiftly rode through the burning city.

Everywhere Ingrid gazed, there was fire and ruined buildings while ash and smoke filled the air turning day into night. People formed lines whilst they passed buckets of water to put out the flames of one structure after another. Their faces were streaked with soot and sweat. Children cried out for their parents. Merchants attempted to save what they could from their marketplace stalls. All around her there was complete wreckage and chaos. Theobald was right… there would not be much left to save if the bishop's men continued this rampage to burn the city to the ground.

They stopped for no one, and Ingrid's heart went out to those who appeared frightened and bewildered about what they should do next. She wanted to halt her horse and help these poor souls, but Theobald and his men gave her no such opportunity. Their mission was clear. Get to the castle. Protect the Empress. Anything else was of little consequence, no matter how much the villagers' situation broke Ingrid's heart. She would have thought she was made of sterner stuff considering the lives she took whilst upon the battlefield. But suffering inflicted on children and the elderly was a different matter. Mayhap she would be able to help them in some other capacity once inside the protective walls of the castle.

Burning embers floated in the air like dangerous fireflies. On more than one occasion, Ingrid swatted the hot specks away from her face and exposed skin. But soon, their fast pace had them leaving the fires behind. They reached the castle without incident, the barbican gate opening as though by magic when Theobald hailed the guards above. The intimidating portcullis, with its wooden spikes to kill any enemy, fell back into place once they were through the barrier to the outside world. Theobald was expected, this much was clear, proving to Ingrid the Empress held her knight in the highest regard. She trusted him to obey her orders and keep her safe. But where would this leave Ingrid?

Uncertain what her future might now hold, Ingrid led her horse into the bailey still surrounded with her trusty knights. She looked over to Oswin who rode to her right, surprised when she found him gazing upon her.

"You are worried," he murmured. Turning his head forward, he appeared as though he was embarrassed to be caught staring in her direction.

"I did not say I was worried." Her head lifted as she tried to rouse her courage for whatever she was about to face.

Oswin reached over and patted her hand before straightening upright in his saddle. "You did not need to speak the words, Ingrid. I can see your emotions written all over your face."

She gasped. "You can?"

"Do not worry," he chuckled with a wink. "Your secret is safe with me.

Easygoing Oswin. Leave it to this knight to put her fears to rest with but a few simple words. She wanted to say something to let him know she appreciated his kindness, but they came to a halt before she could voice anything. Theobald dismounted first, immediately coming over to her. He raised his hands to assist her from the saddle. The moment she rested her hands upon his shoulders, a zing of emotions caused her heart to lurch inside her chest. He lowered her slowly down his body, the simple gesture only serving to heighten her emotions as she felt every glorious inch of him. Good heavens! What this man did to her senses.

Their horses were taken away to the stables, yet he still held her close. He inspected her as if for injuries and instead chuckled.

"What amuses you so?" she asked, curious what could be so humorous about the situation they had just fled.

He took off one of this leather gloves. His finger slowly ran down her cheek before showing her the dirty mark it left behind. "I am afraid, Ingrid, we are covered with soot and ash…"

"…and in need of a bath, I suppose," she finished for him with a devious smile. Her eyes roamed over his visage taking in his own disheveled appearance after their flight to the castle. Her teasing caused his laugh to boom over the noise in the courtyard and she realized her words could be misconstrued to imply that they should bathe together. Heaven forbid! She was bold but not that bold… yet!

She fingered his shoulder length hair, twirling one of the dark tresses with her fingertips. Licking her dry lips, his eyes became wide at her action. He leaned forward to kiss her. She closed her eyes in anticipation, for she craved his lips upon her own.

"Sir Theobald!" a voice called out breaking their shared moment together. A low groan rumbled in his chest before they broke apart. An emissary for the Empress stood at the steps to the keep. "Our Empress requests your presence in the great hall."

"We are coming," he answered before tucking Ingrid's hand in the crook of his arm.

Terrified of meeting the Empress looking like she just crawled out of a hearth, she pulled Theobald's arm bringing them to a standstill. "I cannot meet the Empress appearing like this, Theo," she said in alarm.

"You have no need to fear, Ingrid. If you but look closely, everyone around you is unfortunately in the same predicament. Now come along. 'Tis best not to keep Empress Matilda waiting."

She glanced over her shoulder to Richard, Oswin, Blake and Kingsley. No help was forthcoming from them. A last silent pleading to Reynard only rewarded her with a bright smile. His teeth looking snow white in a face covered in black soot. Dear Lord! If she appeared just as filthy, she would surely pass out from complete humiliation!

CHAPTER SEVENTEEN

THEOBALD ENTERED THE keep of the royal castle. His stride was confident, knowing he was about to meet with the Empress. A brief glance down at Ingrid confirmed she was terrified. Mayhap the best recourse was to attempt to keep her out of view. But he would not assume such a course without first asking Ingrid if that was what she desired, too.

He bent forward to whisper in her ear. "Would you prefer to stay hidden behind the rest of the men? I cannot promise our Empress will not notice you anyway, for she is very astute, but 'tis worth a try if you are not comfortable in her presence." Relief appeared to flood her visage.

"Aye!" she murmured raising tormented eyes to his. "I do not wish to give her such a bad first impression."

A chuckle rumbled inside his chest. He squeezed her hand to give her the comfort she stood in need of. "Nothing could be farther from the truth, my dear. You are as suitable to be one of the Empress's guards as any man here standing. You have proved yourself on the battlefield. Do not forget your own worth."

Her eyes glistened with gratitude. "Aye… the fighting I can handle and is not my concern."

His brow rose. "Then what is causing your obvious distress?"

Ingrid sighed, then squared her shoulders back. "Fitting in at court."

He nodded, understanding how ill at ease she might feel in such an unfamiliar environment. He took her elbow before turning to the men who had been following directly behind him. "Keep her behind you and out of direct sight of our Empress. Reynard, up front with me."

The men made a path for Ingrid, Oswin in particular seemed entirely too pleased if the smirk on his face was any indication of how he felt about the situation. Theobald had no time to reconsider his request nor to chastise the man. In his heart, he knew Oswin had good intentions toward Ingrid just as he, himself, did. She was as safe as she could be with any of the knights who now provided a protective shield in front of the lady. But he doubted Ingrid would be out of sight for long. Her red hair was still just as much a problem as when he himself first espied the woman, even though her tresses were covered in ash and soot. The color was still a beacon, drawing attention to her. And once anyone with half a brain in their head took the time to look closely at her, they would be sure to notice the lady's gender.

They entered the great hall without ceremony for what was there to celebrate with the city ablaze all around them? There were few people in the room—merely the Empress, three lady attendants who stood behind her, and a few guards. Normally, there would be any number of people paying court to the Empress, but on this day, they were nowhere to be found. Theobald and Reynard were waved forward. They dropped to one knee and bowed their heads.

"My Empress," Theobald said. "How may I be of service to you?"

"The Norwood brothers, ever faithful to my cause," Empress Matilda replied looking over their shoulders to the men behind them. "Is that Grancourt I see as well?"

Richard stepped forward. "Aye, my Empress."

"Come closer so that I might see you better," she ordered, and Richard also fell down to one knee. "Still following the Norwoods, Grancourt?" she asked. A corner of her mouth lifted with a knowing grin.

"Or they are following me, Empress. In either case, I willingly fight by their side as I did when I followed Lord Wymar into battle at Lincoln."

"Aye, and such a glorious battle that was with the capture of that usurper, Stephen. I wish I could say things here at Winchester were going according to my plans. But alas, such is not the case." She waved her hand and the men rose to their feet.

Theobald placed his hand on the hilt of his sword. "I am certain 'tis but a temporary setback, Empress Matilda. We would willingly lay down our lives to help place you on the throne."

The Empress nodded her head. "Let us hope the situation does not come to that. I have no doubt as to the faithfulness of those who currently surround me. You and your brothers have served me well this past year. Grancourt, as well. 'Tis my hope that we may still yet win the day and this city."

Reynard inched forward. "We shall do all in our power to make it so."

The Empress held out a hand and a chalice was placed in her grasp. She took a sip and then handed the cup back to her attendant. "And tell me, young Reynard, how was your older brother faring since you were the last to see him? Is he enjoying marital bliss?"

Reynard nodded with a slight bow. "Thanks to your graciousness in allowing him to marry Lady Ceridwen."

"They were a good match despite the lady's refusal to follow my orders to stay at Norwich originally. I assumed that they would learn to love one another and would make an amicable union," she said, talking as though she had initiated their first meeting. "I was sorry to hear of her father's passing, but I know the lands are in good hands with her steward."

"I ensured all was in order before leaving, Empress Matilda," Richard stated before he was waved back into place with the other knights that stood behind Theobald and Reynard.

"I had no doubt such was the case, Grancourt," she murmured before glancing behind Theobald.

Theobald leaned to the side, hoping to distract the Empress.

"Mayhap you can inform us how we might serve you better whilst residing inside the castle?" he inquired praying that his ploy would work. Her next words told him that he had failed.

"Who is that you are all trying to hide? Hopefully 'tis not more rabble like those outside my gates."

Theobald frowned at her words. "You mean the rabble that makes up your army, madam? The same rabble who fights in your name or protects you? Is this the rabble you speak of?" he fumed.

The corners of the Empress's mouth turned upward in amusement. "You have some nerve, Norwood, to be so miffed with me or at least speak your thoughts aloud. And here I thought to bestow lands and a title upon you upon my success in gaining the throne." She sat back in her chair waiting for the apology she knew he would utter.

"I meant no disrespect, my Empress, only that those who serve you do so with a loyalty—"

"—that I demand of all those who surround me," she finished with a frown. She turned her attention once more to Ingrid, and Theobald knew he was unable to stop whatever would happen next.

"I am but your humble servant," Theobald replied with another bow of total obedience. He could do no less, and Reynard silently followed his actions.

"Of course, you are, Norwood. Now… Come forward, young man with the red hair, and address your Empress," she demanded.

The knights parted and Ingrid made her way forward. Theobald and Reynard made a space between them, and Ingrid fell to her knees. "My Empress," she said in a hushed town. There was no mistaking her voice as anything other than that of a woman.

"Good heavens! Another lady fighting for my cause," Empress Matilda uttered in disbelief. "What is it with you Norwoods? Can you not leave these women where they belong—at home and not on the battlefield where they risk their lives?"

Ingrid quickly rose to her feet. "'Tis not their fault, Empress. I am here of my own accord."

The Empress lifted her brow in what could only be termed curiosity. "Are you now? No one has forced you to follow the camp to become—"

"Nay, Empress!" Ingrid shouted at the implied reference she was one of the whores who serviced the men.

"Quiet!" the Empress ordered those in attendance in her court as the whisperings became louder. She returned her gaze to Theobald. "And is this woman competent enough with a sword to hold her own during the fighting?"

"More than capable, my Empress, else she would not be found on the battlefield. I myself ensured she could wield her blade as well as any man who serves you," Theobald answered honestly.

The Empress drummed her fingers on the wooden arm of her chair. "I see," she murmured whilst her eyes once more scanned Ingrid from head to toe. "What is your name, girl?"

"Ingrid Seymour," she answered.

"Seymour… And from where do you hail, Ingrid Seymour?" the Empress inquired.

"A small farm outside of London," Ingrid answered.

The Empress remained silent for a moment. "Interesting… I once knew a knight who went by the surname of Seymour but he was certainly no farmer and his lands were in Wales," she stated, turning her gaze to Theobald.

"And what is this woman to you, Norwood?" the Empress asked.

"I have offered her my protection," Theobald said. He tore his eyes from the Empress to look down upon Ingrid whilst a smile etched itself across her face. A moment passed between them until the Empress cleared her throat. Theobald shook himself out of the spell Ingrid had temporarily cast upon him with just one look.

"I see…" the Empress said. With a wave of her hand, she

motioned for Ingrid to step closer. "I can ascertain for myself the temptation you might cause my knights if you were to continue to fight by their side, no matter how great my cause."

"But, my Empress," Ingrid began. The Empress raised her hand and Ingrid looked back upon Theobald with wide eyes.

"Norwood, I release you from whatever vow you have made to this woman," the Empress said. Before he could reply, he was silenced with another gesture and clamped his mouth shut. "This woman shall now become one of my attendants. 'Tis a far greater honor than hefting a blade that might cause her to lose her life, not that I do not appreciate her efforts on my behalf."

"I am honored," Ingrid replied before kneeling down once more in homage to the Empress who held out her hand. Ingrid took her fingertips and kissed the signet ring. The Empress then stood and all those in attendance dropped to one knee and bowed their heads.

"Now rise, young lady, and follow me. The rest of you will be shown to chambers to await my orders."

Ingrid held back in order to catch Theobald's gaze and when their eyes met, he witnessed her look of anguish that showed how terrified she truly was. Given no other alternative, Ingrid was quickly whisked away from his view. Theobald's audience with Empress Matilda was at an end as was his duty to watch over the fair Ingrid.

◆━━━━•━━◦◦◦━━•━━━━◆

CHAPTER EIGHTEEN

INGRID SAT BEFORE the hearth in a bedchamber she had been assigned to by one of the Empress's lady attendants. Wrapped in a blanket to hide her nudity after her bath, a servant was drying her hair. The bedchamber itself was grand… far grander than anything Ingrid had ever been in. Her gaze swept the room from the large bed to a sturdy oak chest along one wall. A table and chair were placed near the shuttered window that could serve as a desk. Another small table holding a cup of wine for her pleasure was situated between her chair and the one opposite her now occupied by Lady Eden Howlande.

Ingrid's hand shook as she reached for her wine, the chalice encrusted with jewels worth a small fortune. Taking a sip, she observed the lady across from her with lowered lids. Eden… She certainly appeared as though she belonged in Eden for the woman appeared as beautiful as any heavenly garden brought down to earth by God himself. Blonde hair hung loose to below her waist. Her gown was covered with jewels that would see a village fed for an entire year. Blue eyes rivaling the clearest sky were framed in a face with creamy white skin. The woman looked as if she belonged in a painting and not sitting in a castle with a fire burning outside its gates and throughout the city.

As if the lady knew she was being inspected, their eyes met, and Lady Eden gave Ingrid a soft smile. The woman reached for her own cup and gave a silent salute. Placing her goblet back down, she folded her perfectly shaped fingers in her lap and Ingrid could only ponder how she would be judged. After all, a lady such as this had nothing in common with a woman who spent her life on a farm or hefting a sword in the Empress's name. Ingrid did not have long to wait for her answer.

"You have been blessed to be selected as one of the Empress's ladies. You must have questions," Lady Eden said in a kindly manner, surprising Ingrid.

"Blessed? I am not certain the Empress has chosen wisely, my lady. I am far from what is expected of a lady who attends court." Ingrid took another sip of her wine to fortify herself. What the devil was she doing here and when would she see Theobald?

"The Empress rarely makes a mistake when choosing those she keeps close to her. As you can probably surmise, there are few of us she trusts—with good reason," Lady Eden answered quietly before continuing. "The tasks of attending our Empress can be taught, but you cannot teach someone to be loyal."

"Aye, but I am a commoner and not some titled lady. I have no notion on how or what I must needs do to become one who follows her court. I am a simple woman with simple needs and am far more comfortable with my sword in my hand."

A short laugh escaped the lady. "I am certain the days of you swinging a blade are over, Mistress Ingrid, along with remaining in the company of men."

A groan escaped her. "I suppose I can somehow manage whatever may be thrust my way once my clothes have been laundered and returned to me." Ingrid's hopes of being back in her hose and tunic were quickly dashed when Lady Eden's sweet, bubbly laughter burst from her lips.

"Oh, Ingrid! You are truly a delight. You shall not be wearing the clothes you arrived in, my dear," she said before patting her hair back into place, not that even one strand was amiss.

Before Ingrid could reply, the bedchamber door opened and in walked Lady Rovena Eatone and Lady Petula Wintere. Ingrid had been introduced to the pair prior to her bath and now they returned with enough fabric to make the dead groan in fear. They began placing a dress and other under garments on the bed.

Ingrid's eyes became wide in horror. Not a gown! Good heavens. She could not even remember the last time she had donned one. "Where are my clothes?" she asked biting her lip.

Lady Rovena's gaze was torn from the pretty dark blue fabric to stare upon Ingrid as though the answer was obvious. "This will be yours, now. Lady Petula and I thought this gown would fit, and we can alter the fabric as necessary, can we not, Petula?"

Lady Petula nodded whilst she set various threads and needles on the desk. "Aye. I came prepared to either take the hem in or out. Shall we get started?"

Ingrid clutched the fabric of the blanket closer to her chest. "Started? Started with what?"

"Making you presentable for our Empress." Lady Eden stood and motioned to the servant. "You can leave us now. We can take care of the rest."

The servant bobbed a curtsey and with a hasty *milady*, left the room.

Lady Rovena came over and began braiding some of Ingrid's hair but left the majority of her red locks to flow in heavy natural curls down her back. Once she was finished, she took Ingrid's hands and *tsk tsk*ed over them, muttering how the calluses that took years to form made Ingrid's hands rough. A soothing balm was rubbed into her palms by Lady Petula whilst Lady Eden made her way to the bed.

Oh no! Ingrid thought when each of the lady's took up various pieces of what could only be termed torture devices that would make her completely miserable. "Honestly, my ladies, I cannot wear such clothing. 'Twill be stifling and not allow me to breathe properly. Also, it may impede the healing of my recent injury," Ingrid insisted when Lady Eden came forward in an attempt for Ingrid to drop the blanket.

Lady Petula halted her progress across the room whilst Lady Rovena's eyes widened in concern.

"You have been injured in battle? No one mentioned this to

us." Rovena scowled coming before Ingrid and making an attempt to lift a portion of the blanket she held close to her chest. "Let me assess the damage so we might call a surgeon to look upon the wound if necessary."

Ingrid pulled the material closer to her body and swatted the woman's hands away. "I have had a surgeon see to the wound. Theobald and his friends saw that the injury was well looked after."

Rovena placed her hands on her hips. "Bah! What do men know? They probably stitched your wound with no care to avoid leaving you with a nasty scar afterwards."

Petula placed one of the undergarments back upon the bed. "Mayhap we can leave off one of the layers," she suggested.

Ingrid still winced at the thought of wearing a gown. "I would rather don the garments I arrived in."

"You have little choice, Ingrid, and you may as well get used to your new life for 'tis about to drastically change… for the better, I hope," Lady Eden stated. "Now drop the blanket so we may get started. We will do our best to ensure we do no further damage to your wound, but we must work swiftly. The Empress does not like to be kept waiting."

"But, my lady…" Ingrid began to protest only to be cut off by Lady Petula.

"And you must call us by our first names… none of this *my lady* business. We shall be spending a fair amount of time in each other's company so there is no need to be so formal unless in the presence of Her Majesty." Petula's look was one that she would not take no for an answer and before Ingrid could voice another objection, the three ladies took matters into their own hands.

She shivered when the blanket keeping her warm left her body. Yet she had little time to contemplate this new hell she had been thrust into. Rovena *tsk tsked* when she carefully examined the wound and then told the other ladies they could proceed. A thin white chemise was quickly placed over her head and fell over her body reaching to the floor. Next came a light blue undertunic.

Ingrid pushed her arms through the sleeves that came to points over the back of her hands. Already she was dreading the weight of the full-length dark blue gown. Her apprehension proved to be well placed when the weight of the garment nearly consumed her. She took deep gulps of air to try and calm the rising panic inside her chest. Would this torture never cease?

Rovena placed two pairs of soft leather slippers on the floor for Ingrid to step into. Looking at her choices, she instantly knew one set would be too small, so she placed her right foot into one of the others. A perfect fit. She lifted her left foot into the other. Next, a golden chain with a sparkling blue gem at the end was fastened at her waist. A matching necklace was efficiently clasped around her neck with the bauble landing perfectly in the center of her cleavage. Rovena secured earrings to the lobes of her ears, completing their efforts to make her appear ladylike. Ingrid felt certain in her heart that they failed until Eden clapped her hands, apparently satisfied.

"Beautiful!" she replied before motioning with her finger for Ingrid to turn so they could observe the full effect.

Petula grinned. "You were right, Rovena. Your gown fit her perfectly!"

"I told you it would," Rovena answered as she, too, smiled, "and your jewels were the perfect addition to her ensemble for the night."

Ingrid smoothed the soft fabric of the gown and then reached for the end of the chain at her waist to inspect gem attached at its end. "These are yours?" she asked watching them both nod. "You are too kind and generous."

"'Twas nothing," they replied in unison before bursting out in a chorus of giggles.

Ingrid was humbled at their efforts to make her appear, at least on the surface, presentable. "I do not know how I shall be able to repay you."

Eden stepped forward to clasp her hands in Ingrid's. "There is nothing you must repay. We take care of one another along with the Empress. You are one of us now."

Rovena clapped her hands together "You will turn all the men's heads tonight at the evening meal."

"Oh, aye! She will indeed," Petula chimed in.

Ingrid's eyes widened again. "But I do not wish to turn anyone's head. I would rather stay out of sight."

Eden linked her arm through Ingrid's, and they began to make their way toward the door. "No more hiding, Ingrid. You are now one of the Empress's ladies in waiting. You are meant to be seen, elsewise the Empress would not have chosen you. Now come, we must attend Her Majesty and see that she, too, is adorned in her very best."

A short walk down the torch-lit passageway and soon they came to another bedchamber with two guards standing at its door. One of the knights gave a brief nod before he opened the wooden portal. If Ingrid thought her bedchamber had been grand, 'twas nothing compared to the room she now entered. Wealth was in abundance in every corner of the room as though the Empress traveled with her entire treasury. Gold objects glimmered in the candlelight and Ingrid gawked until she heard the Empress's voice.

"You four took long enough. The water grows cold, so attend me," she ordered, and the three other women quickly snapped into place as if this was a well-practiced dance. It was clear they had performed their duties hundreds of times in the past. Ingrid felt out of place and unsure what she was required to do so she stood out of their way whilst they assisted the Empress from her bath.

Eden caught her attention whilst she nodded to a pitcher holding what Ingrid assumed was wine. She hurried over to the table, picked up a silver encrusted goblet and began to fill the cup. She went to hand the wine to the Empress who took the chalice and peered at Ingrid over its rim before taking a sip. She handed the goblet back and Ingrid placed the cup back on the table.

"You clean up very well, Mistress Ingrid," Empress Matilda

stated. "Turn around so I may see the full effect." Ingrid did as she was told and once she faced the Empress again, she lowered her eyes. "Aye… very well indeed."

"You are too gracious, Your Majesty." Ingrid's voice was so low she wondered if the Empress had even heard her reply. But there was no further time to ponder such matters. Not when the ladies began to dress their monarch for the evening meal. Whereas Ingrid felt as though she herself was highly overdressed for any occasion, the Empress's attire was nothing short of magnificent as the lady should appear before her subjects, right down to the diamond band that surrounded her headpiece. Once she was completely gowned, she took a seat near the hearth and motioned for Ingrid to take the vacant chair opposite her. Ingrid's eyes widened as she realized that she was expected to sit next to the Empress.

"Sit down, girl, for heaven's sake," Empress Matilda ordered. "I do not wish to strain my neck while we have a private word together."

Ingrid gulped and once again did as she was told. What else could she do? She waited for the Empress until she began speaking to her other ladies. "Lady Eden, you may stay, the rest of you may leave us and head to the great hall. We shall join you shortly."

Lady Petula and Lady Rovena, along with the remaining servants in the room, left promptly, leaving Ingrid to again wonder why in the world the Empress wanted to have a private conversation with her. Ingrid did not have long to wait, although she did so with bated breath.

"You mentioned your father was a farmer and you lived outside of London," the Empress said holding out her hand. Lady Eden promptly went to the table to fetch the goblet Ingrid had filled earlier.

"Aye, Your Majesty."

"And his name again?" she inquired taking a sip of her wine.

"Harold. Harold Seymour, Your Majesty," Ingrid answered.

"And your mother?"

Ingrid cast a quick glance as Lady Eden who nodded for her to continue. "Jonet Seymour."

"French?" the Empress continued, causing Ingrid to wonder what the monarch was after.

"I cannot say for sure, Your Majesty. She died giving birth to me."

"Interesting." Empress Matilda paused in her questioning before handing Lady Eden the goblet of wine. "Fetch me Mistress Ingrid's sword, Lady Eden. You shall find the blade has been placed near my bed."

Lady Eden did as she was ordered. When the Empress held out her hands, Lady Eden placed the scabbard into her waiting palms. The Empress pulled the sword from the sheath. "These markings on the hilt," she began pointing to the etchings. "Do you know from whence they hail and what they represent?"

A frown marred Ingrid's brow. "No, my Empress. My father never went into any detail about them once he had given me the blade as a present. He said 'twas his from his youth but that is all he would ever say on the matter no matter how hard I pressed for an answer."

"And you know nothing of his childhood? His parents? Or from whence he, or your mother, hailed?"

"I only know he met my mother whilst traveling abroad until they made their home in our village. He would never speak of his upbringing only to say his parents were not pleased when he wed someone not of their choosing," Ingrid replied, curious now as to what her father may not have told her.

"Interesting…" The Empress returned the blade back into the scabbard. "See that this is returned to Mistress Ingrid's chamber. A gift such as this must not be misplaced."

"Aye, my Empress," Lady Eden replied before taking the sword and leaving the room.

The Empress rose, causing Ingrid to stumble as she, too, quickly gained her feet without tripping over her gown. The

Empress took another long look at Ingrid. "I have my suspicions about the truth of your parentage. I will not speak further on the subject until I have confirmed the matter. Needless to say, Mistress Ingrid, I do not think you are only some commoner from an obscure village in my realm. But we shall see."

Ingrid was more confused than ever. This day only continued to become worse and worse. What was the Empress trying to tell her and more importantly what had her father kept secret?

CHAPTER NINETEEN

THEOBALD AND HIS men entered the great hall for the evening meal. Noticeably absent was the Empress and, more importantly, her new lady in waiting. He took a place at one of the tables and his friends and brother began filling the empty spaces around him. His day that had begun as a nightmare to see Ingrid to the safety of the castle had become one of inner torment knowing he was no longer bound to her by honor. Mentally, he could in no way shake the emotions consuming him, telling him that he must needs keep his vow to protect her by any means possible.

He ran his fingers down the forest green tunic, one of the last clean garments he owned that was presentable for an evening meal with his monarch. The rest of his clothing had been given to a servant to see that they were laundered. If he were to be in the presence of his Empress for days on end, he would need to appear well-dressed. While the fighting was at an end for the day, Theobald had no doubt 'twould resume come the morn and yet it appeared that for now, his fighting days outside the walls were at an end. He supposed keeping the Empress safe was an honor, but he felt he could achieve more by raising his sword against her enemies. Apparently, the Empress felt she would prefer to keep him close.

Reynard gave him a nudge and Theobald came out of his musings inside his head. "You are too deep in thought, brother. Come now and make merry like the days of old when you were carefree instead of a knight where chaos appears to follow you!" Reynard said thrusting a cup of wine into Theobald's hand.

"*Knight of Chaos*... you give me a new nickname that somehow does not seem to suit me," Theobald said with a sly grin. "Surely, I have not earned such a labeling."

Reynard chuckled. "Look outside and see what is before you."

A low grumble left him. "'Tis hardly my fault the city is burning to the ground."

Reynard took a sip of his wine. "Mayhap not, but trouble does seem to follow you of late, especially since you met a certain red-haired temptress."

Theobald twirled the cup in his hand and then raised the goblet to his lips. Taking a sip, he closed his eyes as the sweetness of the wine worked its magic when the heady liquid slid down his throat. There was something to be said for a good wine.

When he opened his eyes, he saw those around him staring. "What?" he gruffly asked.

Richard was the first to reply. "You appear troubled, my friend."

"'Tis nothing," Theobald replied hoping to brush off any concerns regarding the fair Ingrid.

Blake laughed. "Hardly! 'Tis apparent you are in a foul mood at the loss of your little bird."

"Aye," Oswin chimed in. "But do not fear, Theobald. She is certainly in good company as a newly appointed lady in waiting for our Empress."

Reynard took a long drink of his own wine before setting down his cup. "Best not to aggravate him, if you know what is best for you," he advised. "Trust me, you will not like the outcome."

Kingsley chuckled. "I think he can stand the jesting on his behalf. Afterall, the fair lady has more than proved to us who she favors."

Oswin grumbled into his cup, clearly annoyed he had not

been chosen. "More's the pity," he finally muttered.

Theobald eyed the group not wishing to add to their jesting of him. "I am certain Mistress Ingrid is doing just fine in her new appointment."

Oswin slammed his goblet onto the table. *"By God's Bones!* Do you not know the lady at all?" he shouted whilst coming to a stand. "She will be miserable all dressed up in gowns and whatnots! She belongs with us!"

Theobald's brow rose at Oswin's outburst. "Us?" he asked, his tone low and threatening.

"Aye!" Oswin responded before his gaze swept the group. "Fighting amongst us on the battlefield."

The men began to match Oswin's ramblings and Theobald had to agree, at least silently, that he would miss the woman fighting near his side. Oswin was right. Ingrid would indeed be miserable being forced to act like a lady, quiet and demure, confined in heavy dresses. But he also knew that the woman he had come to admire would find a way to handle the situation she had been thrust into despite any reservations she might hold in her heart.

Theobald, however, continued to eye Oswin warily. "She will adapt as she must, or do you not know the lady at all?" he taunted in return, not bothering to rise to Oswin's bait.

Richard waved at Oswin. "Sit down and calm yourself. From the little I know of the woman, I agree with Theobald. Mistress Ingrid will indeed adapt to her new surroundings—as must we all."

"Aye," Blake chimed in. "Wasting our time inside these castle walls will surely be the death of me."

Kingsley nodded. "I much prefer hefting my sword to our enemies who would do our Empress harm."

Theobald took another drink. "We were ordered to attend the Empress and be on hand if she needed to make a quick escape of the city. We should be honored she asked for us with so many who would jump at the opportunity to serve her directly. Let the matter rest. We must adhere to her demands."

The men grumbled their objections but agreed there was not much else they could do. A trumpet blared echoing in the hall announcing the Empress's arrival. And then there *she* was. Ingrid in all her glory, and it took all of Theobald's willpower to prevent himself from rushing to her side.

If he had thought the woman beautiful before, then her appearance now was nothing short of breathtaking. Her hair appeared as though 'twas on fire as it glowed in the light from the torches in the room. Her dark red tresses fell in waves of heavy curls down her back, bouncing with life with each step she took. Her gown fitted her slim body like the garment had been made specifically for her, and the blue color suited her. Costly jewels hung from her neck and ears causing Theobald to assume they had been given to her from the other ladies. They presented a unified front whilst they strode behind their elegantly gowned Empress.

Ingrid began glancing around the room until their eyes met. A weak smile presented itself across her face even whilst Theobald's hungry eyes continued to devour her with every step she advanced into the hall. She gave the briefest of nods before she once more turned her head forward. She lost her footing when her shoe caught in her dress, and she bumped into one of the ladies in front of her. The woman appeared aghast before she whispered something in Ingrid's ear. Ingrid looked as though she mumbled her apologies before she once more began to follow along like a duckling on wobbly legs attempting to keep in step with her mother. He could see for himself she was uncomfortable in her surroundings, and he could hardly blame her. It stood to reason that a farmer's daughter thrust into the world of court would be struggling to find a way to fit in.

They made their way to the raised dais where all who were present would get a full view of the Empress. Once she was seated, her ladies in waiting joined her and Empress Matilda motioned with her hand that the meal could be served. Wine was poured and Ingrid reached for her chalice and took a long sip of the heady drink. She closed her eyes as if in relief before setting the cup down and proceeding to fill the trencher placed in front of her.

"What a beauty," Oswin whispered whilst a chorus of *aye ayes* followed his words.

Theobald certainly could not gainsay his friend's comment for in truth, Ingrid was a true gem among the women who were currently present in the room. In fact, he only had eyes for her. Although she did not glance in his direction again, Theobald was well aware of her every move.

Richard leaned forward. "You best marry her, my friend, before someone else beats you to the honor of requesting her hand."

Blake took up his knife and stabbed at a piece of venison when the platter was put before them. "Aye," he murmured sniffing the meat before placing it on his trencher. "We know of at least one such knight who would like such an honor. Others in this room will surely follow."

All eyes turned to Oswin who grumbled a reply under his breath. "Best leave it be, gents."

Theobald began to fill his trencher until he realized the silence amongst his friends was deafening. "What?" he growled out again, annoyed that they would not leave him in peace to consume his meal and let his thoughts run amok.

Kingsley swallowed his food before replying whilst pointing his fork in Theobald's direction. "You best heed his words, Theobald, or you shall lose a prize worth more than any gold filling your coffers," he said before he began eating again.

Theobald chuckled in his attempt to turn the conversation to get his mind off the lovely Ingrid. "You all spend too much time worrying about my marital status. Come… there is wine to drink and food to fill our bellies. We should make merry as my brother suggested, given we are now in the presence of our Empress."

Oswin's cup stopped midair and instead of taking a sip he

placed the goblet down none too gently. Wine sloshed over the goblets rim. "You do not wish to wed her?"

Theobald knew he could in no way deny his heart's desire. "I did not say I did not wish to make her my wife," he replied quietly. "I only know that for now, I will not take my situation with Ingrid too seriously for if I do, I am sure to lose her. Life has treated me unfairly where women are concerned and I do not wish for it to repeat itself with Mistress Ingrid."

Richard sat back and studied Theobald for a moment until he replied whilst shaking his head. "I have known you for almost my whole life, Theo, and you judge all women based on one from your younger days. I regret I could not warn you about Lady Millicent once I learned of your feelings for her. She was never worthy of your love. But since the day she broke your heart, you hide behind this façade that life is here for only your amusement. I know better, as do you, if you but take the time to look inside your heart. Do not wait too long to claim the fair lady. Elsewise, you may be in the same situation as Wymar once was... pining away for a woman who will never be yours."

'Twas as though Richard's speech pierced a part of Theobald's heart that he had encased in ice for more years than he could remember. The memory of a woman whom he once thought was the love of his life flitted across his mind. He had been young, too young to realize she merely amusing herself with him. He had not thought of her in many a year, nor had he been willing to even speak her name. Flashes of their brief time together sped unwillingly across his mind until that fateful day when she told him she would wed another—one who could provide her with a home, a title, riches—but that she had enjoyed their short time together. From that day forward, he refused to let another woman get close enough to him to allow even a dash of hope that love might find him. At least until now.

And even now, his instincts shouted at him not to move too fast. Surely it would be better to wait until he had proven himself to the Empress, had won an estate for himself, before making his offer. Why would Ingrid ever agree to marry him if she did not believe he could provide her with a comfortable life?

Female laughter from the next table brought Theobald out of his sudden melancholy mood. His friends were once again eating their fill, but Richard's gaze remained on him. He lifted one brow in a silent question and Theobald only shook his head and instead began to eat his fill. There would be time later to figure out how his life might proceed with or without the fair Ingrid. With her newly elevated status as one of the Empress's attendants, it seemed all the more important that he secure his fortune before asking for her hand. He'd need the Empress's blessing to marry one of her ladies, and she would not be likely to give it until he had proven himself.

The evening meal progressed without any further jesting from the men around him. Soon, the tables began to be moved to allow for the eve's dancing. Minstrels tuned their instruments in a corner of the hall. The Empress waved her hand in permission for the entertainment to begin as ladies and knights began pairing off and taking their places in the center of the hall.

Theobald found he could no longer restrain himself when the prospect of taking Ingrid into his arms lay before him. He rose and strode toward the dais, making his bow before Empress Matilda. "With your permission, I would like to ask Mistress Ingrid for this dance."

The Empress nodded her approval and Theobald went over to the lady of his choice and held out his hand. Ingrid rose from her place and made her way around the table. Her cool fingers slid into the palm of his warm hand, and he began to escort her across the room.

"I do not know the steps," she confessed quietly.

"I shall teach you," he stated whilst his gaze swept her body until a rosy blush caressed her cheeks. "You are beautiful tonight."

"'Tis just these garments and jewels that make me so," she said lowering her eyes.

His finger lifted her chin, so she had no choice but to gaze into his eyes. "Nay. Your beauty has always been there for all to see if one only cared to look close enough."

She bit her lip. Theobald wanted to kiss her mouth until those lips were as rosy as her blush and she lost her breath. "I want things to go back to the way they were." Her honest reply that she wished they were together melted a piece of his heart.

"As do I."

"Whatever shall we do, Theo?" she asked in a tone that conveyed her unhappiness.

"Whatever we must," he said for he could give her no shred of hope they would be together any time soon. He did not know what the morrow might bring.

He had no time for a further reply as the music began and he concentrated on teaching the steps of the dance to the lady at his side. She was a quick learner and once the pattern of steps came easily to her, she relaxed. Her laughter rang out and once again another piece of ice was chipped away from his heart. She was a joy to be around, and God help him, but he was falling under her spell. His heart would never be the same.

⎯⎯◆⎯⎯ · ⎯⎯❧❧⎯⎯ · ⎯⎯◆⎯⎯

CHAPTER TWENTY

*S*TRANGLING SMOKE MINGLED *with the fog layering the dew-covered ground. She gasped for air even whilst her boots dampened as she hastened across the battlefield. The sounds of the dead and dying were all but silent now, and yet the voices inside her head screamed for her to hurry to reach the castle and the safety she would find within.*

She stumbled, sliding across the ground where mud mingled with the blood from those who had fallen in their attempts to win the day. A corpse stopped her from skidding further causing a cry of anguish to be yanked from the depths of her soul. Her eyes squinted shut and yet she could not remain this way forever for she needed to continue her way before the gates were closed for the eve.

Finding her courage, she stared once more into the sightless eyes of the dead knight. 'Twas a grim reminder he would forevermore stare up at the morning sky and yet see nothing. Thankfully, a priest would come soon with the rising of the sun to bless the dead, along with those who would carry the bodies away to be buried. Rising to her feet, she cared not that she was covered in mud and blood from her fall. She was yet alive. She had survived the battle. 'Twas all the mattered! But as she began to run once again, the morn started transforming as though someone had turned time against her. Day became night in the time it took her to blink, and she knew she had little chance of gaining entrance to the keep if she did not hasten her steps.

She ran as fast as she was capable. As she approached the barbican gate, no knight called for her to proclaim her allegiance to the Empress. Nay! She walked unhindered straight through the entryway and beneath the deadly portcullis. Making her way into the inner bailey, the place was as quiet as the battlefield had been. There were no servants rushing to and fro with their daily chores, nor did anyone guard the entrance to the keep. She walked up the steps and entered into the foyer to an eerie silence that was deafening. 'Twas as though she was the only occupant on the entire estate. The thought caused her to run toward the turret stairs that would lead her to the one man who held her heart.

Climbing the stairs two at a time, she reached his open doorway, out of breath. Her chest heaving from her efforts to reach his side, she at last saw him in his bedchamber. He was a welcome sight to behold, and she sighed in relief that he, too, had lived to see yet another day. But there was something wrong with him as she stared at his solitary figure inside his chamber. He looked dejected. Alone. Distraught. He held his head in his hands whilst sitting in a chair near the hearth. And then she heard his words and understood his fears…

"She is gone. Dead! I have failed her," he cried out before he took a nearby cup and threw it toward the hearth. The goblet loudly clanked when it smashed against the stone wall before the dark red wine slowly trailed down to puddle on the floor.

She entered the room almost afraid to reach out to offer him comfort. "I am here," she said resting her hand upon his shoulder.

He flinched. Raising his head, his gaze flitted across the room and yet he did not see her. How was that possible?

"Now I hear her voice as if I was dreaming," he murmured. "How shall I ever go on without her in my life?"

She knelt before him, gently placing her hands upon his knees. "I am here, my dearest love. Open your eyes and see me," she pleaded to no avail.

"I shall never be the same without you," he whispered, "but forever will I cherish your memory."

He took a deep breath to collect his inner most thoughts before he rose. She also stood, waiting for him to finally acknowledge her presence. But 'twas not to be for he walked right through her. Her once whole body disintegrated into a vague smoky cloud until she was miraculously pulled back whole. Panic filled her when she looked down and noticed she floated above the floor. My God! She was dead!

INGRID AWOKE FROM her nightmare disoriented. She clutched the linen night rail around her trembling body whilst her gaze took in her whereabouts. How the devil did she manage to leave her bedchamber and find herself in one of the many passageways of the castle? She had heard that there were some who walked about restlessly in their sleep, but she had never experienced the affliction before.

Distressed that she would be found in such a state, she tried to get her bearings as to her location inside the keep. She shook her head in wonder as she stared in disbelief at the door that was in front of her. She knew who slumbered inside—Lady Eden had given her an account of who was in each room when she had walked the passageways with Ingrid to get her acclimated to the castle. She knew she should not wake him. Yet she could not bring herself to walk away. She felt torn between what she knew was right inside her heart, and what she knew was now expected of her. What should she do?

A strangled sound left her lips. The answer to such a question was obvious, was it not? She should get her sorry self back to her own bedchamber before her reputation was ruined any further. Had not last eve at the banquet proven that most of those who attended the Empress's court thought of her as nothing more than a whore? Whispers followed in her wake when she had made her way through the great hall. Most of these elegantly gowned knights and ladies were well aware Ingrid had spent her time as a knight fighting for the Empress and living unwed in a tent with a man. She tried to ignore their gossiping. She cared not what they thought of her. They knew nothing of her life and 'twas none of their business what she did now or in her future.

Pondering her memories of earlier this eve did not solve the dilemma that was now put before her. The wooden portal that beckoned to her loomed at her as though the man inside was her salvation. But if she were to be found in his bedchamber, any chance of pleasing the Empress would be ruined. She should return to her own room and forget how she came to be standing in front of *his* door. That was what she should do.

Common sense and the responsibility of being prudent again warred with what her body craved. But she had not come this far in her fight to become her own woman to back down now. Inside her heart, she knew where she belonged and 'twas not as a lady in waiting for the Empress. Nay! She was meant to be with him!

Her feet cold from the stones beneath her, she took a hesitant step forward and then another. Biting her lip in indecision, her hand poised itself over the large wooden door. All 'twould take would be the briefest of knocks and she would then be in his arms. Safe. Protected. Warm. So why could she not make her presence known? She hesitated. Waiting. She told herself that she was not certain why…but that was not true. She waited because she wanted to know if he could feel that she was near. If he, too, had some inner sense that she had come to him. She had her answer when the portal was flung wide, bringing joy to her heart.

Ingrid gasped at the view before her, the sound echoing down the drafty passageway. Theobald stood there in all his glory and her eyes devoured every glorious inch of him. From his broad shoulders and bulging biceps, down to his furred chest where the hair disappeared into his braies. Her eyes continued their descent to the shapely toned legs and bare feet. He was magnificent and her fingers itched to reach out to skim their way down his glorious, muscled body. He had the physique of a warrior, and her dreams of him were now a reality.

He thrust his sword forward, scanning the corridor for danger before he realized that none presented itself. Setting his blade aside, he reached for her hands. His thumbs made small circular motions across the tops of her skin, causing the rest of her body to shiver in delight.

"By God's Bones, Ingrid," he swore whilst searching her face, "whatever are you doing outside of your own bedchamber at this

hour?"

"I had a bad dream," she murmured stepping closer to the warmth of his body.

"A glass of wine would have settled your nerves. You should not be here. What if you are discovered?" he asked letting go of her hands whilst stepping back from her. A frown marred his features that became shadowed in the darkness of his room.

"I must have walked in my sleep for I awoke outside of your chamber. Surely such a course of action must mean something."

"Aye! It means we are both fools to be in each other's presence with barely a stich of clothing on between us." He went further into the room and Ingrid shut the door, sliding the bolt into place. The sound disrupted his footsteps and his head swiveled in her direction before a growl of outrage left him. "Are you mad, Ingrid? Open the door!"

"Theo—"

"Where is my damn tunic?" He began searching his room for his missing garment when Ingrid rushed to his side, wrapping her arms around his waist. Her head rested on his back whilst she tightened her hold. *By St. Michael's Wings!* The warmth of his skin was like an inferno causing desire to rush through her veins.

"Please, Theo... I wish to be with you... in all ways..." Her heartfelt plea must have softened his mood for his body rose as he took a deep calming breath. His calloused hands from holding a sword for years slid over her arms.

"Ingrid... the Empress will not—"

"—I care not what the Empress may wish for *my* life!" she finished before stepping around his tall body to stare up into his face. She reached up to cup his cheeks. One fingertip traced the white line of his old wound running down his face. "Are you not at least a little bit happy to see me? To have me here?"

He hesitated for only a moment before one hand wrapped around her waist and pulled. Her eyes widened at what was obviously apparent when his erect manhood pressed intimately into her body. She may not have the experience of coupling with a man but she had been raised on a farm and was not ignorant of the breeding practices of their animals. Aye! He was more than glad to see her.

"You have your proof how much I want you, Ingrid," he murmured with a clenched jaw.

She gulped, raising her chin to challenge whatever doubts he might yet have that would surely pass his lips. "Theobald…" His name, once it left her mouth, lingered in the air between them and she waited to hear what she knew was coming.

"But I am no saint, as I have told you before. If you stay here much longer, I will no doubt forget about any sense of chivalry I have left in me and take you to my bed," he warned with a gleam in his eyes that all but told her he was barely hanging on as it was now.

"Take me," she answered honestly. "I freely give myself into your tender loving care."

His free hand came up to weave its way through her hair, down her cheek, until his fingers started to leave a trail above the mounds of her breasts. "You have no idea how tortuous it has been to not touch you. I have longed for you since we laid together in my tent."

Her hands found their way around his neck. "We have waited long enough, Theo. Make me yours in every way," she purred with a seductive smile.

"Once we start this journey together, we can never go back," he said, giving her one last opportunity to change her mind. "You will be mine, forevermore."

"I know," she whispered softly. The slight pressure on the back of his neck had him leaning down until his lips were just inches from her own. "Kiss me. Kiss me and show me how much you want me, too."

She could see his uncertainty flash across his visage, struggling between his scruples and his desires. A low moan left him when the last of his restraint collapsed. Arms of steel lifted her up on her toes when his mouth descended upon her own taking full possession of her mouth. His tongue darted inside to dance with hers as she followed his lead, intent on proving that they belonged together.

He yanked at the linen covering her body before he grew frustrated. Another gasp escaped her when the fabric was ripped from her body leaving her shivering when the coolness of the air hit her naked flesh. His braies came next and before she could make any sort of comment as to the magnificent view in front of her, he lifted her up in his arms, carrying her effortlessly to his bed. The need to have him inside her was urgent even though a part of her feared the pain she knew their coupling would initially cause. But her love for the man whose hands started to explore every inch of her suddenly hot skin outweighed her anxiety of the unknown. How could anything that felt so right be so very wrong in the eyes of those who might condemn her and her wanton actions?

Theobald seemed to no longer be in such a hurry whilst he took his time touching every inch of her body. She trembled in delight at this exploration. The wait was unbearable and yet all Ingrid could do was moan in pleasure when his lips left a trail from her neck and moved ever downward. Then he moved lower still. Horrified at what his destination appeared to be, she grabbed a hold of his wavy brown hair, halting his progress between her thighs. Those fascinating green eyes pierced her into place upon the bed.

"You would deny me?" he asked. His breath left her trembling in anticipation of what he was about to do to her. He kissed her inner thigh whilst awaiting her answer.

She shook her head even though she was unsure of what to expect. "Nay… never," she whispered even as she began to tremble in anticipation.

"Then surrender to me and let me taste you as I have wanted to do for weeks," he said before placing another kiss upon her other thigh.

"But Theo—"

"Shhh, Ingrid. Lay back and enjoy the moment," he ordered.

She did as she was told until his mouth touched her most inner, private place. She almost bolted off the bed until his large hands held her back down in place. And then she could no longer think because of the pleasure that coursed through her entire body and all but consumed her. Never had she felt this way before. 'Twas all because of Theobald. He took her higher than the heavens and when she could almost stand this sweet torture no longer, her body shattered all around her. She called out his name and heard his deep rumble of laughter while her body slowly came back down to earth.

He kissed his way up her body until he was laying down beside her, his fingers trailing over her hot skin once more. She peeked at him between her lowered lashes and saw he continued to watch her closely until her breathing returned to normal. She was so embarrassed to have had him down *there*—at such an intimate part of her body—that she turned away from him. Her cheeks must be flushed as red as her hair.

He took a firm hold of her chin, turning her head so she had little choice other than stare into his mesmerizing green eyes. "Do not hide yourself from me, dearest Ingrid. We have only just begun to play," he said with a roguish grin. His tone was calming, and she could only ponder what he had in store for them next.

"Wine?" she asked through a parched throat.

"Of course," he murmured giving her the opportunity to watch his magnificent backside when he left the bed and strode across the room. He poured wine into a chalice, taking a large sip for himself, before he turned the rim and held the cup out to her.

"A lover's gesture," she remarked knowing the custom of placing her lips where his had just touched. She took a drink, handing over the goblet before coming to kneel upon the bed.

"Aye, although you have yet to know me fully," he said staring down upon her. He was every inch the warrior she expected him to be without his garments and she was enjoying the view before her.

"May I... touch you?" Her words caught in her throat knowing she had never been this bold in her entire life.

He took her hands, placing them on his naked chest. "Anywhere you wish, my sweet."

A slow grin spread across her face whilst her fingertips began to explore every rigid muscle beneath her hands. She traced the ridges of his stomach, marveling at the difference between his body and hers. And then she explored even lower. A hiss left him when she reached for his manhood. She swiftly let go thinking she had hurt him until his hand wrapped around her wrist and brought her fingers back so she could continue her exploration. The skin was silken and far softer than she'd thought it would be for something hard and ready to take her.

She continued to run her hand up and down until a moan left him and she quickly found herself beneath her handsome knight.

"I cannot wait any longer, dearest Ingrid. Forgive me for the pain that I am about to cause," he whispered in her ear.

Theobald entered her until he met the barrier of her virginity. He began to kiss her, and she was so lost in what he was doing to her mouth that she forgot all else until he plunged fully into her body. A sharp cry passed her lips and he patiently waited until the pain subsided and she became accustomed to his size.

'Twas not long until he began to move, and she began matching him in the rhythm known throughout all time. If Ingrid had thought Theobald had taken her to the heavens before, then now was no comparison. Higher and higher did they soar together until she came alive for him like white hot lightning exploding across a midnight sky. He called out her name when he, too, found his release, and she felt his seed pulsing inside of her.

Her breathing coming in short gasps, Theobald rolled over next to her whilst he pulled her up against his body. Her head rested upon his chest, and she could hear for herself his heartbeat beneath her ear. The rapid staccato more than told her how affected he was by their coupling. She smiled in satisfaction that she had pleased him.

"Theo…" she began whilst her fingers once more ran over his heated flesh. "That was wonderful."

He bent forward and kissed the top of her head. "Aye. 'Twas better than I had hoped our love making would be for your first time. Now, sleep. The morn will come soon enough and with it our obligations, which will take precedence over my desire to keep you in my bed."

Ingrid yawned. "I like the idea of staying in your bed."

"'Tis good because I have no intention of letting you leave it, my dear."

Content that she was safe in Theobald's arms, Ingrid slept. And when she dreamt this time, 'twas of her handsome knight and a life that they began to live together.

CHAPTER TWENTY-ONE

T HEOBALD AWOKE TO the sound of someone banging on his bedchamber door. Whoever was on the other side of the wooden portal better have an extremely urgent matter to be causing such a ruckus and disturbing him at such an ungodly hour. After being up most of the night with the fair Ingrid, Theobald had had little to no sleep.

Moving the arms that were gently wrapped around him, he placed a kiss on the inside of Ingrid's wrist and watched when a beautiful smile crept it way across her features. She was lovely in the morn, and he decided there was no need to wake her as yet. She would need to leave soon to begin her duties attending the Empress...but there should still be a little more time for them to spend together first. Leaving the warmth of his bed, he quickly grabbed a robe. Wrapping the linen around his body, he took up his sword, and slid the bolt from the door. He opened the portal a crack to peer into the corridor. Reynard and Richard stood waiting none too patiently.

"We are summoned to have speech with the Empress," Richard said with a lifted brow. "That is if you can tear yourself away from your companion."

"At this hour?" Theobald inquired knowing the sun had not fully risen.

"Aye. 'Tis obviously an urgent matter" Richard replied.

"The great hall?" Theobald asked knowing he must needs hurry.

"Nay," Reynard answered with a nod of his head. "Her solar. 'Tis up on the next floor and down the passageway—"

"I was told last night where the Empress's solar is located," Theobald interrupted irritably before lowering his voice so as not to awaken Ingrid. "I shall join you shortly."

The two men looked as if they were going to further comment on what would cause Theobald's delay. He shut the door in their faces even as he heard their laughter echoing down the corridor. The damn taunting curs!

He quickly made his way to the hearth to throw wood onto the dying embers. There was a chill in the air this morn and 'twas no wonder. He had no idea where the time had gone when August had turned into September. Soon winter would be here, and snow would cover the ground once more. He could only ponder how much longer they would remain in what was left of the town of Winchester.

Grabbing his garments, he quickly donned them. Strapping his sword into the scabbard at his side, he leaned down and kissed Ingrid's cheek. Her eyes flickered open whilst a frown formed on her brow.

"You are dressed," she murmured covering her yawn with her hand. "What is amiss?"

"I must needs attend the Empress. Hopefully I will not be gone long."

Her eyes grew wide. "The Empress! I should get dressed so I can attend her if she calls for me."

He ran a hand down her flame-colored hair, tucking a strand behind her ear. "Nay. 'Tis still early enough that you will not be missed as yet. Stay in bed and dream of me, my sweet," he whispered. He kissed her lips and watched her close her eyes once more. Although he would rather join her in his bed, he had no further time to dally. One did not keep the Empress waiting for too long.

He took the stairs two at a time to the next floor and made his way down the passageway. A guard stood outside the solar and opened the door for Theobald. 'Twas clear he was expected. The Empress sat in a throne-like chair; Richard and Reynard stood off to her right. Her half-brother, Robert of Gloucester, was pacing the room as though he was caged. This could not be a good sign.

"You took long enough, Norwood," the Empress said through clenched teeth.

"My apologies, my—"

"—there is no time for groveling," she interrupted him with a wave of her hand toward her half-brother. "Robert, you may begin your report."

Robert quit his pacing of the room and came to stand next to the Empress. "As you are most likely aware, Queen Matilda and her one thousand strong militia have set up camp on the east side of Winchester. I suppose she is representing her husband, the usurper Stephen, and acting on his behalf. With her descent upon the city, our forces are now unfortunately blockaded inside. My scouts inform me that the queen's men are well provisioned while ours suffer from lack of food. I tried to weaken the blockade by attempting to fortify Wherwell Abbey, but we were defeated and sustained heavy losses.

"Our supply situation is dire, and I have proposed to our Empress that we must leave Winchester. We can plan an orderly withdrawal with an advance guard of our best knights designed to protect the Empress. I will command the rearguard and hopefully draw them away whilst she makes her escape."

"What of the main body of men?" Richard asked.

Robert began to pace again. "They will be used to guard the baggage."

"And the advance guard? Where are we to head?" Theobald inquired with the assumption he was to lead the Empress to safety.

The Empress tapped her fingers on the arm of her chair before she pointed to two men standing next to her chair. "This campaign will be led by my close associates, Brian fitz Count and

Reginald of Cornwall. Norwood… you and your men's focus will be to guard me and scout out the area ahead as we make our escape. We can use the road that crosses the River Test at Stockbridge. From there, we will head to Ludgershall about twenty miles away. We can rest there overnight before continuing onward to Devizes Castle. Another forty miles will then have us arriving at Robert's home in Gloucester where we will finally find a safe haven."

Theobald was about to voice his concern for the distance the Empress would need to travel, but his brother spoke up first.

"Stockbridge is… what… eight miles from here? Will that be far enough away to make our escape unseen?" Reynard inquired raising his hand to his chin whilst he contemplated their situation.

Robert at last stood still. "I have every faith in you to keep the Empress safe. You will need to ride hard and fast initially. 'Tis nigh unto fifty miles to reach Devizes and even further to Gloucester. 'Twill take several days before you arrive and I am certain the Empress will be exhausted whilst traveling at a pace to which she is unaccustomed. But the rest of us bringing up the rear will be enough of a diversion to give you ample time to see that the Empress escapes capture."

Theobald bowed. "We will not fail you," he said with his hand over his heart. What more could he do? He had his orders and could only follow them.

The Empress rose from her chair. "See that you do not, Norwood. I am trusting you with my life and those of my ladies. Now, go and see that everything is prepared for our departure," she ordered before she took her leave of the men with Robert and a small entourage following close behind her.

Richard gazed upon Theobald. "Will it work?"

Theobald shrugged. "Let us hope so, but there is only one way to find out. I pray the Empress is prepared to spend several days traveling without the comfort and luxury of a wagon."

They left the solar to make their way to their chambers to begin packing their gear. Theobald gently woke Ingrid and explained the plan whilst she, too, began to scurry about the chamber collecting her things that Theobald had kept for her in a chest. He could only pray that time would be on their side when their escape was put into motion. He did not relish being captured by that Queen Matilda's men. God only knew what revenge she might enact upon the people who continued to hold her husband captive.

⟡

CHAPTER TWENTY-TWO

L EAVING THE ROYAL castle before the sun had risen, the advance guard avoided watchmen posted by Queen Matilda far easier than they had expected. Once away from the perimeter of the castle, they rode hard and fast. Thankfully, Ingrid was once again comfortable in her attire after gaining permission from the Empress to return to the clothes she had previously been wearing. She had made her point that she could serve her better with sword in hand whilst they made their escape. The Empress had reluctantly agreed but only until they reached Gloucester.

A brief memory flited across her mind when the Empress saw her other ladies in waiting outfitted in their expensive jewels and gowns as though they wore everything they owned. They obviously did not wish to leave anything behind once they fled. The Empress had pointed to Ingrid, already fitted in men's garments, and told her other ladies to change accordingly. All three had sputtered their objections but there would be no gainsaying the Empress and the women had reluctantly done as they were told.

Aye… Ingrid felt her old self again now. Gone were the costly gems adorning her throat and ears, including gowns that stifled her ability to freely move without tripping. She could breathe again whilst back in her hose, tunic, and boots. True, the chainmail upon her body weighed her down as though she had never worn it before, but this mattered little to her. For the first time in the past several weeks, she felt useful again. Her sword strapped to her side, her trustworthy steed beneath her, protecting the Empress was once more was her main goal… as long as they evaded capture, that was.

Theobald and Richard had led the way through the city and over the River Test, scouting far ahead of the rear and middle guard. Fitz Count and Reginald of Cornwall came next. They were men of few words and Ingrid kept her own council as to the measure of their efficiency with a sword. 'Twas of no matter. The Empress trusted them, so Ingrid could only do the same.

She peered over at Blake riding next to her. He gave Ingrid the briefest of nods before his attention went to the surrounding area. He looked over his shoulder where the Empress and her ladies rode. Oswin, Kingsley, and Reynard brough up the rear, a perfect barrier for any foe who might wish to attack them from behind. All in all, their escape through Winchester went for the most part, unnoticed. Yet they were unsure what awaited Robert and the rest of the Empress's army who had been left far behind. Her scouts would surely catch up with them once they reached Gloucester and would give her further reports.

Theobald raised his hand, and their company slowed their mounts. A stream was nearby, and Ingrid jumped from her saddle to lead her horse over for a drink. The rest of their company did the same with Richard walking over to the Empress to help her dismount. Theobald remained in his saddle alongside his brother, deep in conversation. If the frown marring Theo's brow was an indication of what he was feeling, then Ingrid would say that any time for their reprieve from their reality would be short. Ingrid would take full advantage of the gift.

Whilst Valor drank his fill, Ingrid made her way to Eden, Rovena, and Petula who appeared as though they had had enough of their wild escapade through the woods.

Ingrid scanned the ladies and did not care for what was evident in their weary faces. "You realize we still have many hours in the saddle," she stated whilst her hand went to the hilt of her sword. She scanned the woods around her to ensure they were not about to be ambushed.

Petula moaned in agony. "My weary backside will never survive," she complained bitterly.

Eden rolled her eyes until she ran her hands down her hose. "Better to have a sore backside then to be captured or dead," she warned. "Besides, look how fetching our legs are in this hose. We should wear men's garments more often."

A laugh escaped Rovena. "The Empress would never allow it," she said whilst her gaze went to the Empress who was speaking with Theobald and Reynard. "The men who ride with us are most handsome. Do you think perchance one of them might favor me?"

Ingrid had a moment of jealousy sweep through her. Odd that, considering the woman did not mention which knight she was interested in. Since her gaze went to each man individually, it appeared she was not too picky. Ingrid was about to reply when the ladies broke out into laughter. Ingrid frowned, curious what could be so humorous between the women.

Eden quickly gave her the answer. "We certainly know of one knight who is already spoken for, do we not, ladies?" She smirked knowingly. All eyes turned in Ingrid's direction.

"You know?" she asked, aghast that others knew of her relationship with Theobald. She *knew* she should have snuck back to her own bedchamber that night before the entire castle had risen.

Rovena placed her hand on Ingrid's shoulder. "Of course, we know, silly. We are all close in the Empress's court. A person can barely keep a secret for very long. Did not someone tell you this?"

Petula huffed. "I learned this the hard way. Why, I still have not lived down the gossip that surrounded me when I first joined the Empress as one of her attendants. 'Twas foolish of me to give myself to a man who only wished to bed me but how was I to know he would not take me as his wife?"

Rovena placed her hand on Petula's shoulder. "You were young and trusted him. 'Tis not your fault he abused your faith in him."

"We have all had experiences that left us a bit… jaded," Eden replied, honestly. "Mayhap this is why she chose us in the first place."

Ingrid ran her hand over her eyes. "Are you telling me that the Empress knows of my current… sleeping arrangements?"

Eden laughed once more. "Sleeping? Are you really getting much of that, my dear?"

Their merriment erupted again, and Ingrid could only shake her head in shame. "I am mortified."

Rovena once more began to console her by patting Ingrid on her back. "Do not worry overly much, my friend. The Empress is very understanding when it comes to her ladies and when they find love. She handsomely rewarded those who came before us when they left the Empress's service in order to wed. We hope for the same when love finds us some day."

Love… That word held so much meaning. Ingrid could only ponder when her and Theobald's lives might become something that might resemble whatever a normal life might look like. When would their lives settle down to this new reality? Would Theobald be rewarded some grand estate by Empress Matilda? She knew that was what he wanted. But would Ingrid then have to become the lady of the manor? She trembled at the thought. She would be ill suited for such an undertaking, having had no training for such a monumental task. They had rarely spoken of what their future might hold, and they had made no plans together. And yet even though he had not proclaimed himself completely, she believed that one day they would become husband and wife. When that day came, where would they live? In a manor house somewhere? Or would they live in a palace, continuing their service to the Empress? The possibilities were endless.

"Good heavens! Just look at her face," Petula called out rushing over to Ingrid and giving her a fierce hug. "You should not worry so, my friend. We are certain your handsome knight cares for you. Enjoy being in love and take each day as it comes."

The ladies all nodded their heads and yet Ingrid could not find any words to offer them. Her cheeks flushed to be caught fretting over her future life when she should be more aware of their surroundings. Yet the men in their group appeared as if they had their situation well in hand. Even Theobald and Reynard had alit from their steeds to give them a much-needed break. But when he caught her gaze, his hand raised and made a circular motion that Ingrid knew signaled that 'twas time to once again be on the run.

"We best return to our horses, ladies. I have no doubt we will be leaving momentarily," Ingrid said leaving them as Petula began complaining once more.

Ingrid returned to Valor, running her hands over the horse and then double checking that the cinches were still secure. Theobald came to stand next to her. He leaned down to place a kiss upon her cheek.

"You and the ladies are doing well?" he asked warily and with a lifted brow full of concern.

"They shall manage, for the most part. What other choice do they have?" she replied with a weak smile.

"The Empress has also fared well, all things considered."

Ingrid scanned the women in their group. "We are barely out of Winchester and have only just begun our travels," she grunted in response.

Theobald nodded. "Aye. I have no idea how the Empress will endure multiple days in the saddle."

"She has little choice in the matter if she wishes to evade capture."

"I do not wish to linger here any longer. The horses are refreshed but I fear our enemy is not too far behind us. We shall need to ride most likely into the early eve before we can make camp for the night," Theobald stated. He reached out to caress her cheek.

She leaned into his palm. "I have missed you," she whispered, wishing they were alone so she could show him how much he meant to her.

"And I you," he said. Bending forward, he quickly kissed her lips. "Now mount up on Valor and let me see if Buttercup will be as accommodating. He has been especially stubborn this morn. I fear he may just buck me off and trot away to find the nearest stable."

Ingrid stepped closer, taking hold of his hand. She was about to demand a kiss, not caring who would witness their affection, when they were interrupted.

"Norwood... I grow impatient," the Empress warned. "Should we not be on our way?"

"Aye, my Empress," Theobald answered before he gave Ingrid a wink. "Duty calls..."

Ingrid could only watch him depart. Aye... duty called, and she must also adhere to the dictates of the Empress. After all, they had an army that could surround them at any given moment. Ingrid would not be at ease until they were safely ensconced at the earl's castle.

CHAPTER TWENTY-THREE

FAR INTO THE night did they travel. Finally, when they were far enough away that Theobald deemed 'twas safe, they made camp. Reynard and Oswin had been able to hunt, and several small rabbits were roasting over a fire. A slow-moving stream provided both water for drinking and bathing for those brave enough to withstand the icy cold.

Theobald reached out for the Empress when she tripped over a hidden root on the forest floor. He tucked her hand into the crook of his arm and continued their stroll. She had asked him to accompany her so that they could have a private word. *Merciful God!* What more would she ask of him?

"You are no doubt wondering why I asked you to walk with me, Norwood," she began as though she had heard his innermost thoughts. Her eyes turned upwards as though she was assessing his worth. One would have thought she had already found him more than capable of performing his duties. If the Battle of Lincoln had not proven his allegiance to her, then surely their safe flight from Winchester had done so.

Inwardly he sighed. "I am yours to command, my Empress," he said whilst they continued to walk. They did not go far from their campsite, nor did he think they would be gone long from the company of the others.

"You have had my attention for some time, Norwood. I am more than aware that you are trustworthy, or you would not be here with me now," she said patting his arm as though to soothe any troublesome thoughts he had running amiss inside his mind. "I am confident that you shall listen carefully when I ask what your attentions are toward Mistress Ingrid."

"I wish her to be my bride once we have fulfilled our duty to you and your cause, Empress," he stated without hesitation.

"And will that be before or after you fill her belly with your babe?" She stopped walking and took her hand from his arm waiting for his reply.

"I cannot in good faith offer to wed her when I know not what the morrow will bring. Our journey is filled with the threat of being accosted upon every turn of the road. I could be lying dead upon it on the morrow for all I know."

"What the morrow will bring?" she fumed with an angry scowl. "'Twill bring you into the state of fatherhood whether you are ready for the responsibility or not, you fool! God forbid if you were to perish in your service to me—but at least if you were married first, Ingrid would become a widow and her child would not be labeled a bastard."

"'Tis not my intention to take unfair advantage of Ingrid, Empress," he declared placing his hand over his heart.

"And yet you bed her without the bonds of wedlock. How is this treating her fairly? You have not even asked permission to wed her nor have you sought out a priest to bless your union!"

"I had every intention of doing so once our situation became more stable. Surely you cannot expect me to take a wife when I have naught to offer her." He stood his ground. Even though the Empress clearly considered him to be in the wrong, he was unsure how to right the situation.

Her brow rose. "So, you seek the riches only I can offer you. Title? Lands?" she asked warily.

"Only if you deem me worthy, my Empress," he stated with a bow. "I am, after all, only your most humble servant."

A snort left her whilst she continued to stare up at him. "Only time will tell if you continue to be worthy, Norwood. However, I expect you to do right by one of my ladies in waiting. I will not have her pregnant at court without having vows spoken between you."

"As you wish, Empress," Theobald said wondering how he would bring this issue up to Ingrid.

"'Tis not what I wish, Norwood," she said quietly, "but what I *hope* you will do on your own terms."

'Twas Theobald's turn to be surprised at her words. "My Empress?"

"I have another mission for you, Norwood, once we have reached Gloucester, you have been properly wed, and your horses have adequately rested from our journey." She began pacing back and forth across the forest floor and Theobald waited for whatever she would now ask of him.

"As always, I am yours to command," Theobald replied waiting for her words that would undoubtedly change his life.

"I have been pondering the paternity of Mistress Ingrid since you first brought her to my court. I have no doubt that she is far more than some farmer's daughter."

"She has never mentioned any of this to me," Theobald replied with a shake of his head.

"Nor would she for I have the notion that she knows nothing of what I am about to tell you. The sword she carries with her has some interesting markings on the blade, and I have studied it whilst we were at the royal castle."

Theobald frowned. "I did not think anything of them only that mayhap her father had thought the etchings would be pleasing to his daughter."

"Aye, 'twas my thought as well until I studied the sword further. I believe Ingrid is none other than the lost heir of Calbridge Castle," Empress Matilda said before she gave a heavy sigh.

"Is that not near Penhow in Wales?" Theobald asked, mulling over what the lady was telling him. Ingrid's parentage was beginning to come to light.

"You know your geography well, Norwood. Penhow is part

of the estate although 'tis located several miles from the main castle. 'Tis a small keep but still part of what would be her inheritance."

"But that would make her—"

"—Lady Ingrid de St. Maur."

"*Bloody Hell!*" he swore before raking a hand through his hair. "How is this possible?"

"'Tis hardly uncommon. 'Twas the usual story of feuding brothers who each wanted the estate coming to blows, although why the younger thought he had a claim is a mystery. One brother stayed and then died without leaving any offspring to take over. The other departed, vowing never to return. No one could find him. There had been rumors that Ingrid's father changed his name to Seymour. Clearly, he told his only daughter nothing of the fact that she was to inherit a vast fortune that would see her, and her children's children, settled comfortably for years to come."

Theobald stood there stunned and then thought about their conversation but moments before. "Yet you still wish me to wed her?"

A smirk lit her face. "'Twould be advantageous to all those concerned. I shall give you the title you so richly deserve. You shall marry the woman you obviously care for, if not already love. There is a steward currently watching over the land. Once you and the lady are wed, you shall both maintain the estate in my name and in doing so, gain my favor. What could possibly go wrong?"

A sound of disbelief left him. "What could go wrong? I can think of one main thing that is almost certain to go wrong—she will think I marry her only for the coin and wealth she will bring to our union. 'Tis not the way I had hoped to propose to the woman."

"I care not how you go about making her your wife only that you do so upon our arrival at Gloucester. I will, of course, approve of your union and we can have the local priest perform the ceremony."

"Is this a request or a demand?" he snarled not caring for the cool calculation with which the Empress arranged their lives. She cared little for the feelings or preferences of two people who would have eventually found love together on their own. Nay, she only cared for the fact that another estate would be governed in her name. He should not have been surprised for truly what else did a reigning monarch wish for but more land to rule? He supposed he should be grateful the Empress was willing to allow Theobald to marry Ingrid instead of giving her to someone else in her court.

"Does it make a difference?" She took up his arm again and they began making their way back to camp.

No answer was needed. He would perform his duty and ask Ingrid to marry him. He could only pray that she would agree so that they would not be forced to wed. He had no doubt the Empress would hold them both at the point of a blade if they thought to defy her.

CHAPTER TWENTY-FOUR

INGRID PACED THE forest floor, pulling her mantle around her to keep the cold from her body now that she was no longer in front of the fire made at camp. Theobald had asked her to walk with him after they had partaken of their evening meal. She had been more than happy to share a private moment together. That was until he started informing her of his conversation with the Empress.

"Surely you are jesting with me." Ingrid fumed to the sound of dry leaves crunching beneath her boots. "My father would never have kept something of such import from me!"

"Mayhap he thought to protect you," Theobald offered.

"From the truth of my own birth?" she shouted.

Theobald reached out for her arm, halting her pacing. A heavy sigh left her when his arms wrapped around her waist bringing her close. Her emotions were running amok. Betrayed by her own father! How could he not tell her she was in truth an heir to an entire estate? By rights a *lady*! Tears leaked from her eyes from the knowledge that her own father had not trusted her with such information. 'Twas not as if she would have left to go seeking the riches she presumably had a right to own. Perchance this was what he had feared but she would never know. 'Twas not as if she could go ask him why he had kept something of such import to himself.

"I wish with all my heart I could give you the answers your father did not impart to you, Ingrid." Theobald stroked her hair, and she tightened her arms around his waist. At least this man would give her the comfort she stood in need of.

"I do not understand why he would keep this from me. I would not have left our farm, no matter what awaited me in Wales. He should have had more faith in me. 'Tis not as if all the riches in the world would have changed who I am as a person," she said whilst wiping away her tears.

Theobald reached down to cup her cheeks. His thumbs caressing her skin caused goosebumps to raise up on her arms. She tried to see his features, but the darkness of the night kept them hidden from her.

"There is more…" he said, stepping away to now do his own pacing.

Heaven help her, there was more! What further torment could be uttered this night that had not already caused her world to spin out of control?

"I am afraid to ask what more you could say to me after you have already informed me that everything I have ever known about myself has been a lie," she stated whilst his pacing continued. A frown marred her brow. 'Twas clear there was another matter of grave import that Theobald had not as yet confessed to her.

"'Tis the Empress…" he began. He came to a sudden halt then returned to her, taking her hands.

She raised one brow at his tone. "What *about* the Empress?"

"Ingrid…" He cleared his throat as though whatever he was about to say was difficult for him.

"What about the Empress?" she repeated wrenching her hands away.

"She demands we marry once we reach Gloucester," he blurted out.

A gasp of surprise left her lips until the situation became clear inside her head. Anger replaced her startled reaction to his words, and she lashed out at the man standing before her. "Oh, does she now? I suppose the land and riches I bring with our union will be beneficial to her and her cause. And what of you? You get out from beneath the shadow of your older brother with an estate large enough to see you comfortable for the rest of your life. What about *my* wishes?"

The moon revealed itself by creeping into view from behind the clouds. Hurt flashed across Theobald's features until concern filled his eyes from her words. "I understand you have your reasons to be angry, but you are being unfair, Ingrid," he said quietly before turning his back on her. "I have never once been unkind to you and your assumption that I only wed you for the monies you bring to fill my coffers is beneath you."

She had the decency to inwardly cringe that her words had caused him pain. But still, she pressed on. "'Tis not true? Will you not become lord and master if we were to wed?" she asked attempting not to cry at the injustice of her situation.

But she knew his answer before he could even respond. If what Theobald had briefly told her of Calbridge Castle was correct, she was a very wealthy woman. A prize for the taking. Any man would welcome the opportunity to become her husband. With their marriage, she would lose everything the instant she said her vows. All her wealth would be her husband's to manage.

"You know I care for you," he hissed before picking up where he had left off moments ago… pacing the forest floor.

"But you do not love me…" Her words, once whispered, lingered in the air between them like the bitterness that crept into her voice. A sour taste filled her mouth and still she could not stop her words from spilling past her lips.

He skidded to a halt. "Ingrid, I—"

She held up her hand to stop any further words from tumbling from his mouth. "I suppose there is no need to answer my question. For I will now never know if you, in truth, love me for who I am or if you are just fulfilling an obligation to our Empress. Either way, I am the loser in a game played by those who have the most to gain."

He turned abruptly, coming to her so swiftly she barely had time to catch her breath. He took hold of her upper arms and gave her a shake. "Again… you are being unfair and go too far, Ingrid. If you look deep inside yourself, you know that I care for you. Do you think I could honestly take you to my bed if I did not wish for you to become my wife?" he said, scolding her.

A sob unwillingly escaped her. "You would not be the first to take advantage of a woman by pulling at her heart strings while concealing your dishonorable intentions. I suppose you will not be the last."

He let go of her arms as if in defeat. He seemed as though he was as upset with their situation as she was. "Then you do not know me at all," he scowled turning away from her.

Tears leaked from her eyes. "We are like two different worlds colliding together in a sea of chaos," she whispered.

"I have no notion what you speak of. We are of the same worlds," he growled out in frustration.

"Are we?" she asked pleading with him to somehow understand the torment she was suffering. "You were born into nobility. I am but a simple farmer's daughter. Do you in all honesty think I will ever be able to fit into a world where I am naught but an ornament to be dangled from some lord's arm? I will never fit into such a world. Just look at me!"

He came to stand before her. "I *am* looking at you, Ingrid, and I see *you*. Not the wealth you might bring to our union, but you," he replied, his tone crestfallen. "I may have been born into a noble house, but I have been on my own with my brothers as a mercenary longer than under the watchful eyes of those who might think to rule me."

She lifted her chin. "And yet the Empress has ordered you to wed me, so you are obviously under someone's rule now."

"And you would demand me to disobey her?" he asked in annoyance.

"Mayhap in this instance," she replied knowing she could not expect him to defy the Empress any more than she could do so herself.

He raked his hand through his hair and Ingrid pondered what she should say to ease the tension between them, but the words would not tumble from her mouth. She watched his shoulders heave. He at last turned back around but once more she could not see his expression. Mayhap 'twas for the best.

"Theobald—"

He held up his hand as she had done moments before, and she snapped her lips shut. "I think you have said enough. I understand you are upset but for now, I do not think I could stand to hear you say another word that would tarnish my feelings for you. We should return to camp."

He did not wait for her to proceed first. Instead, he left her alone with their conversation running rampant inside her head. Standing in the dark shivering, she could only wonder how her life could suddenly turn out so very wrong.

※

CHAPTER TWENTY-FIVE

T HEOBALD FIDGETED WITH his tunic as though the garment was strangling him. The past several days without Ingrid to talk to had felt like hell on earth. He missed her presence by his side, the sound of her laughter and voice, and even her anger. The good Lord above knew Theobald's heart was true but how was he to prove such to Ingrid if she refused an audience with him? And now this... a wedding before he could even honestly voice how much he had come to care for... nay... love her. Ingrid's words from the forest rang inside his head and he vowed to prove his love if it took the rest of his life.

Upon their arrival at Gloucester, the Empress, completely exhausted from their race across the countryside, had to be lifted from her horse and carried inside. After several more days of recuperating, she was finally well enough to resume worrying over those she had left behind in Winchester. A runner soon came from Winchester. The news was not good. The Empress's reaction to learning her half-brother had been captured had caused the woman to remain behind closed doors as she plotted her revenge on the usurper's wife, Queen Matilda. The woman meant to trade the earl for her husband, Stephen. Empress Matilda had no notion to comply.

Theobald had no idea what would happen next but was not surprised when the Empress entered the chapel with her attendants to witness his marriage to Ingrid. He gave a short bow when the Empress took her place, and she returned it with a nod of her head. However, 'twas the sly smirk that briefly crossed her lips that caused Theobald to clench his teeth and fists. She was getting what she wanted.

His eyes scanned the back of the chapel waiting for his soon-to-be bride. The room was barely filled. Only his brother and the knights closest to Theobald and Ingrid occupied the pews behind their Empress and her ladies. 'Twas a sad situation especially when he had always envisioned his wedding as a large, joyous event. Mayhap at some other date he would be able to make this up to his lady. *His lady…*

He gave a heavy sigh. Theobald and Ingrid had been given no choice but to comply with the Empress's wishes… nay… demand. Theobald could not think of their situation as anything other than being forced. This was no way to begin a marriage, especially when he had held such high hopes of telling Ingrid how he felt about her. They should be full of joy while celebrating their special day. Instead, Theobald would be lucky if Ingrid would, at the very least, not attempt to cut his heart out. She was *that* upset, and he could not blame her.

Yet all thoughts of how angry she had been left him the moment he espied her gracefully striding into the chapel. A dark green gown framed her body to perfection while a golden chain swung from her hips with each step she took. Diamonds hung from her neck and sparkled from the torches in the room. Her red hair had been tamed and braided forming a crown around her head with most of its length falling in soft curls down her back. She was glorious and most certainly befitting her new station in life. A lady by any means and he meant to tell her so the instant she was at his side.

She made her way to stand before him and he reached out his hands to take her own. Her fingertips were icy cold, and he prayed he could make her feel the warmth of his love again soon.

"You are radiant, my lady," he said with a bow. His green eyes bore into her hazel ones and for the briefest of instants he saw love shining in their depths. But it was quickly masked as though she had no wish for him to see her emotions, let alone her love for him. Still… the love that had begun to bloom between them was hiding right beneath the surface of the irritation now etched upon her visage.

"You are handsome, as well, my lord," she softly murmured giving reference to the title the Empress would bestow upon him once they were married. Being the Earl of Calbridge would take some getting used to, he supposed. Somehow the title did not hold much meaning if Ingrid could not see for herself that he loved her for the woman she was and not the wealth and prestige she brought to their union.

"Your gown matches my eyes. Well planned," he teased and saw a spark ignite in the depths of her eyes. Aye… that attraction they had for one another was still there. He only needed to remind her of what had begun between them.

"An accident, I assure you. I had nothing to do with the gown I wear any more than I was given a choice on who I was to marry." Ingrid lifted her head, defiant to the bitter end. But no matter. They would perform their duties as was required of them. 'Twas unfortunate they would need to settle their differences tonight once they were alone together to consummate their marriage.

"Whether an accident or not, you are always beautiful in my eyes," he said in a husky whisper. She gulped, clearly not believing his words until the priest cleared his throat. With one more look at the lady next to him, he reluctantly turned his attention to the man waiting to make an honest man of him. "Please proceed, Father," Theobald replied, tucking Ingrid's hand at the crook of his elbow.

"We come here today…" the priest began and then droned on about the weakness of the flesh. Theobald tuned him out only to come around when the priest asked the couple to stand before the altar and say their vows. He did so in a strong and steady voice while Ingrid's cracked in misery. Once the priest proclaimed them husband and wife, Theobald bent forward to seal their vows with a chaste kiss. 'Twas nothing compared to how he really wished to show his affection, but they had an audience, and he would not embarrass his bride by making a public display.

Empress Matilda stood and clapped her hands. "Well done!" she exclaimed, coming to stand next to the priest. Theobald bowed while Ingrid curtsied. The Empress waved her hand and Eden stepped forward holding a sword. She handed the thin, ceremonial blade to the Empress then returned to her place in the chapel. "Take a knee, Sir Theobald."

Theobald knelt and bowed his head whilst the Empress tapped the blade on one shoulder then the other. "I dub thee the Earl of Calbridge, rightful lord of Calbridge Castle and its lands. Arise, Lord Calbridge, and sign your marriage documents with your new title."

"My Empress," Theobald, said kissing her ring when she held out her hand. "You are too gracious."

"You have earned the right to your title by serving me valiantly. Continue to do so as I have previously commanded you," the Empress ordered. She motioned to the altar awaiting their signatures.

"Shall we, my dear?" Theobald asked waiting for Ingrid to proceed him.

"I suppose the damage has already been done and there is no turning back," Ingrid fumed until the Empress took her hand, having overheard her words.

"You will do well to not only obey me but your new lord and master," the Empress hissed.

Theobald could see for himself how Ingrid struggled to hold back her temper, but her eyes still blazed with fury.

Ingrid defiantly raised her chin. 'Twas obvious to any who observed her that she would cower to no one. "With all due respect, Empress, I have no master," Ingrid stated through clenched teeth.

The Empress's brow rose at this blatant show of Ingrid's strength and courage to speak up for herself. Or was it stupidity?

There were not many who would face the Empress when she was speaking. "You do now, and he is your husband. I expect you to go and claim your lands, Lady Ingrid—"

"—I have no lands that are my own," Ingrid interrupted until the Empress stepped forward, clearly done with Ingrid's insolence.

"Aye, you do. They are as much your lands as they are your husband's. Claim them and your people, and do so in my name," the Empress warned.

"Aye, 'twill be done, my Empress," Ingrid murmured, finally bowing her head in submission.

The Empress leaned forward to speak softly so only Theobald and Ingrid could hear her words. "You will thank me one day for this service I have done for you. I have no doubt Norwood would have eventually proposed his desire to wed you. However, I would not have a lady in my keeping be spoiled because a man could not keep his hands off her."

"I will endeavor to heed your words, perchance given some time for me to come to terms with my new… situation," Ingrid retorted.

A snort left the Empress. "You will have you hands full with this one, Norwood. I pray you are up to the task of taming her."

Ingrid's eyes widened but Theobald took her hand raising it to his lips. "I would not dream of taming such a fierce creature, Empress. She is perfect just the way she is."

He saw the briefest of smiles light up Ingrid's face until she moved ahead of him to sign the parchment declaring they were wed. Once their signatures were written on the document, red wax was dripped onto it and the priest took his signet ring and made it official. They were wed. Mayhap not how he had planned but married all the same. He could only pray they could somehow find a common accord to move forward in their future life together.

⬥

CHAPTER TWENTY-SIX

INGRID SAT IN Theobald's bedchamber near the hearth, awaiting his arrival to consummate their marriage and the vows they had taken this day. 'Twas not as though they had not previously made love but now Ingrid's soul cried out for what had been. Long gone were the days when they occupied a tent together getting to know one another when they were not lifting their swords in battle for the Empress's cause. Nay! She had been forced to wed so the brute could claim a title and strip away her lands that by right belonged to her! How would she ever forgive him or know that he truly loved her for who she was and not the wealth that would now line his coffers?

Bitterness consumed her leaving a sour taste in her mouth. Reaching over for a goblet of wine, she took a sip hoping some kind of magic might overturn the iciness of her cold heart. But 'twas no use, she thought putting the cup back down. How quickly life had changed. One moment she was happily in love and now… Ingrid shrugged, covering her face with her hands. Now, she had no idea how to move forward with the knight who was now her husband.

A heavy sigh left her. She was probably being ridiculous and should search her heart for her earlier feelings of Theobald and what they had shared together. They had been happy… at least for a few brief, stolen moments. She had fallen in love with him and deep down she knew he cared for her too… Did she not? But for some stupid reason all that had changed the moment he had told her of her birthright. Confusion wracked her head to the point that she did not even trust her own feelings. 'Twas not the best way to start a marriage together.

The door opened and there Theobald stood filling the entryway with his magnificent body. The rush of excitement seeing him was just as familiar to her as when he first found her hiding in the forest. She had never believed in love at first sight until she met this warrior who stood at the doorway.

Her attempts to remain uninterested to him would fail. She knew it with the next breath she took and, by the look upon his face, so did Theobald. As much as she might try to hide her feelings for him, the love she bore him would overrule whatever wrong he had done to her. Wrong at least in her overactive mind. In truth, what had he honestly done wrong? And yet, doubt still lingered in her mind and 'twas most unwelcome.

He closed the door, sliding the bolt into place. His stride across the room to her was like a lion stalking its prey. Towering over her, he took one finger and ran the warm digit across her cheek causing her to shiver in delight. Aye… her body would betray her faster than whatever else she might attempt to keep hidden from him. *Bloody Hell!*

"You are not in bed," he said and her heart once more betrayed her knowing what awaited her beneath the coverlets.

Ingrid shrugged as though his words mattered little to her. "I waited for you. I thought we could have speech together," she murmured raising her tormented hazel eyes upward.

"Aye. There is much to talk about but mayhap such a discussion can wait until the morn. The day has been long."

His words only confused her further about how they could proceed from this point forward. She wished to have this conversation cleared once and for all. Otherwise, she was unsure if she would ever be able to trust him.

"Theobald…" His name whispered in the darkness of the room lingered in the air as though to pull their two souls together. He took her hand bringing it to his lips.

"You are chilled," he said pulling her to her feet. Once close to his hard, well-formed body, she could feel the heat of this man. His strength and the warmth that was radiating from him were enough to curl her toes in anticipation of what would happen between them once abed.

"Am I?" she asked not realizing he spoke the truth.

"Aye." He took her hand and walked her toward the bed, throwing back the covers and waving his hand for her to get in.

Her fingers trembled when she tried to undo the ribbons of her robe at her throat. He saw her dilemma and with a husky *allow me*, he swiftly took care of the problem including slowly drawing the robe from her body. His warm hand caressed her shoulder before he replaced his fingers with his lips until he took her robe and placed the garment on a nearby chair. Now Ingrid only stood there with the lightest linen outlining her body from the fire in the hearth. His hot gaze roamed the length of her before he once more motioned to the bed.

Ingrid would not be reminded a third time, so she went to lay down and he pulled the coverlets over her quaking body. 'Twas not from the cold this time. Nay! 'Twas from the anticipation of Theobald joining her in their marriage bed and what would come next.

He went around the bed to the side nearest the door and sat on the edge. Ingrid watched his broad shoulders when he stretched and saw his sword stood near at hand. With a quick check of the room, she saw her own blade was also near the head of the bed as if it but awaited her need to use it for her protection.

His boot as it thumped upon the floor caused Ingrid to return to the present, and she watched in fascination when Theobald drew his tunic up and over his head. The rippling muscles of his back made Ingrid's fingers twitch in desire to touch his skin. Aye… she would most certainly fail in keeping up this pretense that she was angry with him for deceiving her. For in truth, 'twas not Theobald's fault they had been forced to marry. The Empress did in fact do her a favor by having them wed. She could not stay mad at him, and she was being foolish for even trying. She loved him and deep down in her soul, Ingrid knew Theobald cared for her too.

Her decision made, she threw the coverlet from her body and crawled across the bed to mold her body up against her husband's. He flinched in surprise but recovered quickly by looking over his shoulder into her eyes. Taking her hand, he kissed the inside of her wrist, and she gave him a smile.

"I thought you were angry with me," he murmured, turning slightly to look upon her fully whilst she sat back on her legs.

"I was," she replied. "I was hurt and confused. I am certain you can understand my predicament if you think of how you would feel if the situation had been reversed."

"Aye. 'Tis not exactly how I would have chosen to begin our lives together, Ingrid. I did not care that the Empress forced my hand, but you must know I would have offered for you once we had completed our service to her," he said humbly whilst he took a lock of her hair between his fingers. Its length took on a life of its own as he caressed her tresses, and it wrapped around his fingers as though taking possession of him. "You must know I care for you… nay… love you."

She gazed up into his eyes and there was nothing in their depths that told her he spoke a falsehood. He loved her and her heart soared hearing those beloved words escaping his lips.

"As I love you, Theobald." Her hand reached up to skim down his face, the scratchiness of his stubble causing friction to add to the excitement of what they were about to share.

He stared at her for another moment before returning to the task of undressing. She was only allowed a glimpse of his magnificent body before he joined her in their bed, drawing the coverlets over them. He pulled her into his side, his arm wrapping itself around her shoulder keeping her close.

With the steady rhythm of his heartbeat under her ear, she ran her hand along his chest until he took her hand once more and kissed it.

"Go to sleep, Ingrid," he murmured before kissing the top of her head. "I suspect the morrow will be just as long as today."

Confusion wracked her bed. Go to sleep? On their wedding night? She raised herself on her elbow to stare at the man in bewilderment.

"But are we not going to—"

"Nay, we are not," he answered and then settled her back into place, tucking the covers around her.

"But why?" she gasped out. He moved quickly, placing her beneath him. Bending forward, he kissed her gently as though giving her a promise of what would be. When he at last broke off their kiss, he caressed her cheek.

She gulped. "But why?" she repeated.

He returned to his place in the bed bringing her close against his side again. "Because although you may not voice them, you still have your doubts about my motives to marry you. If I must needs prove my feelings in order for you to trust me completely, then so be it. I will not make love to you until I am satisfied that there is no doubt in your heart that we have wed for all the right reasons."

"But—"

He kissed the top of her head. "Go to sleep, wife, and I will see you with the rising of the new sun."

A small smile lit her face at his words. She would have raised her head to look into his eyes, but he kept his hand upon the top of her head until his fingertips ran down the length of her hair. He wanted her trust. Now, this might be the start of a good beginning between them after all...

CHAPTER TWENTY-SEVEN

INGRID MARCHED HER way across the outer bailey, searching for her husband who was training with the other men upon the field. For her part, she was dressed in tunic, hose, and boots. She had refused to be gowned in a dress this morn and had shooed away the servant assigned to her. The poor girl had appeared as though she were amid a full-blown crying fit, but Ingrid had stayed resolute. For the morning, her decision to dress how she normally did was her choice. In the afternoon, she would be attending the Empress and would force herself to wear the gown and jewels, as was expected. But the afternoon was soon enough for that.

Once she had left her bedchamber, the Empress's attendants had been her second obstacle to obtaining her freedom. Eden, Rovena, and Petula had gasped in dismay to see Ingrid clothed thusly again. They did their best to deter her and make her change her mind to dress in a more ladylike manner, given her new position as the Lady of Calbridge, but Ingrid stayed true to her course. She meant to spend the morn training with the men. How else was she to keep fit to raise her sword for her Empress?

She made her way to the edge of the training field whilst Eden caught up with her. The two women remained silent as they observed the scene before them. The knights were all well-trained, but Ingrid only had eyes for one knight in particular. He swung his sword in a well-practiced move and she shielded her eyes when the steel caught the sunlight making it appear as though 'twas blazing. Sweat gleamed from Theobald's skin from his training causing Ingrid's heart to race with thoughts that he belonged only to her.

"Your husband is a fine-looking man. You are lucky to have him," Eden said softly whilst her gaze swept over the men.

"Lucky to have a husband who married me at the Empress's command? Theobald only wishes for the title of my heritage," Ingrid said, surprising even herself with the words that had come out automatically. She thought she had reconciled herself that such was not the case, but mayhap Theobald had been correct when he had told her last eve that she still had hidden doubts about the truth of his feelings.

The sweet sound of Eden's laughter rang out causing several knights nearby to stop their training. "Surely you know you speak a falsehood," she said whilst waving to several of the men who now showed her some interest until she continued. "He is devoted to you and you alone."

"We truly do not know each other well enough for me to determine if his eyes will wander to another someday," Ingrid replied as her gaze once more traveled to her husband.

An unladylike sound left the woman's lips. "I suppose you know him better than any other. If you do not have feelings for him, then there are plenty of men here who would be willing to take his place in your bed."

Ingrid scowled. "Did I say I had no feelings for Theobald?"

"'Twas the suggestion I heard in your words. If you do not care for the man or trust him, find another to replace him. He will surely do the same."

"We are wed," Ingrid said fiercely whilst watching Eden's eyes freely roam over Theobald's body. There could be no mistaking the hungry look this woman had on her face.

Eden laughed. "As if that ever stopped an illicit affair before..." She turned her back to the training field to stare directly at Ingrid. "Really, my darling girl, have you never been to court before now? 'Tis most common for courtiers to share partners when their husband or wives become… preoccupied."

Ingrid's fingers twitched on the hilt of her sword at her side. "You know very well that I have never been to court, nor do I have any desire to stay here any longer than necessary. I only await the Empress to release my sword from her service."

"But she has already done so, my friend, when she took you in upon your arrival in Winchester and then had you marry the man of her choosing. She will be most displeased to see you thusly attired," Eden said raising a hand to her nose as though an offensive smell was in the air.

"She never told me I could no longer train in order to keep myself fit," Ingrid proclaimed. She watched Eden carefully when the woman once more stared at one man in particular upon the field. If Ingrid was not careful, she just might lose her husband to the beautiful lady at her side. Jealousy reared its ugly head telling Ingrid that no matter what came from her lips, she did care for Theobald and greatly disliked the idea that he might take a lover.

"She should not have to. You have the clothes given to you by me and the other ladies. Wear them. They were a gift for you to enjoy," Eden stated before she continued. "You should decide your feelings for your husband, or you might lose him."

"To you," Ingrid hissed as though the woman had read her thoughts.

"Perchance… or to another. If you do not want him, there are plenty of women here who would be more than willing to take him to their bed."

"'Tis clear you would readily take my place."

"Do not let jealousy cloud your thoughts, my friend. I am not saying I would make an attempt to gain your husband's attention, only that he is a handsome and gallant knight. There are not many who continue to hold onto their beliefs of righting all the wrongs of the world. That man is full of valor, which makes him a prize for the keeping."

"And you think I do not know this?" Ingrid asked whilst she continued to assess Eden and her words.

Eden placed her hand upon Ingrid's arm. "I am only telling you all this so you can open your eyes and see what is before you. Theobald is yours. All you need to do is claim him. The rest will fall into place as is meant to."

As though the heavens were giving Ingrid a push in the direction her life would now be led, Theobald at last noticed her. He nodded to the knight he had been training with and crooked his finger for Ingrid to join him. She began making her way to her husband even whilst another knight went to Eden and began having speech with her. Ingrid shook her head wondering how fickle the lady was. One moment she was flirting with several men, the next implying she could have Theobald with a wave of her hand. Ingrid had no notion what to think of the woman, but she left that situation behind when Theobald sheathed his sword and took her hand.

"Come to train, my lady?" he asked in a husky whisper. His tone was one that belonged in their bedchamber. Her heart raced at the sound.

"With you?" Ingrid asked with a teasing grin.

"Of course. 'Twould be my pleasure to spend the day with my beautiful wife," he said with a chuckle.

Ingrid stepped back, pulling out her sword and waving the weapon before her. "Then you do not mind being bested by a woman."

Laughter erupted from her husband. "I see my wife is a wee bit cocky today. Let us see how you manage to defend yourself against me."

"Then let us begin your downfall, husband!" she taunted.

The sound of their swords clashing together was barely muffled by their combined laughter. And as the morning wore on, Ingrid swore 'twas one of the best days in her memory. Theobald gave her his best and did not coddle her as they trained which was exactly what she needed. He had eyes only for her, and 'twas how their relationship could now begin again.

CHAPTER TWENTY-EIGHT

F OR NIGH UNTO a fortnight, Theobald did everything within his powers to not take Ingrid each night in their bed. 'Twas becoming harder, as the eves passed into the next, to keep his hands to himself and retain the vow he had made to her and himself. What had he been thinking? His promise had seemed like a good idea at the time. Win his lady's trust and with it her heart. He had no notion that she would become such an enchantress, seducing him effortlessly with every look and every touch. Damn his sense of chivalry!

Their days together had found them on the training field. The Empress had voiced her displeasure to Theobald that he could not control his wife, but he in turn had politely informed the Empress that if he was to win his wife over, then he must needs allow her to do as she saw fit. If that included dressing in tunic, hose, and boots, then so be it. The Empress had waved him away with her bejeweled hand saying she would leave the taming of Ingrid up to him. 'Twas obvious his monarch disapproved and would rather have Ingrid dressed as the lady she needed to become.

Yet, Ingrid knew the role she must needs play and would change her attire accordingly each evening. She may have appeared the docile woman standing next to their Empress, and yet a person only had to take one look at Ingrid to know she was completely miserable. Her words in the forest haunted Theobald. How would she fit in at Calbridge as the lady of the keep? His only thought would be to give her more time here at court to accustom herself to the ways of the nobility. But while the passage of time had made her more adept at the tasks of serving the Empress, she remained entirely miserable in the role, showing no liking at all for life at court.

Thus far, the Empress appeared in no hurry to see them on their way to their new home, and Theobald was thankful. The more time he was able to spend with Ingrid, the more time he had to prove she could trust him. And so, they trained together during the daylight hours and dined and danced together in the eves. 'Twas a good way for them to get to know one another further and yet he was growing more and more uncomfortable that he could not have his wife completely whilst in their bed. 'Twas a conundrum of his own making.

He watched as Ingrid performed the intricate patterns of the dance with Oswin, of all people. The knight appeared to be more attentive than one should be of a friend's wife and yet Theobald refused to intervene. After all, Ingrid had her own free will to choose with whom she would dance. Theobald had already had his turn several times, and Richard had teased him that if he did not allow Ingrid to dance with another, the men might think he was actually in love with his own wife.

Theobald had refused to take the bait causing Reynard and Richard to laugh until Theobald excused himself. He found his arm taken by Lady Eden and he had no recourse other than to allow her to do so. He would not wish to cause a scene nor anger the Empress by treating one of her attendants with discourtesy.

"How may I be of service, my lady?" he inquired, dreading her answer for she appeared as though she would ask more from him than he was willing to give.

She pressed herself into his body and looked up batting her eyelashes at him. "I thought I could do you a favor."

"A favor?" He tried to remove her arm, but her grip was like a vise. This woman was on a mission, though only she knew for certain why she was acting in such a seductive way. He had never given her any reason to believe he might desire her company.

"Aye. To make your wife jealous, of course. Unless 'tis your wish for her to dance her way through the entire room of knights, excluding only you?" Eden inquired whilst running her fingertips across the front of his tunic.

"Ingrid may dance with whomever she wishes," Theobald said with clenched lips. This woman was making him uncomfortable, and he had no desire to further their association.

She giggled. "Smile. At least appear as if I hold some appeal to you. Elsewise, this ploy shall not have the desired effect and will be a waste of time," she purred stepping even closer.

Theobald looked down upon the woman and scowled. "I do not play the games of court life, my lady. There is no need to make Ingrid jealous."

"Mayhap we can continue this in my bedchamber," Eden said pressing on, undaunted.

"Nay," he said firmly prying her fingers from his arm. "You may find another man to conquer this eve, for I am not interested in what you have to offer."

Eden shrugged but once more took his arm, although her fingers now rested lightly upon the sleeve. "You cannot blame a woman for trying. Now, come... My offer to make Ingrid jealous still stands, and I am sure the result will be to your satisfaction."

"You cannot promise anything where my lady is concerned," he grumbled.

"Can I not?" she said taking one delicate finger and pointing across the room. "If you but take a moment to notice, your wife is about ready to tear my hair out. 'Twill not take much to push her over the edge. Mayhap a kiss..."

"Lady Eden... the only woman I will be kissing is my wife," he replied giving her a short bow. "If you would excuse me."

He left her there without allowing her time to comment but 'twas of no use. Somehow, the entire room of women appeared to be on a task to thrust themselves into his arms whether he wished them to or not. One after the other, they came to him, and he was becoming increasingly aware that Ingrid would not take much more. The fierce frown across her visage told him much.

The music of the current dance ended and Ingrid hastily excused herself from her current partner. Fleeing across the crowded room, Theobald caught up with her at the stairs to one of the turrets that led up to their bedchamber. He took hold of her hand in a firm grip.

"Ingrid…"

She yanked away from him. "Do not touch me."

"What have I done wrong?"

She threw up her hands. "Why not ask Lady Eden or any of the other women who have been all but throwing themselves at you this night?"

"'Tis not fair that you judge me for the actions of others. I have done nothing to earn your anger nor did I have any intentions to accept what those women offered," he fumed, running his hand through his hair.

"They are more than willing to have you in their bed. Feel free to take any one of them for all I care!" she yelled out.

"Your behavior is childlike, and your accusations have no merit. I have given you no cause to think that I am attracted to any other woman but you," he said whilst he attempted to take hold of her yet again. Instead, she distanced herself by climbing up another two steps.

"You must be bedding one of them for you are surely not taking me each night!" she cried before running up the rest of the stairs.

Theobald began following her as she fled to their room. He attempted to open the door, but she had slid the bolt into place. Banging his fists on the wooden portal only earned him a sore hand and after several attempts, he finally gave up. Lady Eden may have had a ploy to bring the two of them together, but it had had the opposite effect. The wedge between Theobald and Ingrid had now widened and he had no idea how he was going to pull them back together.

CHAPTER TWENTY-NINE

*L*OST… INGRID WAS completely lost and alone. The friendships that she had started to form with the Empress's other ladies in waiting had deteriorated as the women continued to rush to Theobald's side whenever he entered the room. Ingrid did not understand their sudden fascination with the man who was now her husband but the sly looks they tossed in her direction spoke volumes. *Either claim him yourself or they would gladly take your place.*

Her sour mood kept her from thinking rationally. She knew she was being unfair to Theobald and yet she could not stop the jealousy that coursed through her veins as though they were on fire. She could halt the situation at any time by having a simple conversation with the man. But barring him from their bedchamber that first night had only caused the rift between them to become as large as the ocean was wide, and she no longer knew how to cross it. She could not stop the way her emotions ran amok inside her head any more than she could simply walk across the room to her husband's side.

Ingrid gave a heavy sigh and took a sip of her wine. Should not Theobald be attempting to make the first move? After all, he was the one prancing around with women dangling from his arms. His sudden laughter from across the room pushed Ingrid's anger nearly to the point of erupting.

"You must know he only wishes to be with you, my lady," a man's voice intruded into her muddled thoughts.

Ingrid set her chalice down and turned to stare into Reynard's face. He was striking with his dark brown hair that boarded on black, but 'twas those steel-grey eyes that would one day be some woman's downfall.

"He has a funny way of showing it," Ingrid huffed.

"Those women do not have any hold of his heart, Ingrid. I may call you by your first name, may I not? We are family after all…" Reynard asked with a slight smile.

Ingrid nodded her head. Whether or not their marriage could be salvaged remained to be seen but annulling their union would be hard to do. The Empress expected them to leave soon for Calbridge but traveling there with Theobald suddenly felt as though 'twould never happen. Unless she could get over these confusing emotions, they would never stand a chance of making a go of it. Perchance the situation was as hopeless as Ingrid was feeling. Mayhap her heart would never be able to get over his betrayal.

"*God's Bones!* You are in love with him," Reynard whispered whilst reaching for his own cup to gulp down the contents.

"'Tis *that* obvious?" she asked praying that the tears she was attempting to hold back would not somehow cascade down her cheeks to embarrass her.

"Aye! Why, then, are you allowing those malicious women to fawn all over my brother?"

"Free will?"

Reynard harrumphed. "To hell with free will. If you but care to look close enough, my brother is miserable. He wants nothing to do with any of them."

"His laughter suggests otherwise," Ingrid said, shrugging. "He has only to makc his way to me. A show of good faith."

"The last time he tried, you barred him from your bedchamber. Did you expect him to break down the door in the keep?" he asked with a frown.

She stole another look at her husband before turning her tormented eyes to her brother-in-law. "He told you?" she whispered in shock. Clearly, Reynard was upset with her, but Ingrid felt that anger should be turned to his brother.

"Aye, after several tankards of ale to drown his sorrows. But I will not say more. 'Tis not my place, and I have revealed more than I should have. I only wished to speak my mind. 'Tis clear the two of you belong together. The only question that remains is which one of you will let your guard down long enough to let the other back into your life."

"I do not know if I can trust him," she said quietly knowing her emotions were too raw to make any decision where Theobald was concerned.

Reynard cursed beneath his breath. "I have never met two people who were more suited for one another while also being too stubborn for their own good."

He pushed his chair back and left her to her own solitude. Alone again with her thoughts, she was able to reach only one conclusion. She needed to leave Gloucester and soon. Yet how could she escape without Theobald's knowledge? And more importantly where would she go? Technically, Calbridge now belonged to her husband. She would only be his chattel and nothing more. Once she provided him with an heir, would she perchance be sent away to some unknown destination whilst he reaped the benefits of being the lord of the keep? Ingrid had heard tales whilst at court that this was sometimes the way of the nobility. She shuddered at the thought.

There was no one to give her the answer she needed, and a sob escaped her. She needed help but who would she ask? She knew what awaited a lone woman on the open road. Had she not learned as much when she encountered de Payne at the inn and upon the battlefield? Although she knew she could defend herself, traveling could still be dangerous without the company of men she could trust.

Her gaze swept the room of mostly strangers. The ladies in waiting had become distant and showed more interest in pursuing Ingrid's husband than in remaining friends with her.

The knights had been courteous enough to dance with and fight alongside, but she hardly knew them well enough to ask for their assistance. Oswin would certainly leap to the chance to aid her, but she was certain he would think she wanted more than to remain just friends. Reynard was Theobald's brother and Richard the same, although not blood related. She could not count on any of them to follow her wishes in this.

This only left two men. Blake Kennarde and Kingsley Goodee. Men she had fought with, side by side, for the Empress's cause. Men she could hopefully trust not to go running to her husband and reveal her intentions of leaving the castle.

Her decision made, she downed the remainder of her wine before standing and making her way across the room. The two men stood near the hearth, deep in conversation.

"Gentlemen… may I have a moment of your time?" Ingrid asked, stepping closer to the pair.

"Of course, Lady Ingrid," Blake proclaimed with a bow.

"How may we be of service to you, my lady?" Kingsley asked at the same time.

"Kind sirs… I have a proposition for you…"

Ingrid quietly began to outline her plan to return to her small farm outside of London. Although the two men initially protested, they ultimately agreed to help her find her way back home. With one last look at her husband, Ingrid left to pack the few things she could call her own. She would leave this life behind and never again look back.

CHAPTER THIRTY

THEOBALD ENTERED THE bedchamber he had recently shared with his wife. The fact that the door had been left ajar told him much. The bed had not been slept in, mayhap for the past two nights. Two nights that he had allowed her to think on her hurtful words. Two nights for her to remember all they had shared. Two nights that he had given her for her to come to terms with the truth that he did not wish for anyone other than Ingrid in his bed. Two nights that were obviously too damn long!

His angry stride took him across the room to open the lid of the wooden trunk he had bought for her things. The costly borrowed gowns were neatly folded. The lovely gems left behind glittered in the light from the torches held in the sconces on the walls. Digging into the depths of the trunk told him what he had already assumed. Ingrid was dressed in hose, tunic, and boots again. At least she took her cloak when she fled.

She had left him!

He sank into the nearby chair by the hearth, rested his elbows on his knees, and leaned forward. His hands brushed over his face as if this act alone would allow him to come to terms with the fact that his wife had actually left him. He would have thought she would, at the very least, have left him a note. But there was nothing. *Nothing!* Nothing but an empty room and a cold bed to gaze upon. 'Twas as though she felt that the connection that had been between them since they first met had never existed at all.

Bloody hell.

He stood and began pacing the room like a caged animal. Where would she go? The only logical place that made sense was Calbridge or Penhow Castles. Both now belonged to her and would see to her needs. She only had to make her way there and announce she was mistress of the hall. With the Empress's missive and wax seal, no one would question the authenticity of Ingrid's claim. But surely Ingrid knew Theobald would follow her to hell and back just to ensure she was safe. Or did she?

He shook his head. Considering they had not been talking for nigh unto a se'nnight, Theobald was not sure of anything anymore especially where his wife was concerned. She had become a stranger, and he missed those hazel eyes that used to stare at him with what he had naturally assumed was love. Love! If this was love, he had no use for such an emotion. He snapped out of his sour mood. Nay... love *had* found him, and he was destined to find his wife so that they could work out their differences. He would not denounce his feelings for Ingrid no matter how angry her actions had made him.

Richard appeared in the doorway to the chamber with Reynard and Oswin close behind. Theobald waved them forward.

"You have news of her whereabouts?" Theobald inquired whilst attempting to keep his rising anger in control.

"Aye," Richard said nodding. "She was seen leaving yesterday morn just prior to the rising of the sun."

"Why did no one stop her?" he bellowed.

"She appeared as a young man. The morning guards thought nothing of it," Richard replied taking a seat by the hearth.

Reynard came up to his brother and placed a hand on his shoulder. "There is more..."

Theobald threw his head back in frustration to stare at the ceiling. "Why am I not surprised?"

"She did not ride alone. Blake and Kingsley are also missing, so we assume they have all left together," Reynard finished.

Oswin muttered a curse. "If she needed help, I do not understand why she did not ask me. I would have told Theobald straight away what she was planning and then we would not be having such a conversation."

Richard tsked. "Which is why she did not ask you. Besides, you hold a certain affection for the lady whether she is wed or not. She would not have asked you because of it."

"I would never think to defile her. I would not dally with a married woman—particularly not one who is married to one of my best friends," Oswin swore whilst his hand went to the hilt of his sword.

Reynard took the other vacant seat by the hearth. "I think I know her well enough to know she would not have wanted to put herself into such a position as to travel with you, Oswin."

Oswin began to sputter his protest to defend himself, but Theobald came to stand next to the knight. "Calm down. It does Ingrid no good if we fight amongst ourselves. I am thankful she at least thought to take two very capable knights with her. God alone knows what might have met her on the road had she gone alone." He became lost in his thoughts as his memories of the red-haired beauty attempting to hide in the trees rushed across his mind. That hair would be her downfall.

Richard went to the window to open the shutter. He took several deep breaths before he spoke. "We must needs ask the Empress's permission to leave and search for your wife."

"And make our way to Calbridge as soon as we are able. With a couple days head start, she is likely to lock you out of your own keep if you do not get to her first," Oswin stated.

Theobald began pacing again and became lost in thought. If he was in Ingrid's place, would he truly head to the grand estate that now belonged to him? Nay. She would not, which left only one place for her to go.

"She is not heading to Calbridge," he muttered in annoyance.

"Penhow?" Reynard suggested.

"Nay," Theobald growled out. "She is heading toward London and the farm where she grew up."

Oswin cursed. "Why the devil would she go there?"

Theobald stopped his pacing and one brow arched upwards. "Because 'tis the last place she would expect me to look. Trust me... she is heading home."

Richard nodded and headed toward the doorway. "I will inform the Empress we must leave immediately."

Reynard followed behind him. "I will go ready the horses."

"Pack light. Bring only what is necessary. We travel fast and hard. If you cannot keep up, I will leave you behind," Theobald stated before he went to his own trunk and started to load his things into a leather satchel.

Oswin stood still as he watched Theobald move about the room. He finally stopped packing. "Well? Do you need a special invitation to join us?" he asked.

Oswin grinned. "I just wanted to ensure you wished me to accompany you."

Theobald nodded. "Aye. I might have need of your sword. Besides... I trust you."

Oswin nodded and bolted out the door leaving Theobald to resume his packing. His stubborn wife was in for a surprise when he finally caught up with her... That is, if he could find her. He did not mention to his brother or friends that Ingrid had never revealed in exactly what town outside of London her farm was located. He had a general idea, but the countryside was large and the village could be located anywhere.

He swore he would find her no matter the cost. One thing was for certain... nothing and no one would ever tear them apart again once she was back in his arms!

CHAPTER THIRTY-ONE

INGRID KNELT BY the glowing fire and proceeded to cut up the rabbit that she had been roasting over their makeshift spit. The meal would have to nourish them for the day. 'Twas not much of a meal to feed three people but she gave the larger portions to the two knights sitting across from her. She nibbled at the meager offering on her tin plate. She could barely choke the food down.

The ride across the countryside thus far had been uneventful and Ingrid was thankful that they had not encountered any obstacles—or Theobald himself. She was certain he would head in the opposite direction toward Calbridge... That is, if he attempted to follow her at all.

"He is going to kill us—if the Empress does not get to us first," Blake muttered as he ate his food.

"'Twas a terrible plan to begin with," Kingsley grumbled, too. "Whatever were we thinking? The Empress will not think kindly of us for not asking her permission to leave Gloucester."

Ingrid set her plate aside. "You did not have to agree to accompany me. You could have refused."

"And let you go alone?" Kingsley proclaimed with wide eyes. "That would have been just as bad if not worse."

Blake nodded. "Theobald will not be forgiving. I can almost feel the beating as if his fists have already bruised my body."

"You two are complaining like a pair of old women," Ingrid mumbled whilst attempting to keep her own concerns from her features. "Where are the courageous knights I fought alongside at

Winchester?"

Kingsley chuckled. "They lost their minds and became senile the moment they agreed to help you leave Gloucester. 'Tis obvious whatever sanity we had has left us, my lady."

Ingrid threw a stick into the fire. "Just Ingrid, if you would not mind."

"'Tis bad enough we are here with you," Blake began and then continued, "but 'twill only be worse if we do not respect your station in life. You are no longer Mistress Ingrid Seymour as you once were."

"Aye," Kingsley agreed. "You are from a noble house and must needs remember that, my lady."

"Fine… if you insist." Ingrid gave up trying to convince them of addressing her informally. She should be grateful they had complied with her wishes for aid in the first place.

The crackling fire was the only sound amongst them until Blake at last looked up from his plate to stare upon her. "He will follow, Lady Ingrid. You must know in your heart he would never let you go so easily."

She raised her troubled eyes to the two men and watched Kingsley point toward the road.

"Does he know where your farm is located?" he asked.

Ingrid shook her head. "Nay. I never mentioned the village by name, only that it was outside of London. He will not find us so easily."

A sound left Blake's lips. "You should have more faith in Theobald. As I just said, he will follow—so you must needs be prepared for when he at last catches up to you… and us."

The two men exchanged a look that said much. Theobald would not be pleased with any of them.

A distant rumble in the sky caused her to look upwards. The clouds were beginning to darken as though they, too, were as gloomy as her mood. Another round of thunder answered her thoughts, and she reached over for her plate to finish off her meal.

Blake ate the rest of his food and threw the bones into the

fire. "We are bound to get wet before the morn is over."

Kingsley did the same. "Best get in the saddle and try to out run the storm that is brewing. Is your farm much further, Lady Ingrid?"

Ingrid nodded before she stood. "'Tis still far enough that we are bound to get wet, but let us try to put some distance behind us all the same. There is an abbey in Northaw where we can find shelter if the storm worsens."

She began kicking dirt into the fire to douse the flames and she watched the smoke rise into the sky. The two knights made their way to the horses tethered close by and Ingrid gave a heavy sigh. Blake had been correct. This had been a stupid idea on her part, and all because she had let jealousy consume her. Her childish insecurities had gotten the best of her, and she regretted them. So why was she not heading back in the direction of her husband?

She stood staring up at the heavens as if they would provide an answer and yet none were forthcoming. If anything, the farm was close enough that 'twould provide them shelter this night as long as nothing else besides a storm deterred them from arriving there.

Ingrid mounted Valor and hesitated a moment whilst gazing back down the road they had traveled. Would Theobald follow her? How would he know which direction to go? She supposed she would have her answer soon enough. Either he would be living the high life at Calbridge or she would have one furious warrior on her hands when he at last found her at her father's farm.

She turned her mount to the open road as her mind continued to race with thoughts of the possible upcoming confrontation with her angry husband. She should have stayed with him but there was no turning back now. She had made her decision. For right or wrong, she could only play this out. If she searched her heart, she knew Theobald would somehow find her. She could only pray that once he did, he would forgive her foolishness for leaving him in the first place.

⊱ ❦ ⊰

CHAPTER THIRTY-TWO

FOR NIGH UNTO a se'nnights did Theobald and the men traipse the countryside searching one village after another for his missing wife. His sour mood had not changed since he left Gloucester, and he cursed the rain that continued to pound down upon them as if to match his ugly thoughts. Would he ever find her?

He had thought at one point in their journey that they had been close after seeing smoke rising from the treetops off in the distance. By the time they had arrived at a campsite along the side of the road, the rain had washed away any trace of what might have been Valor's hoofprints. Another dead end but still he had a feeling in his gut he had been close. Now… he was not so sure. Ingrid could be anywhere.

He adjusted the hood of his cloak whilst Buttercup neighed in protest at another day of being soaked to the bone. His companions had stopped voicing their complaints hours ago. He could not blame them. There was nothing more disheartening than leaving another village behind and feeling as though that which you seek is just out of reach. Where was she?

They came to a crossroad and Theobald held up his hand to halt their progress forward and to study the choices before them. Left, or right? 'Twas only a guess on which direction to go and he muttered a curse beneath his breath knowing one way might only take him farther from Ingrid.

The four knights sat on their horses side by side in silence.

Each man was lost in his own thoughts until Reynard spoke first.

"I fear, brother, if we do not find Ingrid soon that I will need to leave you to search without me. Time is running out for when I must return to the Empress as she demanded."

Richard pulled his cloak closer around his neck. "Aye. Another day, mayhap two, at the most, and then Reynard and I will need to depart back to Gloucester as well. Elsewise, we shall incur the Empress's wrath, and I care not to be on her bad side. She is dealing with enough knowing her half-brother is being held in exchange for Stephen."

Oswin spoke his thoughts. "I can continue to travel with you, Theobald, for as long as you need me."

Oswin was the last person Theobald would have thought could stay. If anything, Theobald assumed his brother might be the one to stay with him the longest. "The Empress gave you permission." 'Twas a statement, and Theobald was thankful he would not need to travel alone.

"Aye… until your wife has been found," Oswin replied before pointing toward the open road. "Which way now?"

Which way? Theobald mulled over the two choices before him until some instinct inside him made his decision. "We have been searching the countryside south of London for days. I have the feeling if we continue forward in this direction, we will only be getting farther away from my errant wife," Theobald stated whilst rubbing his eyes to focus on the road again.

"She still may be in this direction," Richard proclaimed.

"We take the road leading to the left," he ordered pulling on Buttercup's reins to lead them in the northern direction. "'Tis a good a choice as any."

"But this way will almost be retracing our path," Oswin complained bitterly.

Theobald muttered a curse knowing Oswin was right. "I stand by my decision. We can look at some of the other villages closer to the outskirts of London just in case she lived closer to town than what I thought. Let us proceed, men."

"We will find her, brother," Reynard exclaimed in encouragement.

"Aye," Richard reaffirmed. "If not today then on the morrow."

Thunder clapped above them, and they brought their horses to a gallop to reach the next village. If they were lucky, they would find shelter for the night and a warm meal to fill their bellies. Hopefully they would also locate Ingrid's farm and the lady herself.

They traveled for most of the day, nigh unto another thirteen miles before they came upon another small village. There was not much here but a few thatched roofs, but Theobald could make out what appeared like an abbey in the distance. He pointed toward the structure, and they quickly made their way to the church. Tethering their horses near a group of trees, they grabbed their satchels before making their way inside for a brief reprieve from the torrential downpour that had plagued them for days.

Puddles formed beneath their feet whilst they stood listening to the song of the monks inside the chapel. Their voices raised to the heavens had a soothing effect on Theobald's frayed nerves, and despite the condition of their garments, he stepped forward to peer into the interior of the small church. One of the clergymen noticed their group and he made his way to the rear of the chapel. His brown robe was modestly made, and a crucifix swayed on the end of a beaded belt at his waist. And still the calming song of the monks continued.

The monk held out his hand and motioned for them to enter. "Welcome, my children. Please come in."

Theobald shook his head and made his way back into the entrance to the abbey. "I am afraid we would only drench the pews with our sodden attire, Father."

"Then how can I help you?" the monk asked.

"We are searching for my wife. She would be traveling with two male companions. She might be dressed as a boy, but you could not mistake her with her red hair."

The monk stared upon Theobald for several seconds before he replied. "I cannot vouch that I have seen her myself, but I can inquire if any of my brothers have come across them. They are at their prayers, however, and will continue for several more hours."

"Is there someplace where we may take shelter for the night?" Richard asked stepping forward.

"All are welcome here, and accommodations can be found for you along with a hot meal. 'Twill be modest, as we live a simple life here at St. Albans, but 'twill break your fast if you have not eaten this day."

Theobald gave a slight bow. "We would be most thankful, Father. Do you perchance have a place for our horses?"

"There is a small stable out back where they, too, will be out of the rain. Come with me," the monk stated and began making his way through a door that led to a long corridor running the length of the chapel.

He showed them the room where they could sleep, and Theobald asked Reynard to see to their horses. Richard and Oswin went with him leaving Theobald to fend for himself. He did not mind the few moments to himself as he went to his satchel and opened the bag. There was one tunic that had managed to stay mostly dry, and he quickly donned it and made his way back into the chapel.

He sat at one of the rear pews, knelt on the cold stones, clasped his hands together and bowed his head to pray. He softly whispered his petitions up to God, asking for the forgiveness of his sins and the strength to carry on to find his beloved wife. Over and over again did he plead for help from a higher being knowing that his devotion in God would restore his faith that all things were possible if you believed in Him.

He at last whispered a soft *amen* and still the monks' song continued giving Theobald the peace he had stood in need of. He left the chapel to find a meal with a new outlook and a better disposition than how he had begun the day.

Ingrid was near… he just knew it!

CHAPTER THIRTY-THREE

Epping Forest
Essex

INGRID SLOWLY MANEUVERED Valor through the towering tress of the dense forest. She felt like they had left the road days ago instead of hours. But the way ahead was well known to her, and she only waited for the moment when they would come to the clearing of fields ready for harvest. 'Twas just ahead… home!

At least the blasted rain had finally stopped beating down upon their weary bodies. Blake and Kingsley had hoped to spend the night in Northaw and in the abbey, but Ingrid had insisted they continue onwards. 'Twas only another eighteen miles or so. What was a few more hours in the saddle after all the days they had already put behind them? She wanted her own warm bed beneath her come this eve.

"'Tis just beyond those trees," she said pointing off into the distance. She could at last see the break in the forest and was elated that home was nearly within her reach.

They broke through the foliage that had been surrounding them and burst into a field of golden wheat. The sun decided to poke its way through the clouds overhead as though to say, *welcome*. Ingrid raised her head to feel the warmth of the rays falling down upon her. The sun had never felt this good.

They skirted the edges of the fields and began making their way to the village. News quickly spread that Ingrid had returned and they soon became surrounded by the village folk once they reached what could be considered the town square. She gazed upon familiar faces until she espied one in particular who was pushing his way through the crowd. She easily jumped down from Valor's back and was immediately crushed in a fierce embrace.

"I knew you would come back to me," Charles whispered whilst holding her tightly in his embrace.

Ingrid peered over her shoulder when she heard the sound of steel leaving a scabbard. She shook her head and Kingsley replaced his sword before he and Blake dismounted.

"Charles… please let go of me," she said softly.

He ignored her subtle request, kissing her cheek and holding her again. His hand skimmed her hair in a gentle caress. "I told them all you would be back, and now here you are. Safe in my arms where you belong."

"Charles, please release me," she tried again. She did not wish to crush his spirits now any more than when she left months ago, but nor could she allow him to take such liberties. She would need to gently inform him she was now married but not here. Not within the hearing of everyone in the village.

"My lady," Kingsley's address caused a hush to fall over the crowd around them.

Ingrid frowned at the man. "Not now, Kingsley."

"But Lady Ingrid—"

"I said *not now*, Goodee," she replied, interrupting him. Kingsley and Blake exchanged silent glances and continued to stand by their horses, holding the reins while they waited for what would come next.

Charles slowly raised his head to stare upon her. The golden tints to his amber eyes stood out before he gave a fierce frown whilst turning his attention to her riding companions. "Who are they?" he growled out.

Ingrid watched the play of emotions running rampant across Charles's features. *God's Bones!* Was this how she had appeared when jealousy had clouded her judgement? She would be hard pressed to explain herself to Theobald once they met again.

She took Charles's hand as she had done a million time before in their youth. He mistook the gesture as something more as happiness swept across his handsome features. She hastily withdrew her grip. He appeared crestfallen once more and his mask of jealousy rose again to the surface.

"Well?" he scowled at her and her friends. "Will you not tell me who these two men are that you have been riding with?"

"Aye, I will once we see to our horses, I have a fire lit in my hearth, and we have had some time to fill our empty stomachs. We have been riding long and hard, and I must needs rest my weary self before I tackle another obstacle in my life," she proclaimed looking upon her friend in sympathy. "I am most certain you understand my plight and will give me the time I need."

A blush of embarrassment flushed his face. "Aye, Ingrid, of course. Take what time you need," Charles said stepping away from her and crossing his arms over his chest.

His arms bulged with muscles, reminding her that he was not the same scrawny youth from their younger days together. Nay. This was a man who was used to hard labor, and he had the body to prove it… just like the men she was with, along with her husband. She could see Charles would demand answers from her soon and would not wait long for her to settle into her dwelling. Her life here had been so much simpler in her youth. Now that Charles was a man fully grown, he appeared to think he had the right to claim ownership over her. He would be hard pressed to accept the truth.

"Thank you for understanding, Charles," she finally murmured, although from the looks he was giving her, her words were a falsehood. He was far from understanding anything concerning her and her traveling companions. "Come by my hut in about an hour. That should give me enough time to get myself settled."

The crowd parted giving Ingrid, Blake, and Kingsley a straight path in the direction of her home. She wasted little time pulling Valor toward the small barn in the backyard. 'Twas not much in the way of a stable, but large enough for the three trusted steeds. They made quick work of taking off the saddles and bridles. Combs were found to brush the horses down and one of the villagers came to bring several bags of oats. Whilst Ingrid thanked the man, he informed her that a hot meal would be brought over so they could eat their fill. Ingrid was thankful for this as well. She had no provisions for a lengthy stay here and would have to rely on the generosity of others. Another part of her plan she had not thought completely through.

Blake and Kingsley took off to clean themselves in a nearby stream, giving Ingrid the moment of privacy she had not even realized she needed. She slowly opened the cottage door. Memories of her father flooded across her mind in wave after wave. She could almost feel a physical manifestation of the love that he had for her washing over her as she remembered all the good times they had shared. She could envision him sitting by the fire sharpening a knife or eating a meal she had prepared for them. A sob caught in her throat as she recalled that, despite how close she had considered them to be, he had still kept her birthright a secret from her. Why had he done that? The lie still did not sit well with her. She wanted to demand answers, but there was no one who could give them to her. Not anymore.

A knock sounded upon the door, and Ingrid assumed Blake and Kingsley had returned. She opened the door only to see Charles standing on the other side. He was earlier than expected, but she could do nothing but allow him entrance.

Before she could protest, he kissed her cheek as he swept by her, making his way over to the hearth to start a fire. Once the flames were ablaze, he at last stood to stare upon her.

"You look different," he stated, taking a seat on a wooden chair whilst motioning for her to do the same with the vacant one across from him.

Inwardly she sighed. If he had given her the time she had

requested, she would have at least had the opportunity to wash herself and change into clean garments. Instead, now she was having to entertain a guest in her own home still feeling the dust and grime from days in the saddle.

"You are early," she said, crossing the room to sit. "I asked for an hour."

"I could not wait that long," he mumbled, looking sheepish. "I have missed your company."

"I would have preferred you to wait until the appointed time. I have yet to change and clean myself from my travels. I have only had the time to see to my horse," she said with firm lips.

"There was no need to clean up just for me but I appreciate that you would like for me to see you looking your best," he said whilst inspecting her.

She cursed beneath her breath. "I have been traveling for days in the rain, Charles. My desire to be presentable was not with the intention of being pleasing for you or anyone for that matter. 'Twas a desire to see myself clean and to settle back into my home after being gone for so long."

"You should have never left," he replied.

And there it was… the dig she should have expected from him.

"I had a mission to fulfill and a duty to the Empress Matilda." She looked directly into his amber eyes, watching whilst a multiple of reactions crossed his features before he masked them.

"I apologize for not waiting the hour that you requested. But as I said, I could not wait knowing you were home. Besides, no matter what you look like, you are always beautiful to me, Ingrid," Charles proclaimed with a bright smile.

"That is kind of you to say, Charles, but there is much that needs to be said between us," she began but halted once he reached across the space between them to take hold of her hand. She allowed it but briefly before she pulled her fingers from his grasp.

He sat back in his chair and a frown marred his handsome

brow. "You have changed."

Ingrid nodded. "War will do that to a person. I have seen and done… much."

"So, you did catch up with the Empress's army. Hiding your identity must have taken a lot of convincing on your part."

A blush rushed across her cheeks. "I am afraid my ploy did not last for long. I was seen from the start for that which I am… a woman wielding a sword for a cause."

"They knew you were a woman and still let you fight beside them?" he asked with wide eyes.

"Aye."

"And you were not… harmed?" He leaned forward and rested his elbows on his knees whilst waiting for her answer.

Ingrid swallowed hard. "I was given protection."

"Protection? From whom?" he bellowed, coming to a stand and almost knocking over his chair.

"If you cannot keep your voice down and be civil, Charles, then this conversation will soon be at an end. I am too tired to try to appease the angry jealous thoughts running through your head." She waited until he growled out a curse and then returned to his seat.

"Then by all means, please continue to tell me who offered you his protection," he said through clenched teeth.

"His name is Theobald Norwood, Earl of Calbridge…" Her voice trailed off. Ingrid closed her eyes. This had been the first time she had said Theobald's complete name and title aloud. She was almost disappointed when she opened her eyes once more and his was not the face staring back at her. She gulped before she finished her thoughts. "… and he is my husband."

Charles's face appeared as if he were going through a range of emotions from her words. Ingrid could not blame him. 'Twas hardly what he would have been expecting. She did not have long to wait for his anger to erupt.

"Husband? You are gone but a few months and you marry a man who's practically a stranger even though you knew I was waiting for your return?" Charles shouted and slammed his fists on the arms of his chair. A crack echoed in the room from the force.

"I never asked you to wait for me—and I never gave you cause to believe I would return your affections. You know that I've always considered us to be nothing more than friends. I could never come to terms with our relationship becoming anything more than that," Ingrid said calmly. She knew her friend was hurting and did not wish to rub salt into his wounds, but nor would she indulge his fantasies.

"But I love you!" He stood and began to pace the small room until he went to lean an arm on the mantle of the hearth. His head then rested on his arm.

She rose for her chair and went to him, placing a comforting hand upon his shoulder. When he looked up, his amber eyes were brimming with unshed tears. "Charles... I love you like a brother... nothing more," she whispered.

"I had such hope for us, and now 'tis all for naught." He straightened himself up and wiped his eyes with the back of his sleeve. "I suppose one of those men you traveled with is this husband of yours?"

Ingrid shook her head. "Nay, he is not here."

He scowled. "Do you love him?"

"Aye."

"Then where is he? How could any man leave you to your own devices?"

She tried to think of the best answer. "He will be here soon."

"You do not sound overly confident, and I believe there is more you are not telling me," he said with a raised brow.

"My husband and I have much to... reconcile," she softly stated.

"I will not ask for you to clarify what is going on that would cause you to travel without him." Charles headed toward the door. "I do not think I can handle more today than what you have already confessed. Mayhap later we can continue this conversation when I have a clearer head. I do not wish to say something I may one day regret."

Charles did not wait for her reply and instead left her there alone with her thoughts. Aye… there was still much to tell him, and she could only hope that her words that Theobald would be here soon would ring true.

CHAPTER THIRTY-FOUR

Much of the morn had dwindled away until one of the monks had found Theobald and his men sitting outside beneath a tree. The man recalled Ingrid and the others staying for a night to get out of the rain. He had overheard Ingrid mention that they were heading toward Epping Forest and her farm on the eastern edge. So now Theobold at least had a direction in which to head—though inwardly he cursed knowing he had spent days backtracking when he could have taken the road to the right and arrived there possibly sooner. His gut instinct had failed him but at least now he knew where to go rather than wandering aimlessly. He would find his wife before the day was at an end.

They had wasted little time saddling their horses and getting back to their mission to find his wife. Soon she would be back where she belonged. That is, if he could only convince her of his feelings for her and her alone. She was a stubborn as he was. Clearly, they were made for one another.

The eighteen or so miles it took to travel to Ingrid's village felt like 'twould take a lifetime. Time passed as it tended to do and soon, Theobald and the men arrived in the tiny farming community. Thatched cottages appeared in his vision, much like those they had already visited. But these seemed different because this time, Theobald knew that this had been Ingrid's home. She had played here as a child and grown up here into the beautiful young woman she had become. His clear mind after the day before spent in prayer had helped Theobald let go of much of his anger with Ingrid for running from him in the first place. Now he was filled with hope that they could be happily reconciled.

His eyes searched ahead into the faces who were hesitant about strangers entering their village. Some scurried to gather up their children, others huddled together in apparent fascination to learn what their business here might entail. Yet, there was only one face Theobald longed to see and 'twas the one person he did not encounter. He could not miss, however, the two knights who quickly pushed through the crowd to reach their side.

Theobald tried to keep his temper in check as he slid to the ground from the saddle. His face surely showed any who cared to look close enough that he was going to fail once Blake and Kingsley were in his reach.

"Thank the heavens, Theobald, you made it," Kingsley announced in relief but held up his hands in defeat. "Do not take out this matter on us. We kept her safe!"

Blake stepped forward. "Aye. She is safe and that should be your main concern."

Theobald cursed. "Safe? My concern should be that she is safe? I have been at my wits end trying to find her since she left. By *Saint Michael's Wings* you two are idiots to have aided her in leaving me!"

Kingsley wagged his finger at Theobald. "You would rather she go alone?"

"Of course not," Theobald sputtered in anger.

Blake nodded. "She would not be talked out of her decision. Be thankful we came with her. She has no sense of direction and we became lost several times. What should have only taken a few days took double that, but we knew you would eventually catch up with us."

Reynard inched his horse forward. "Brother... you are creating a spectacle. Mayhap this conversation could be taken elsewhere?"

Richard dismounted. "I hope there is a stable somewhere for the horses. They have earned a rest."

Kingsley nodded. "'Tis not much but 'twill provide shelter."

Oswin also dismounted. "We could use a reprieve from our travels, but you had best tell our friend where to find his wife or he just might take his frustration out on all of us."

Blake pointed off into the distance. "There's a path into the forest past the fields where you'll find a stream. She went in that direction to wash some of her garments."

He handed Buttercup's reins to his brother. "See to my horse and then find yourself some place warm to rest your heads. I have matters of import to impart upon my missing wife."

His stride was one of pure determination. She was so close. He continued onward through the fields of wheat and entered the forest, plunging himself into its shadows. He stopped to listen to his surroundings and heard the sound of the creak nearby. He followed the sound but stopped short of leaving the tree line when he espied Ingrid talking with a blond-haired man.

When Theobald heard his wife call the man *Charles*, he knew this was her childhood friend, although from the looks of things, this man wanted more than mere friendship. Theobald began listening to their conversation. He knew Ingrid was more than capable of handling the situation and protecting herself but he still worried. His eyes scanned the surrounding area. Where the bloody Hell was her sword? Theobald clenched his fists at his side when Charles stepped a little too close to Ingrid.

"This is hardly the place to continue our conversation, Charles," Ingrid hissed dropping the sopping wet tunic onto a nearby bolder. "I have work to do, and I need to figure out how I will feed myself and my two friends. What little monies I had were given to the monks at an abbey where we took shelter from the storm. I cannot continue to take advantage of the generosity of the two knights I traveled with, nor can I keep taking handouts from the villagers. Not when taking their food might mean that their own families go hungry."

"I care not for the villagers, only that you admit that you care for me," Charles growled out.

Ingrid put her hands on her hips. "I *do* care for you, Charles, like a *brother*. When will you get that through that thick skull of yours?"

"How can I convince you to see me otherwise?" he pleaded whilst attempting to reach for her hands. Ingrid stepped back.

"You cannot. I do not understand why you continue to push this matter. You know very well that it matters not how you may wish our relationship can be closer. I am now married," she said taking hold of the wet tunic and wringing the water from the fabric.

"Mayhap a kiss would change your mind." Charles reached around to grab her waist in an attempt to pull her close. Ingrid once more dropped the garment to place her hands firmly on his chest.

She pushed hard but Charles barely moved. "Are you mad?" she said angrily. "The only man I will be kissing is my husband. Now, let me go!"

A smile of satisfaction at his wife's words spread across Theobald's face. Having heard enough, he came forth from the trees. "Am I interrupting anything, wife?" he asked attempting to hide his amusement when the two people suddenly broke apart.

Relief appeared to sweep across Ingrid's face. "Theobald!" she cried out.

"Have you missed me?" he asked whilst holding out his hand. A sob escaped her as she ran into his arms and buried her face in his chest. "I will take it by such a welcome that you have," he said chuckling.

She gazed up at him with tear filled hazel eyes. "I have no ken what you find so amusing."

"We can discuss that later once we are in the privacy of your home. Now, tell me who this is who thinks to take advantage of my wife," he asked even though he already knew Ingrid's answer.

She clutched his tunic. "'Tis not what you think."

Her frightened eyes told him that she worried about what he might have seen or overheard. Court life and how she must have viewed the scenes played out for her benefit came to his mind.

He took a finger to tip her chin up. "I know that you have been faithful," he said before leaning down to whisper in her ear. "Just as you should have known nothing would happen between me and those women at court before you decided to flee."

She had the decency to look a bit ashamed that she had taken flight. He watched as she gulped. "I am sorry, Theobald."

"There will be time for that later. After crossing the breadth of England, I am content that I have at last caught up with you. You have given me a merry chase, my dear," he said good naturedly. "Now, who is this that I have yet to meet?"

"This is my childhood friend, Charles. Charles, this is my husband, Theobald Norwood," Ingrid said by way of introduction.

Theobald nodded and stepped toward the younger man who most would consider a rival for Ingrid's affections. But he and his wife had spent enough time apart and he would in no way allow a man from her past to attempt to lay some claim to a woman who already was his wife.

Theobald held out his hand and Charles reluctantly took his forearm. They stood almost toe to toe as if assessing each other's worth.

"A pleasure, Charles," Theobald said as he continued to stare upon the younger man. "Thank you for ensuring Ingrid's safety until I could arrive."

A sound left Charles's lips. "'Twas not hard. She has been my… friend… for many a year now, my lord."

"I know what a handful she can be, stubborn woman that she is, but that is why we love her, is it not?" Theobald asked with a raised brow, knowing this man before him cared very much for the lady. Charles nodded his reply.

"Aye… I suppose this is true," Charles finally declared turning his gaze upon Ingrid. He gave her the briefest of nods before taking his leave without another word.

Theobald crossed his arms over his chest whilst keeping his

glare upon Ingrid. "Will we have further problems with that one declaring himself?" he asked, attempting to keep any annoyance from his tone.

"I cannot even imagine why Charles would want to make some kind of claim on me in the first place," Ingrid answered taking a step closer.

"Can you not?"

The silence grew between them with only the sound of the nearby creek as the water rushed over the boulders and riverbed. She didn't answer his question and he finally crossed the distance between them.

His hand caressed her cheek. "The fact that you cannot in truth see that you are a treasure that any man might covet is a true testament of the rarity that is all *you*, my dearest wife."

She leaned into his palm. "Then you forgive me?"

A muffled laugh escaped him. "Forgive you? Surely not that easily, my dear."

Her eyes widened. "But I thought—"

He went to her quickly, picked her up, and tossed her over his shoulder, landing a playful slap on her bottom. "That was your first mistake, my pet. Or mayhap 'twas your second. I believe I lost count in the se'nnight I have been traveling trying to track you when you should not have left me in the first place."

"Theobald! Put me down this instant!" she bellowed pounding upon his back with her fists. Her feeble efforts went without success in getting her way.

Another gentle slap landed on her other buttock. "Nay, my disobedient wife! I think perchance to ensure you cannot escape me, I shall have to hold you captive until I have had my wicked way with you. Only then will I be able to prove that you are the only woman who shall ever be invited into my bed again."

Ingrid calmed down until she finally answered him with the softest whisper. "Do you promise?"

"I promised you there would be no other on the day we wed. You just never gave me the opportunity to prove myself to you when those women began to play their games. You should have listened to your heart, Ingrid—or rather, you should have listened to mine, for then you would have heard that it will forever and always beat only for you."

"Oh, Theobald," she said with a catch to her voice.

Theobald pulled her down from his shoulder to stand before him. He took hold of her arms bringing her into his embrace and proceeded to kiss her. 'Twas a kiss with a promise—one that he hoped would erase any further doubt she had left in her mind. She was his just as much as he belonged to her. His kiss was a vow that they would never be parted again even if the world around them was filled with chaos.

$$\longleftarrow \quad \bullet \quad \text{◦⦿◦} \quad \bullet \quad \longrightarrow$$

CHAPTER THIRTY-FIVE

INGRID HAD RISEN early knowing they would be traveling again this morn. A small repast was left on the table for Theobald and the men to partake of once they finished attending the horses. She had already broken her own fast. Their gear had been packed the night before, and there was little left in this small place she called home that she wished to take with her. There was only one thing left to do… mayhap two.

Her reunion with Theobald had been… magnificent. She gave a shy smile as she remembered how attentive to her needs he had been with her that first night when he had at last finally found her. That was until she begged him to take her. Gentle was one thing and had its time and place, but they had been apart for too long. Her desire that they be as one overtook all common sense of acting the genteel lady. She had wanted Theobald in ways she never thought possible, and he had proved to her that he could take her to new heights.

She would certainly not complain with him teaching her what he liked in their marriage bed. And she learned a few things in their play she had not known she was capable of. One moment the shy kitten, in the next she became a temptress who reveled in hearing him moan and call out her name. Aye… she had learned quickly what he liked, and she had enjoyed their coupling, too! She could only hope that the other knights—camping out in the fields to give the married couple some privacy—had not been close enough to hear the racket they had made.

She picked up the two small bouquets of wildflowers tied with ribbons she had gathered yesterday and made her way across the village to the cemetery. The graves of her parents were not hard to find. It seemed as though it was just yesterday that she had buried her father next to the mother she had never known. She had been loved. That much her father had told her about the woman who died giving birth to Ingrid. Yet there was so much he had kept from her. How could he have gone to his grave knowing he had hidden such vital information as to the origins of her birth from her? That question would always remain a mystery. He certainly was not going to rise from the grave to impart any final words of wisdom.

She placed one bunch of flowers at the head of each headstone. The carvings in the stone had their names but nothing else. Kneeling between the graves, she looked upon her father's and could only ask herself why. *Why did you not tell me I was born into a noble house?*

"You may never have closure to your question, Ingrid," Charles's voice answered behind her as if he had read her very thoughts. But Ingrid knew that Charles had no knowledge of the inner turmoil, since she had decided to keep secret from him and the villagers the true circumstances of her birth. In the little bit of time she still had with them, she hadn't wanted her rank to get in the way or make anyone feel uncomfortable. She had not spoken the truth even to Charles. He likely just thought she had unfinished business since her father had died so suddenly.

She wiped her tears and stood taking one last look upon the graves not knowing when or even if she might ever return this way. Ingrid turned her attention to the man who had seen her through the worst of her childhood. He had always been there to right the wrongs of the way she had been treated... or rejected... by the other village girls. He had wiped her tears away as a child and she in turn had held him in the very highest esteem even though she knew someday she would break his heart. She had always known he had romantic feelings for her but she could never have those same emotions, even as she appreciated the wonderful man Charles had become.

She ignored his comment, redirecting the conversation. "I am sorry I could not give you more, Charles. You deserve better than what I could have offered you," she murmured coming to stand next to him and taking his hand.

His thumb ran over her skin in a gentle caress. "You mean only half your heart?"

"Aye. If you look deep enough, you will see that we never would have been happy together in the way a husband and wife should be," she said, hoping he would understand.

"I would have been willing to try," he confessed whilst squeezing her hand.

She gave him a weak smile. "I know you would have. I hope you know I only wish for your happiness, Charles."

He gave a half laugh, half snort. "Happiness… what is that?"

"You will know it when you see it with the right person at your side," she answered him brightly in the hopes he, too, would find love someday.

"And does your husband make you happy?" he asked whilst looking in the direction of Ingrid's home. Theobald stood there as if waiting for a sign she was in need of rescuing.

"Aye, he does."

Charles nodded. "If such is the case, then I am happy for you, Ingrid."

"Thank you for understanding."

He offered her his arm to take, which she did. They began making their way toward the tethered horses. "I am not certain I understand anything, these days, Ingrid. Only that I lost you."

She pulled on his arm to halt their progress. "You have not lost my friendship, Charles. You must know this. That is the one thing that will never be taken away from you. If you ever have need of me, you can always send word to Calbridge Castle."

He gave a slight grin. "A lady and her castle. Who would have ever thought such a thing was possible for you?"

She gave a shrug knowing such words would have been out-landish if spoken but months ago. "Certainly not me. I still consider myself a simple woman with simple needs."

He patted her hand and then continued forward. "That will all change once you arrive at your new home. I hope you are prepared for all that will entail."

"I can only take things one step at a time." She made every attempt to appear the confident woman Charles had always known but inside she was still quaking in fear of the unknown. Nervous knots filled her stomach when she allowed herself to imagine what awaited her in her future but she knew Theobald would help her along the way.

"Then I wish you and your husband well and Godspeed, dearest Ingrid," Charles said. From the look upon his face, he appeared resigned to her situation.

She placed a chaste kiss upon his cheek. "I wish you all the happiness life can offer, Charles," she replied knowing this could also be the last time she saw her friend. 'Twas perhaps best that things were left this way. Her future lay ahead of her, not behind her in the past.

Theobald waited patiently for them to arrive. Oswin came from the cottage with a piece of bread and cheese in his hand. He waved his hand in Ingrid's direction as though giving her thanks for the simple meal before taking another bite and heading toward his horse. Blake and Kingsley came next, followed by Reynard and Richard. All in all, they would be quite the traveling party as they made their way back to the Empress in Gloucester.

Theobald stepped forward to take his wife's hand. He nodded to Charles who returned the gesture. "Are you ready, my dear?" her husband asked.

"Aye, I suppose. As ready as I shall ever be," she answered looking once more at the cottage. She had previously spoken to Charles about keeping the place for himself or giving it to anyone who was in need of a place to stay. The choice was up to him. She no longer needed it or the memories that went with it. She had given the cottage and its belongings to Charles to do with it as he pleased.

Theobald helped her into her saddle after checking the cinches one last time. He gave Valor a pat and the proceeded to mount Buttercup who neighed in protest. Ingrid giggled hearing her husband call his steed an ornery beast before he called out to the men to proceed.

"Godspeed, Ingrid," Charles murmured once again, and Ingrid gave him a nod before flicking the reins of Valor.

Her horse kicked forward, and she looked back upon her past one last time. Charles waved goodbye, and she did the same. She made a vow to herself that her past would no longer haunt her future. She was now heading home and to her new life with Theobald at her side where he belonged.

✦ ⬥ ❧ ⬥ ✦

CHAPTER THIRTY-SIX

THE TRIP BACK to Gloucester and the Empress did not take as long since there were no wrong turns this time, but it was unfortunately just as wet as their previous journey. Once more the sky decided to voice its displeasure by pouring water from the heavens down upon them for days on end. This made the going slow and treacherous, but they had at last reached their destination. Theobald could see for himself that Ingrid was weary, and he longed for a warm, dry bed along with a cool drink to slake his thirst.

Word spread through court life quickly of the arrival of Theobald's party and how he finally caught up with his disobedient wife. Rumors quickly took flight how he had beaten Ingrid for leaving him. Theobald lacked the energy to reprimand those who spread such falsehoods. He was too tired and only required a life of leisure where this bloody war was over. But that, too, was denied him. Once they had changed into dry clothing, they were all summoned to attend the Empress.

With Ingrid at his side and their traveling companions directly behind them, they entered the great hall where the Empress sat in her throne-like chair. Bejeweled and gowned in her finest, her ringed fingers drummed on the arm of her chair whilst waiting for their approach. The men bowed whilst Ingrid curtseyed. Silent, with lowered eyes, they awaited either their condemnation or their new instructions.

"You test my patience, Lady Ingrid," the Empress began

before crooking her finger for Ingrid to come further. "What, pray tell, were you thinking to leave here without permission?"

"I was not of sound mind, my Empress."

"Sound mind? You fool! My best knights were required to go traipsing across the countryside searching for you," she said with a fierce frown before she pointed to Kingsley and Blake. "And you two… Goodee and Kennarde… what do you have to say for yourselves?"

"We only offered to protect Lady Ingrid, Empress," Kingsley answered with a bow of respect.

"Aye. We were bound by our honor to not allow Lady Ingrid to travel on her own," Blake added.

"Ack! She was more than capable of fending for herself," the Empress murmured. "Have you not seen her these many months fighting against my enemies for my cause?"

The two men began sputtering a reply, and the Empress waved them off as her attention came back to Theobald. "Well, Norwood? Have you tamed this runaway wife of yours yet?"

Theobald could only grin. "Probably not, my Empress."

"A shame, but I should not be surprised. I said it at your wedding, and I will say it again… you will have your hands full with this lady," the Empress stated, holding out her hand for a chalice. Wine was poured into the cup and the Empress took a sip before handing the golden goblet back to a servant.

"How may we be of service, Empress?" Theobald asked with a feeling that his time with the Empress was at an end.

"I have come to a decision," the Empress said whilst rising to her feet. She came to the edge of the dais's steps. "Lord Theobald… you, your wife, and Lord Grancourt will head to Calbridge Castle and take your place there."

Richard stepped forward. "But my Empress… would I not better serve you here, offering my sword for your protection?"

"Your stop at Calbridge will be brief, Grancourt. Since I am now missing one lady attendant with the marriage of Lady Ingrid, I wish you to bring your sister Beatrice to court."

A sound of disbelief left Richard and his gaze traveled between the two Norwood brothers. Theobald held back his amusement. Bringing Beatrice to court was asking for disaster. She would most likely flirt her way through the men here. In the end, she would find herself compromised and the culprit at the end of Richard's sword for defiling his sister.

Reynard burst out laughing. "I do not envy you such a task, Richard. You will be hard pressed handling such a rebellious woman."

"Shut up, Reynard."

The Empress stepped forward again. "I am not finished."

The group once more lowered their heads.

"Reynard Norwood, you will remain here with me to see to my protection along with Kennarde and Goodee. I should think the three of you will do well as my personal guardsmen."

Reynard gave a courtly bow. "As you wish, my Empress."

"Do not attempt to flatter me by appearing contrite, Norwood. I know you for who you truly are—but hopefully under my supervision, you will lose some of that cockiness that tends to overrule your rational thinking, resulting in the trail of havoc you leave behind."

"Aye, my Empress."

Theobald's gaze traveled to his brother. They were getting reputations. First his older brother, Wymar, had been called the Knight of Darkness. Then Reynard had laughing accused Theobald of being surrounded by chaos. Now the Empress was telling his younger sibling that he left behind a trail of havoc. Who was next? His eyes met Richard's... a brother of his heart who appeared as though a cloud had formed over his head with thoughts of his sister at court. A laugh threatened to escape him, and he masked his face into one he hoped would testify that he had been listening to the Empress even though he had not heard a word she said.

"In the meantime, we are preparing to leave for Oxford and make arrangements for Robert's release even if I must needs let loose that usurper as a condition," she growled out. She began waving her hands at her attendants. "Must you have a special invitation? Leave me and get to packing your things. We ride with the break of the new day."

Theobald took hold of Ingrid's hand and brought her fingertips to his lips. "It appears, my dear, there is no delaying your arrival at Calbridge Castle."

He watched when her shoulders slumped. "I would have preferred to put off the inevitable," Ingrid replied softly. "I thought perchance we might persuade the Empress to allow us to continue our service to her within her court—or better yet, back on the battlefield. My sword arm is still as good as it ever was even though I am now wed."

"If the Empress has her way, your fighting days will now be behind you," Theobald said tucking her hand in the crook of his elbow.

Ingrid raised her eyes to peer at him. "If it were up to you, you would allow me to continue to fight for a cause I believe in?" she asked in apparent wonder.

His hand wound around her neck and into her hair. "I would rather you fight beside me on any occasion just as long as you wish it, dearest wife," he declared before leaning down to seal his words with a kiss.

Her hands inched up his chest and clutched at the fabric of his tunic. A soft moan for his ears alone left her, and Theobald wished they were already behind a closed door. They had a lot of time to make up for. Besides, there was little to pack since they only just returned from the journey to Ingrid's farm. They broke apart when someone cleared their throat, and Theobald's brow rose in annoyance at his brother.

Reynard chuckled. "I suppose we are to separate once more. I had prayed we would continue to remain together."

Theobald slapped his younger brother upon his back. "I am certain our paths will cross again soon, but married life will rule me now, Reynard."

A growl left his brother's lips. "First Wymar and now you… God forbid if some wench crosses my path and expects me to marry her. I have better things to do than be saddled with a woman for the rest of my life."

Richard laughed. "Said every man who is now contently married."

"I certainly would not change anything given this particular lady is now my wife. But mark my words, brother, your time will come. 'Tis only a matter of *when* the right lady crosses your path," Theobald replied whilst his hand rested on his wife's back. He watched her intently when she took the few steps forward to face Oswin, Blake, and Kingsley.

"'Twould appear that our service together is at an end," she murmured softly. "'Twas an honor to fight beside you all."

Oswin bowed low. "The honor has been ours, my lady."

Theobald went to clasp the arm of each man knowing they would someday meet again. He wrapped his brother into a fierce hug and whispered a quick word to take care.

Theobald took hold of Ingrid's hand and together they went to their bedchamber to collect their few remaining things. The night was spent in each other's arms—and with the rising of the sun, they began making their way to their new home.

CHAPTER THIRTY-SEVEN

Penhow Castle

INGRID SLID OFF Valor's back and gave the horse a pat on his neck. He neighed and pushed his nose against her body looking for a treat. She reached over to her saddlebag, pulled a bright red apple from the sack, and offered the fruit to her horse. He had earned it and more with the number of miles they had traveled. She had been through so many changes these many months. She would have never thought she would be married at the start of her journey to join the Empress's army.

But that was all behind her now. She would no longer need to lift her sword to protect herself, although Theobald had stated he would train with her any time she chose. It would keep her fit, if nothing else and she looked forward to the time when she could enjoy her husband's company in the privacy of their new home. She was still apprehensive about what awaited her at Calbridge, but she would deal with it as she must. She gazed upon the rolling green countryside. This region was lovely and would be the perfect place to raise a family.

Her eyes went to the four-story sandstone tower house with its stone-tiled roof. The place was far simpler than what she had been expecting. Ingrid's conversation with the Empress flashed through her mind. Penhow may have belonged to Ingrid, but they were only stopping briefly at this property where the steward lived. Ingrid and Theobald would learn all they needed before traveling the rest of the way to Calbridge Castle.

Theobald came up to her and took her hand. "It needs a curtain wall," he mumbled in apparent concern.

"That and most likely other improvements as well," Ingrid replied before gazing up into her husband's eyes. "Do you think Calbridge will be in need of development in its defenses, too?"

"We will find out soon enough," he said shrugging. "What do you think of the place?"

"I have the notion that this simple keep will be more to my liking than whatever grandness awaits us at Calbridge," she answered honestly. "But I suppose we will make the best of things."

"As long as we are together, then that is all that matters. I will not allow anything to drive us apart again," Theobald vowed.

"I will hold you to such a promise, my love," Ingrid replied raising her hand to caress the stubble on his cheek. Her finger traced the white scar and she realized he was lucky he had not lost one of those gorgeous green eyes. "You never did tell me how you got this scar."

"Later, my dear, but 'tis not hard to guess given I have been a trained knight for most of my life," he answered, before a chuckle from Richard had Theobald looking uncomfortable.

"Is that the story you tell all the ladies fawning over you?" Richard finally asked.

"'Tis better than the truth," Theobald replied with a sheepish look at his wife.

Ingrid crossed her arms over her chest. "Now you have my full attention. Tell me what happened."

Theobald growled a curse. "'Twas a silly mistake."

Richard chuckled again. "Aye, and one that almost cost you your sight!"

"I was attempting to prove my worth at catching a blade whilst it flipped end over end…"

"Aye… to a group of pretty maids if my memory serves me right," Richard interrupted.

Theobald scowled. "Are you telling this story, or am I?"

Richard gave a jaunty salute. "By all means, continue."

Theobald ran his hand across the back of his neck. "Suffice it to say, I winked at one of the young women present. The two others became upset…"

A giggle left Ingrid. "Naturally. I cannot blame them."

"… a scuffle broke out between them, and they bumped into me when I had tossed the knife again into the air. I lost my balance, the knife came down, and I missed the blade. However, the steel did not miss me with its downward plunge. It cut open my cheek and I have had the scar ever since."

"The ladies must have loved it," Ingrid said with a smirk. "It makes you appear dangerously roguish."

"Roguish or foolish. I only remember the pain when the blade slashed my face."

Richard laughed again. "Aye, he was also in too much pain to appreciate the women who began to coo all over him. If I recall, he wished to have nothing to do with them afterwards, saying they were bad luck."

Theobald cursed again. "They went on to others without much hesitation on their part, proving to me they were not worth my time."

"You must have been young," Ingrid replied since she could see the scar was not something that recently happened.

"'Twas from my youth when I was trying to prove my worth and place in life. My older brother, Wymar, had always sworn we would remain together once our parents passed away. He kept us together for many years until but recently. Now we will be scattered to the four corners of England."

"Unless the Empress ends up back in France," Richard said mumbling a curse. "I must admit, I have no desire to return there."

Ingrid patted his arm. "And yet I know your devotion to our Empress will take you wherever she may ask you to go."

Richard gazed down upon her before he nodded in acceptance. "Aye. You are right on that account."

Ingrid returned her gaze to the keep. "I suppose we can no longer put off the inevitable."

Theobald pointed toward the entrance as the wooden portal opened and a man came forward to stand near the steps leading up into the keep. "As you can see, my dear, they are well aware we have arrived. Let us go announce ourselves. Hopefully, they will have had bedchambers aired out for us."

Theobald offered Ingrid his arm, and she took it as they made their way up to the front of the keep.

Ingrid stepped forward. "I am Lady Ingrid Norwood, formally de St. Maur."

The man wearing simple garments, bowed. "We have been expecting you, my lady. I am John Roberts, the steward of Penhow Castle."

"A pleasure, sir. This is my husband Theobald, the earl, and a dear friend Lord Richard Grancourt."

John bowed again. "My lords… Come in, come in. I am certain you are weary from your travels."

They entered into the foyer where the keep felt cool after being outdoors with the warmth of the afternoon sun. Torches held in ordinary sconces on the walls lit the interior but there was not much in the way of decorations to prove this was a house of a noble. Considering the splendor she had witnessed in Gloucester, Ingrid had expected to see at least costly vases with small golden trinkets adorning the tables. There were no portraits hanging on the walls showing her ancestors. In truth, it looked so bare that it had her concerned. She could see where things *had* hung, where there had been decorations at one point, but all was gone now. Ingrid gave a quick glance toward Theobald and he, too, wore a frown of disapproval. There was much going on here that the Empress had not warned them about. Or mayhap she had not known of the conditions into which she would send them.

A woman appeared, mayhap from the kitchen since she had flour on her gown and was wiping her hands on a towel she had tucked in a belt at her waist. John introduced her as his wife,

Lena. The woman bobbed a curtsey before calling to another servant who quickly ran up the wooden stairs to light fires in what would be their rooms.

John began to usher them toward the stairs. "Once you are settled, we can talk in the solar. Then I can inform you of all that has happened recently at Penhow and Calbridge."

"The place appears as though it has fallen onto hard times," Ingrid stated the obvious.

"As I said, 'twas but a recent occurrence but with no one here with authority to govern the estates… well… I will not burden you with the details until you have rested from your journey."

John halted at the first door. "You can use this room, Lord Grancourt. The next is somewhat larger and reserved for the lord and his lady."

Richard nodded, and Theobald reached over to lay his hand upon his friend's shoulder. "We will see you shortly."

Once Theobald and Ingrid were in the privacy of their bed-chamber and the bolt had slid into place, she threw herself into Theobald's arms. The strength he exuded wrapped around her, making her feel safe, and she breathed a sigh of relief that he was here with her.

"Barely in the front door and already chaos is following us here," she murmured into his chest.

He rested his chin on the top of her head. "Aye. I had hoped we would be able to have a leisurely stay here until we continued onward. A cup of cool ale… a good meal. We may only get a bit of bread and cheese this night if we are lucky."

"I can only pray they will be able to offer more than that. If that is truly the extent of what they have, I may have to refuse eating as I do not wish to take food from their own bellies."

Theobald took hold of her arms before leaning down to kiss her forehead. "If such is the case, Richard and I will scour the land until we find something for our table. I will not see a wife of mine go hungry."

A smile crept along the edges of her mouth. "I *am* hungry, but it has nothing to do with food."

A chuckle escaped him. "My wife wishes to play..." he said with a wicked grin of his own. He pulled his tunic up over his head all the while keeping his gaze focused on her eyes.

Her hands tingled to touch his skin that was now exposed for her viewing pleasure. Broad shoulders, a light dusting of fur across his chest that disappeared into the tight hose hugging his lean hips. She licked her lips and listened to Theobald's response. His moan of desire mirrored her own inner thoughts.

He did not take long to gather her back into his muscled arms. The bed beckoned for them to make their way to the softness of the feather mattress. Their bodies sank once Theobald laid next to her upon the coverlets. There was no need to rush in their play this day. Anything beyond their door would wait for when the lord and his lady were ready to face what awaited them. For now, the only thing that mattered was just the two of them. Theobald and Ingrid... home at last.

CHAPTER THIRTY-EIGHT

THEOBALD HAD BEEN listening intently to the steward's account of the happenings at Calbridge Castle. Ingrid's expression was as harsh as his own. There was never an end to the turmoil that continued to plague them. Mayhap Reynard had been right… Theobald would be known as the Knight of Chaos if things did not improve in his life. He was tired of it all.

Richard muffled a curse. "And this knight just showed up one day and staked his claim upon the land, stripping this house of most of its valuables?" he asked with a fierce frown.

"Aye, my lord," John replied. "He claimed the castle in the name of King Stephen."

'Twas Theobald's turn to curse. "He had some nerve considering most nobles in the west claim Empress Matilda as their sovereign."

John nodded. "The people understand that, my lord, but there was none there to gainsay him. But you are here now to put an end to his tyranny."

Ingrid began to pace the solar. "I have no notion to lay siege to my own castle," she huffed. "They are costly both to the lands resources and the people barricaded within."

"'Twill not come to that, my dear," Theobald said although he had to admit he was not certain that his words were true.

She halted her frantic pacing to stare down at the drawing of the grounds of Calbridge. The castle itself hugged a steep cliff with a fast-flowing river below it so Theobald did not have to worry that they would be attacked from that direction.

"Must we send for reinforcements? How many knights did he bring with him?" Ingrid finally asked.

John took a seat. "Not many, or so I have been informed. I've heard tell that the original knights of the garrison are not overly fond of the man and have not pledged their fealty to him as yet."

Richard took a chair as well. "Does this individual have a name? Mayhap we know of him."

"He goes by de Payne."

Theobald, Ingrid, and Richard all shared a look. Could it be possible?

"Roger de Payne?" Theobald inquired before he took Ingrid's hand and they both took the remaining chairs set by the hearth.

"Aye. That is him. You know him, then?" John asked.

"*Bloody Hell!*" Theobald bellowed.

Ingrid covered her face with her hands. "Of all the people in this world it had to be de Payne. That rat bastard."

John's brow rose in question and Richard spoke before Ingrid or Theobald could chime in. "The lady had an altercation with the man on the battlefield at Winchester. He tried without success to… take advantage of Lady Ingrid."

"De Payne was surprised when I told him that the lost heiress to Calbridge had been found and that she and her husband would be arriving soon to run her estate," John said slowly.

"I assume that information did not go over well if he thought to take over the land without any contest," Theobald replied, angry at the thought of what awaited them at their new home.

John nodded. "His temper became out of control, and he demanded to know who the heiress was, but at the time I had not been privy to your name. The message from the Empress did not have a lot of details as to your identity, only that you would be arriving soon," John proclaimed before he stared at the group before him. "But as I mentioned, I do not think you will have much of a fight against him. He does not have many who are on his side and will be easily routed from the place."

"As long as we can get through the front gate," Theobald replied. John stood and went back to the table that held the map, and Theobald followed him as the two men studied the drawing.

"There is a cave down river," John said pointing to the parchment. "It runs the length of the castle and will bring you up from the cellars into the kitchen outside the great hall. The way should not be heavily guarded. Only those who know Calbridge will have knowledge of the secret passageway."

"That is our plan then," Theobald said returning to his wife. "We should make haste. Mayhap we will have the element of surprise on our side if he is not expecting us this soon."

Richard drummed his fingers on the arm of his chair. "We could send for Wymar. He is somewhat close and would come to our aid."

Ingrid shook her head. "We do not have time to spare to send runners to Brockenhurst and wait for a reply. Nay. I agree with Theo. We should gather supplies and head straight away to Calbridge. The sooner that worthless cur is off our lands, the better I will feel for our people's safety and wellbeing."

Theobald nodded. "I agree. The sooner he is gone, the sooner we can begin our new life together."

Richard and John excused themselves and Ingrid stood before she plopped herself down into Theobald's lap. His arms went around her waist, and he felt her shudder. She curled herself into his embrace, her head resting on his shoulder. He stroked her hair until he heard her give a heavy sigh.

"I will not let him hurt you again, Ingrid," he murmured until he continued, "not that you need help protecting yourself."

She raised her head from his shoulder and her fingertips caressed his cheek. "You are the only one I would wish to come to my aid if I ever was in need of rescuing."

A soft chuckle left him. "Ah... sound words to soothe my manly pride."

"'Tis the truth," she whispered before bending forward to kiss his lips. "I swear once this is all over, I only wish to live a comfortable life with you by my side."

"No more running off?" he asked quietly.

"Nay. I should have never doubted you and the love you have for me." She kissed his lips again and he tightened his hold about her body bringing her closer. "Do you forgive me for my foolishness?"

"You did lead me a merry chase, wife."

"Aye, I know. Say you forgive me."

His hand wove its way through her glorious unbound hair. The red tresses curled around his fingers as if taking possession of him. "There is nothing to forgive. But next time, let us, at the very least, have a conversation before you decide you are angry with me."

"I promise," she said softly before laying her head back down.

"Then I shall look forward to a life of bliss with my wife by my side. No man could ask for more," he said, enjoying having his lady in his arms.

They spent the remainder of the day packing for the short ride to Calbridge. Theobald could only pray that de Payne would leave peacefully allowing Theobald and Ingrid to begin their lives together. If only life could be that simple…

CHAPTER THIRTY-NINE

NOTHING WAS EVER easy.

At least of late, Ingrid mused. The spiked portcullis had been closed at Calbridge so the opportunity to make an easy entrance was nonexistent. At the very least, she had hoped that there might be a knight standing guard above on the parapet who might be on her side and who could be persuaded to raise the gate for her. But there was no one to call. Everything was eerily silent, especially for a castle this size.

Ingrid sat on Valor, staring up at her inheritance, knowing they would need to go around the place and find the entrance to the hidden passageway. Such an option made her feel vulnerable as if she were putting herself and those with her into a dangerous situation. She was not one to do well in enclosed spaces, and the thought of being in a cave made her shiver.

She looked again at Calbridge. The stone walls were not going to be falling down any time soon even if she wished for such a miracle. Nay. They had been well made. The portcullis was just as strong, and unless someone came to work the wheel to raise up the heavily spiked gate, then they would not be entering this way. She gave a heavy sigh of frustration.

The main keep rose high beyond the walls at least six stories tall from what she could guess. What would she find once she was finally able to enter her home? What would de Payne have done in the fortnight since he had taken possession of it? Would everything of any worth have already been stripped from her and sold for de Payne's whim? Or perchance he had hoarded all the treasures, thinking of them as his. There was little she knew about de Payne, aside from his grudge against her. But that was enough to tell her that he would not easily give way to her if she tried to claim ownership of the land. It would matter not that she carried the Empress's seal with her. Despite Theobald's belief that he would be able to make de Payne see reason, Ingrid knew they would have a fight on their hands before the day was done.

"We shall need to go around," Theobald proclaimed once he rode Buttercup up next to her.

"Obviously," Richard drawled. "I still think we should have sent for Wymar."

"What could my brother do other than what we already know must be done? We need to head down river and find the tunnel to gain entrance." Theobald leaned an arm on the pommel of his saddle whilst he appeared lost in thought.

"We shall have a battle on our hands once we reach the great hall." Ingrid voiced her thoughts aloud, and her husband grimaced.

"Aye," he agreed. "As much as I would have liked us to enter Calbridge peacefully, such will not be the case."

Richard cursed. "We already knew we would have a fight on our hands. Any man who would attempt to take advantage of a woman has no honor. Why would he leave here willingly if he thinks of himself as king of your castle?"

Ingrid pulled on the reins turning her steed around. "There is no sense in us sitting here, pondering life's mysteries. The way is barred to us here. Let us go find another way to enter—unless, of course, the two of you would like to continue whining about the matter," Ingrid smirked with a teasing wink to Theobald.

"Saucy wench," her husband laughed. "I shall make you pay for that comment later this eve."

"Let us hope the eve will find us in the lord and lady's bed-chamber and not beneath the branches of a tree. Let us away," Ingrid said kicking her heels into Valor's side and sending him into a trot.

They left the castle grounds far behind them as they continued to follow the river downstream. The cliffside that Calbridge sat up against slowly began to descend until the land and the river were at last on the same level. They reached a small beach area with more stones than sand. 'Twas there that they dismounted, knowing they did not want their horses to stumble on the uneven ground. Bushes had grown up against the cliffside and Richard began poking his sword into the foliage to seek the opening to the cave system.

Ingrid followed Theobald to a nearby group of sturdy trees. They had just looped the leather reins around a tree's branches when Richard called out.

"'Tis here!" he stated whilst waving them forward.

Ingrid and Theobald walked hand in hand. Once they reached Richard, they saw he was already in the process of attempting to light one of the torches that had been left just inside the entrance to the cave. Luckily for them, John had mentioned several would be readily available. Without a torch, they would not get very far in the blackness of the cave.

With their torches lit, they moved aside the branches of the bushes and entered the darkness of the cave. A musty smell of wet dirt and heaven only knew what else hit them first before they were plunged into the inky black surroundings. Their torches threw odd shadows onto the walls of the cave, and they narrowly missed the webs left from spiders hoping to catch their unsuspecting prey.

A sudden fluttering echoed around them as they stood still listening. Before long, the sound became louder. They all ducked, and Ingrid gasped when a whole colony of flittermice flew overhead seeking to exit the cave. They had obviously not cared for the intrusion of humans.

By Saint Michael's Wings, I hate caves, Ingrid thought before rising once more to her full height.

They continued forward, moving slowly to keep from stumbling on the uneven ground beneath them. When they came to a fork in the pathway, they stayed to the right, knowing this way would eventually bring them to the cellars and dungeon of Calbridge Castle. The way heading left was only a dead end, or so John had informed them.

"Will we ever get there?" Ingrid hissed, feeling as if they had been in the cave for hours.

"I doubt we have much further to travel, my dear. Have a bit of patience," Theobald urged as he pushed aside another spiderweb blocking their path.

"I do not care for caves," Ingrid finally admitted aloud as she continued following her husband. "I always have the premonition that the walls will collapse in on me and no one will ever find my body."

A grunt left Richard as he followed behind them. "I understand the sentiment, my lady, but we will arrive soon… I hope."

Theobald reached for her hand and gave it a squeeze. "We most likely have not traveled all that far, my love. 'Tis just the fear of what lays ahead on a pathway we have not tread before that has you feeling uneasy and causes the time to seem to drag."

"Let us hurry and be done with this infernal tunnel. I do not know how much longer I can stand feeling confined," she murmured.

She warily looked above and around her for any signs that the walls would give way, then she continued to follow Theobald. At least if there was a cave in, she would die with her husband by her side. She supposed there were worse ways to leave this life.

There was no sense of how much time passed them by as they continued their way forward. They took a wrong turn at one point, ending up before a blocked passageway where the walls had indeed fallen, cutting off the path. Ingrid refused to give in to her fears as they retraced their steps whilst praying that they would find a usable passage that would finally reach the cellars of Calbridge Castle.

After several more twists and turns, they at last came upon

several crates and barrels stored in the depths of the castle to keep their contents cool. Ingrid shivered when she felt a cold blast of air coming from the room that opened up to them. Bright torchlight blinded her momentarily until she became accustomed to the light. She took a deep breath to calm her frayed nerves. A sound of rattling iron bars had the trio reaching for the hilts of their swords. They pressed forward down a long corridor and came to several cells. One of them held multiple knights. From the standard on their tunics, Ingrid presumed they were a part of her garrison.

One knight stepped forward as the spokesman for the lot. He eyed them with a skeptical look. "Where does your allegiance lie?" he asked with one raised brow. His fingers clenched at the metal bars.

Theobald stepped forward. "I am Theobald Norwood, Earl of Calbridge. This is my lady wife, Ingrid de St. Maur, and our traveling companion, Lord Richard Grancourt. We are here at Empress Matilda's command." The men held hostage began to bow with murmurs of *my lord* and *my lady* as they paid their respects.

The spokesman heaved a sigh of relief. "Thank the heavens. You serve the Lady of England."

"We do," Ingrid replied stepping into the light of the dungeon. "What is your name?"

"Sir Walter Bryche, my lady. Lately, Captain of the Guard until we were taken hostage. Have you come to rescue us from the madman who reigns above?" the knight asked as the other men came closer to the barred door, looking eager at the prospect of deliverance.

"Aye, as soon as we can find the key to release you or pick the lock," Theobald replied looking around at the walls hoping a ring of keys would have been left behind.

Richard pressed forward reaching into his cape. He pulled out a leather pouch and from within two long metal spikes. "Allow me," he said with a smirk.

Ingrid gave a short laugh. "I would have never thought of you as someone who could pick a lock."

Richard knelt on the ground and put both pieces together into the opening where the key should go. "A necessity, I assure you, my lady, that has come in handy from time to time."

"If you say so, Lord Richard," Ingrid replied watching closely as he fiddled with the iron tools in his hands.

Several minutes later, a click resounded in the area and Richard was able to swing the door open for the knights to gain their freedom. They began thanking Richard but looked to Theobald for guidance on their next steps.

"They will need their weapons," Ingrid stated the obvious.

"We will find all we need and more if we can just make it to the blacksmith," Sir Walter said before he continued. "But we must needs tread carefully. The traitor de Payne is certain he will be able to hold off any attack on your part. He has been anticipating your arrival for nigh unto a fortnight."

Theobald nodded. "I would hope he would expect an attack at the front gates and not coming from inside his own cellars."

"*Our* cellars, my love," Ingrid said with a slight smile.

"I stand corrected, my dear," Theobald replied before turning to Sir Walter. "You know this castle better than we do. Tell us what you think the best plan of attack would be now that we have your assistance and have gained access to the castle's interior."

The group gathered into a circle with Sir Walter finding various objects to represent different points of the area. Ingrid, Theobald, and Richard listened intently and suggested alternatives as they crossed their mind. Once they were in agreement, they began to proceed up from the dungeon. Ingrid swore that before the day was out, de Payne would be driven from her lands. That is… if he yet lived when they were through with him.

CHAPTER FORTY

THEOBALD STOOD WATCH at the entrance to the blacksmith whilst the half dozen men they had freed inspected the weapons available to them. That there was only a total of nine of them to hold off however many were loyal to de Payne was of major concern. He knew it had been a blow to Ingrid to learn that many of her garrison had chosen to align themselves with de Payne. How could they fight against nearly an entire garrison of knights with only their meager numbers? Theobald could only hope that the men's loyalty to de Payne did not run deep. He and Ingrid would not last long if there was a large number of knights truly willing to fight to the death to defend de Payne as their leader.

His gazed traveled to Ingrid. She must have had the same thoughts for she turned worried eyes in his direction. She was an accomplished swordswoman—of that he had no doubt. But she had history with de Payne. The man would not accept anything other than a victory over her. How were they to capture de Payne without too much bloodshed to the knights of the garrison? He would need them in order to hold this castle for the Empress and ensure his family's safety in the years to come. 'Twas a conundrum for which he had no immediate answer.

A commotion outside the smithy had everyone holding their weapons before them in anticipation of what they might meet. A horse and rider rode into the bailey followed closely by several knights. They began to dismount, and Ingrid let out a startled gasp when she saw de Payne on one of the steeds. The sound must have alerted de Payne since his head swiveled in their direction.

Dismounting from his horse, he withdrew his sword from the scabbard at his side. "Who is there? Search the smithy," he ordered with a nod of his head.

Theobald stepped forward with Ingrid and their men right behind. "No need to search, de Payne. I believe you have been expecting us."

Roger's eyes widened when he noticed the men who had been held hostage in the dungeon. "How the bloody hell did all of you get free?"

"Does it matter?" Theobald stated before addressing the knights who had been riding with de Payne, along with those who began to gather to witness the happenings in the bailey. "I am Theobald Norwood, Earl of Calbridge. This lovely lady is the missing heiress to this estate, Lady Ingrid de St. Maur, who is now also my wife. Your allegiance to this man has been misplaced as he has no legal claim to this land."

"You speak a falsehood," de Payne shouted. "I hold this land for the rightful king of England, Stephen."

A rumbling went through the crowd when de Payne mentioned the usurper's name. Ingrid stepped forward. "We have legal claim to Calbridge as I am the sole surviving heir to these lands. We also carry the seal of the Empress Matilda, and we hold this land on *her* behalf."

A small cheer rang out until de Payne spoke out. "Silence, or you shall feel the bite of my blade," he warned the crowd.

Theobald's sword swung forward. "You have no right to threaten my people, nor shall you continue to rule here. Let us finish this, just you and I, and let the winner have the final word on who shall reign."

"You are alarmingly overconfident, Norwood," de Payne sneered. A smug laugh left his lips before his gaze traveled the length of Ingrid's body. "I look forward to finishing what we started in Winchester, my pet."

"Is that any way to have speech with my wife?" Theobald snarled stepping forward.

"Once you are dead, that will no longer be an issue," de Payne bellowed. "You heard the man. No one interferes. I have a debt to settle that is long overdue. After today, I will again claim this land and *that* woman as mine."

The clang of steel meeting steel as the two blades clashed together echoed in the air. Theobald continued his attack without mercy, for he would in no way fail Ingrid or his Empress by allowing de Payne to win. But his adversary was a seasoned warrior, and Theobald would not have an easy victory over this knight.

They continued their assault on one another, hacking away until they both bore small nicks upon their bodies where their opponent's blade had made contact. 'Twas not enough for either man to claim victory, so their swords continue to meet repeatedly. And then the unthinkable happened—Theobald lost his balance. He fell to the ground, holding his breath whilst waiting for de Payne's sword to strike the killing blow.

He watched the descent of the steel as though in slow motion, but the blow to kill him never came. His enemy's blade was halted by another, and he looked into the familiar hazel eyes of his wife.

"I think not, de Payne," Ingrid hissed.

"You think to best me?" de Payne laughed in amusement.

"Why not let my sword prove my worth? Let us finish what was started back in Winchester," she taunted as they now came to stand before one another.

An evil chuckle left de Payne's lips. "Kill them! Kill them all!"

Chaos erupted in the bailey as the knights who had sided with them and the Empress took on the dozen men loyal to de Payne. Theobald got back to his feet and resumed fighting for his very life. A quick glance at his wife told him she was holding her own, and for that he was thankful. He prayed that mayhap he had worn de Payne out after their previous altercation. Sir Walter swung a sword in one hand and a battle ax in another as he took on two knights. 'Twas an impressive sight to behold.

One by one, de Payne's knights began to yield until only Ingrid and de Payne remained battling. Theobald watched in horror when Ingrid lost her grip on her sword. She quickly swiveled narrowly missing de Payne's blade aimed at her neck.

"Sword!" she called out and Sir Walter, who was the closest, tossed her his blade.

That she was so readily provided another weapon threw de Payne off, and he stumbled backwards only to find the steel of Ingrid's blade against his neck.

"Yield," she jeered, pressing the steel closer to his skin.

"I yield nothing! You cheated when you took your husband's place. Our battle was to be between the two of us to determine who would rule Calbridge Castle," de Payne replied.

Ingrid inched her blade closer into his neck. "If that counts as cheating then you cheated as well when you ordered your men to kill us all," Ingrid growled out. She would in no way say that she had succeeded in claiming her lands because of foul play.

De Payne took hold of her arm in an attempt to dislodge her sword. "Go ahead and kill me. You will make a martyr out of me when I die for King Stephen's cause," he demanded whilst tilting his head back further as he awaited the killing blow.

"You think too highly of yourself, de Payne. No one will tell your story or mourn your fate. You are nothing but a petty traitor, and you will soon be forgotten." The sound of Ingrid's laughter brought a smile to Theobald's face. Richard came to stand next to him.

"Shall we interfere?" Richard asked.

A chuckle left him. "Nay. I think she has a handle on the situation," Theobald replied, crossing his arms over his chest to watch how Ingrid dealt with the traitor. She continued to hold her sword at de Payne's throat, and he allowed his lady wife to decide the man's fate.

"Kill me, you damn bitch," de Payne swore.

A gleam flashed in those hazel eyes that Theobald loved. He expected Ingrid to slit the man's throat. Instead, she quickly slashed her blade in a downward stroke along the man's cheek. 'Twas just enough of a wound that he would carry the reminder of her for the rest of his life.

"You are not worth the penance I would need to submit to if I took your worthless life. I will have the satisfaction of knowing that we have beaten you and those loyal to the false king," she stated as she stood back to see a thin trail of blood running down the man's face.

Theobald at last came forward. "Men and women of Calbridge. You see before you that we have vanquished our enemy. Any who are loyal to the usurper Stephen will be cast from these gates," he proclaimed loudly for all to hear. He turned toward Sir Walter. "See that this rubbish is gone from our lands. Take a dozen knights loyal to our cause to ensure they are well past our boundaries."

"Aye, my lord," Sir Walter said. He went to de Payne and grabbed him by the edge of his tunic. "Let us away, you worthless cur."

Theobald gathered Ingrid in his arms as they watched men and horses being led through the bailey and, once the portcullis was raised, out the barbican gate. A cheer rose from the inhabitants of Calbridge as they viewed the enemy leaving their home.

Ingrid brushed her fingertips along his body. "You are hurt."

"'Tis nothing but a scratch or two," he murmured kissing the top of her head.

"You let me be the judge of that. We need to find the castle healer," she whispered, wondering who that might be from all the new faces that began to surround them.

"Later, my love," Theobald murmured. "For now, let us enjoy this moment and the reward of knowing Calbridge is now ours."

"Kiss me," she demanded with a bright smile.

"Never let it be said that I did not adhere to your wishes," he said in a husky tone. He bent forward and captured her lips as another cheer went up.

They soon became surrounded by those who would now be a part of their lives. Men and women loyal to them and the Empress. 'Twas a good beginning to the story they would someday tell their children.

CHAPTER FORTY-ONE

I NGRID RACED VALOR on the outskirts of fields of golden wheat ready for harvest. The serfs were busy preparing for a hard day's labor but as for Ingrid, she was enjoying the morning away from the duties that would demand her attention at the castle.

She shot a quick glance over her shoulder, hoping to see that Theobald was far behind. He was closer than she would have liked, especially since she could see for herself that her husband held back on the reins of his mount to give her a fighting chance. She supposed she should appreciate his efforts to let her win, but she would rather arrive first at the finishing point on her own merits.

"You are cheating," she called over her shoulder whilst slapping the leather reins, causing Valor to bolt forward at an even faster pace. She leaned low into the saddle and became one with her horse.

"By giving you a chance to win against me?" Theobald laughed as he easily came abreast of her.

The two horses galloped side by side until Theobald gave a nudge of his knee causing Buttercup to slow. Valor galloped to the finishing line, the victor. Ingrid turned her mount around and watched whilst Theobald and Buttercup trotted forward. Ingrid slid to the ground, looping the reins on a nearby tree branch.

"I won," she stated with hands on her hips.

Theobald smiled down upon her. Still sitting on his horse, he towered over her. She came to Buttercup and patted his muzzle before she gave him a bright red apple.

"You will spoil him," Theobald said before he, too, tethered his horse to a nearby tree.

"Buttercup deserves it since you have saddled him with such an unbecoming name," she teased. "Such a beautiful animal needs a name that befits him."

The horse neighed as if commenting on their conversation. "He may be beautiful, but he is still an ornery beast with the soul of a devil. He is far too used to doing whatever he pleases when given the opportunity."

"He still deserves better," she laughed. She went to Valor and fed him an apple as well before she opened the satchel tied to the saddle and pulled out a blanket and a small repast for her and her husband to share. She placed the blanket down upon the mossy ground and beckoned for Theobald to join her. They ate in silence for several minutes watching the river flow by.

"'Tis not a bad life here, with you by my side," Theobald finally said taking her hand and raising her fingertips to his lips.

"No regrets about no longer serving the Empress in battle?" she asked as she rolled over onto her side and leaned on one elbow. Theobald pushed their meal away and laid down next to her.

"Nay. I have always wanted to place to call my own. A fire next to my feet, good food, and a drink to fill my belly. That this miracle has included a wife whom I love is surely a bonus, do you not agree?" he teased her, leaning forward to capture her lips.

Her arm snaked around his neck, and she held onto him as their kiss deepened. A soft sigh left her. "I left my home for a cause and also gained a husband," she said once their kiss ended. "I suppose the chaos that has surrounded us since we met is finally at an end."

"I certainly hope so!" Theobald laughed. His face suddenly became serious. "Do you have regrets, dearest wife?"

Her hand reached up to caress his cheek. "None. Somewhere along the way of fighting for the Empress's cause, we found one another. You have been a pleasant surprise, my love. I can only pray that nothing and no one will ever tear us apart again."

Theobald took his hand and pulled her closer and she snuggled into his side. "I vow I shall keep you forever at my side."

A small smile crept up at the corner of her mouth. "I could not ask more from you than that."

Theobald kissed her again and they were soon lost in a moment that Ingrid would remember for the rest of her life. With the sound of the rushing river before them, Theobald made love to her as though 'twas their first time together. They were beginning their lives anew. The Lord and Lady of Calbridge. Perchance if they were blessed, children might one day follow.

Ingrid would have smiled if her lips were not busy. Aye… she had captured the heart of the Knight of Chaos and was loved. May peace and prosperity fill their lives from now on.

EPILOGUE

Calbridge Castle
The Year of Our Lord's Grace 1146

THEOBALD PACED HIS solar like a caged animal. His wine had been left untouched for the past hour. Who could enjoy a drink when the screams of his wife could be heard down the passageway? He did not want to get his hopes up again… not when they had lost several babes since they wed five years ago.

"Take a seat, brother. This labor business could go on for several more hours if my own experience with Ceridwen is anything like what your wife is going through," Wymar declared, taking a sip of his wine. "Come… drink! It will make you feel better."

Another scream echoed down the corridor causing Theobald to peer at the open doorway, hoping a servant would appear to give him good news. "How can you possibly drink at a time like this?" Theobald growled out, continuing his pacing.

Wymar stood, refilled his chalice and his brother's, and then held out the cup. "Your wife is about to bring your child into this world. I have never known a better time to drink."

Theobald finally stopped and took the cup his brother offered. He was about to down the contents but thought better of it. He did not wish to have his mind fuzzy with drink in case Ingrid called for him.

He had been shooed from their bedchamber hours ago by the women who were attending to his wife. Ceridwen and Wymar had arrived just in time, and his sister-in-law had immediately stepped in to help see to Ingrid's comfort. As the labor had progressed, Theobald had been told to leave as this was no place for a husband. Birthing a child was a messy business. That comment alone was enough for Theobald to quickly kiss his wife and find his brother to wait until she delivered their child. But the wait had felt endless. Had it been days since she had gone into labor? Theobald had no sense of time anymore.

Wymar ushered him to a chair near the hearth. He sat, numb to everything around him. He knew that many women did not survive childbirth. He could not lose his wife!

"You are having a hard time of it, are you not, brother?" Wymar said. "Tell me what you plan to name the child."

"Rolf, if the child is a boy," Theobald answered running his fingers through his hair.

"A good, strong name," Wymar said. "And if the babe is a girl?"

"Coira." A simple answer was all he could manage when his wife's cries one more could be heard.

Wymar raised one brow. "Coira? Sounds Scottish. Why Coira?"

Theobald gave a slight smile as memories of their discussion on possible names flitted through his mind. "Ingrid has always loved the name. She swore she would tell our children that we met on the Scottish moors instead of me finding her in a forest on her way to fight for the Empress."

Wymar chuckled. "I suppose that would sound far more romantic to a girl. I would not think 'twould matter how you met. Besides, fighting for the Empress is and was a worthy cause."

Theobald shrugged until he placed his arms on his legs and his face in his hands. "I only wish to please Ingrid. If she wants our daughter to be called Coira, then Coira she shall be."

Wymar nodded. "Domesticated life suits you, brother. Do not worry. Ingrid and the child will be fine."

Theobald raised tear filled eyes to his brother. "I cannot lose them."

Another scream had Theobald bolting up from his chair so abruptly that he knocked it over. He was halfway to the door when a servant rushed into the room. "My lord... your wife asks for you."

Theobald did not need any further words as he rushed down the passageway to the bedchamber he shared with Ingrid. He pushed opened the door to find his wife looking exhausted. Sweat poured from her face. One woman put a cool cloth upon her brow whilst another attended to the afterbirth. Ceridwen stepped forward with a tiny bundle held in her arms.

"Would you care to hold your son, my lord?" she declared with a sweet smile before handing him the child wrapped in linen.

So fragile... he thought as he peered down at the face of his son. A crop of dark brown hair protruded from the blanket causing Theobald to grin. His eyes lifted to Ceridwen who patted his shoulder before taking her leave. The rest of the women quickly followed giving Ingrid and Theobald the privacy they needed.

Ingrid patted the bed next to her. "Come sit with me," she said quietly.

"I am afraid I might hurt you," he whispered standing at the foot of the bed.

"I just gave birth, Theo," she said with a weak smile. "I think I can manage you by my side with our son."

Theobald came around the bed and Ingrid held out her arms for their child. He placed the boy into her arms before fluffing up the pillows so he could lay down beside her. "You did well, wife," he murmured not knowing what else to say at a time such as this. "Thank you for our son."

Ingrid nodded. "He is beautiful."

"As is his mother." He leaned forward to kiss her cheek.

"You aim is sadly lacking, my lord. You missed," she teased as she puckered up those lips to receive his kiss.

He chuckled as she patiently waited for him to comply with

her wishes. He would be more than happy to grant her whatever request she might ask of him. He kissed her and she gave a contented sigh. "I love you, dearest Ingrid."

She raised her eyes from their son. "As I love you, Theobald. I pray I did not scare you too much whilst you waited for our son to come into this world."

A snort left him as he downplayed the torment he had been put through. "Nay. I was fine—except for being concerned for you. I would hate to put you to such physical pain again."

Her eyes began to get heavy whilst he waited for her reply. "Nonsense, my love. We still need a daughter to keep this fine boy in line. We shall have another child one day," she said as if she had seen their future.

"God help me," he whispered softly before he plastered a smile upon his face for his wife's benefit. Her eyes had closed, and she breathed, signaling to Theobald that she at last rested. She deserved it and more after all she had gone through. He kissed her cheek again and began to take Rolf from her arms. She jerked awake.

"My baby," she called out as if fearful that someone with ill intent was taking the child from her.

"He is safe in my arms, my love. Sleep and rest," he said and watched her smile.

"I will miss you," she said but he could see for himself she was already halfway to sleep.

"Dream of us, and we shall see you there," he murmured in her ear before standing and going toward the window.

He opened the shutter, noting that the evening sun was just sinking into the horizon. He held Rolf so the last rays of light could shine upon his little face.

"Welcome to the light, my son," Theobald murmured whilst a tear of gratitude slid down his cheeks. Overwhelmed with happiness, he could only stand at the window to see the last of the day with his newborn child in his arms.

The baby yawned causing Theobald to do the same. He only

then realized how long the day had been whilst Ingrid had labored. He put Rolf down in a small cradle they had had made the first time Ingrid had grown big with child. Theobald counted off the years of how long they had prayed a son or daughter would fill it.

He went to their bed and stared down at his sleeping wife. They had known grief in the loss of their children, and yet he would not trade away one moment of their lives together… neither the good nor the bad. He laid down next to his lady and counted his many blessings. A loving wife… a son… and many years to look forward to as a family.

He gathered his wife into his embrace, and she automatically molded her body into his. She was a perfect for him and belonged precisely where she was. As did he. His days of being known as the Knight of Chaos were over. If he were to die tomorrow, he would die a happy man knowing he had the love of a good woman and a son to carry on his name. Ingrid had made a life for them here at Calbridge and with her at his side, Theobald had finally found his home. His life was complete.

THE END

Sherry Ewing needs your help!
Book reviews help readers to find books, and authors to find readers. Please consider writing a review for **Knight of Chaos**, even a couple of sentences telling people what you liked about the story is helpful. Reviews can be posted on BookBub, Goodreads, and on most eRetailer websites. Thank you for purchasing and reading a copy of **Knight of Chaos**. I hope you enjoyed Theobald and Ingrid's journey to finding love.

For links to this book, see Sherry's website at
www.sherryewing.com/books

AUTHOR NOTE

Dearest Reader:

Thank you so much for purchasing a copy of **Knight of Chaos**. I hope you enjoyed the continuing journey of my Knights of the Anarchy series and especially Theobald and Ingrid's journey to finding love.

If you've read my **MacLarens** or **Knights of Berwyck: A Quest Through Time** series, I hope you were pleasantly surprised to learn that Theobald and Ingrid were the parents of Rolf and Coira. Rolf was a significant secondary character in my debut novel, *If My Heart Could See You: The MacLarens (Book One)* and played a pivotal role in *A Knight to Call My Own: The MacLarens (Book Two)*. I won't give spoilers on him but let's just say I've kept him around (even in a couple of my Regency era stories). Coira had her own happily ever after in *The Piper's Lady: The MacLarens (Book Three)*. I thought this was a great opportunity to tie my series together! If you haven't read them, I hope you'll grab a copy.

When I began writing Theobald Norwood's story, I had a vague plot outline in my head. My stories are almost always character driven and it's sometimes not until I'm deep into writing that I come across some interesting tidbits of research or a plot twist I didn't even see coming. My characters will generally let me know what I've gotten right and certainly tell me when I've gotten it wrong.

Let's continue with a little history...

With King Stephen captured at the Battle of Lincoln and his army defeated, Empress Matilda entered London. Unfortunately, her hostile conduct upon her arrival alienated the people. Shortly before Empress Matilda's planned coronation in June 1141, the city and its citizens revolted against her, forcing the Empress and her followers to flee. This allowed Stephen's queen (also named Matilda) to occupy London. But wait... there's more... Stephen's brother was Henry of Blois, also known as the Bishop of Winchester. He had once sworn his allegiance to Empress Matilda's Angevin faction, but at this point, he once more defected and changed sides to support Queen Matilda as she fought for her husband.

After fleeing London, the Empress retreated to the safety of Oxford. The loss of London and the opportunity to be crowned queen was a major blow. At the start of this story, we meet Theobald Norwood on the road to Winchester.

Bishop Henry took a force to Winchester and laid siege to the royal castle garrisoned by Angevins. When the Empress learned what was happening, she was determined to strike back. She gathered her army, and her arrival in the city surprised Bishop Henry. He then fled the city while his soldiers retreated to Wolvesey Castle, which belonged to the church.

Wolvesey Castle was placed under siege by the Empress's Angevin army while the Empress set up her headquarters in the royal castle. Robert of Gloucester (her half-brother) established his command post near Saint Swithun's (now Winchester Cathedral). On August 2nd, the bishop's garrison set fire to Winchester, destroying a large part of the city.

Queen Matilda quickly gathered an army of relief that included mercenaries hired by Bishop Henry, enlisted troops of the queen's feudal tenants, one thousand members of the London militia, and other supports of her husband, Stephen. They proceeded to establish their camp on the east side of Winchester. This caused a blockade of Empress Matilda's forces in the city, which would soon begin to suffer from lack of food and supplies.

In my research, I read how some thought that Empress Matilda remained in the city too long. Their supply situation eventually convinced Robert of Gloucester that they must leave Winchester, and he planned a withdrawal. Earl Reginald of

Cornwall and Brian fitz Count led the advance guard composed of troops selected to protect the Empress. It was the perfect place to put Theobald, Ingrid, and their men. Robert commanded the rearguard along with the baggage.

On September 14th, the Angevins exited from the west side of the city to eventually cross at the River Test at Stockbridge. But once the Angevins left Winchester, the queen's army attacked, advancing past the rearguard to take on the main body of soldiers. The advance guard with the Empress avoided the trap, allowing them to escape captivity. Robert of Gloucester wasn't as lucky. He and his men were captured by Queen Matilda when they were surrounded at the River Test as they tried to cross.

And then I fell into a research rabbit hole because I was determined to learn where Empress Matilda fled after her failure at Winchester. Some of my research led me to believe she went directly to Gloucester, another resource pointed to Devizes Castle, which had belonged to her father. So, I ended up basing my story on a research book I purchased: *Matilda: Empress, Queen, Warrior* by Catherine Hanley, published by Yale University Press. This is a fascinating book, full of all kinds of details that had me turning pages to learn more. The Empress did eventually wind up at Gloucester after two other stops along the way to rest. Her traveling with her ladies was an assumption on my part in order to add further depth to my story.

Ingrid Seymour came as a pleasant surprise when a plot bunny jumped inside my head while driving home one day from the day job. I started to research a name surrounding Penhow and Chepstow Castles. Coming across the owner as Richard de St. Maur, I loved the name and figured I used it. An interesting tidbit of history here… the name was later changed to Seymour and would one day be associated with King Henry VIII's third wife, Jane. I can see another book in here somewhere!

Thank you to Katherine Le Veque and Dragonblade Publishing for allowing me the privilege to write for you.

Thank you to my amazing editor, Elizabeth Mazer, for helping to make this story shine. Your developmental edits have been outstanding!

Many thanks to several of my author friends: Alina K. Field for helping me with the blurb, Jude Knight for taking the time to once again beta read for me when I know how busy she is with her own writing, and Rue Allyn who came up with the name Buttercup for Theobald's horse from a Facebook party we attended years ago. Yes, years. This story and series have been in the back of my mind for years now. I'm glad it's finally on the page!

Thank you, as always, to my family for their continued support, especially when I'm stressing over deadlines. My daughter Jessica continues to inspire me. She came up with the name of Calbridge Castle so I could do whatever I liked with it to fit my story. It is, however, loosely based on Chepstow Castle near Penhow. This castle sits right on the edge of a cliff, but the geography wasn't going to work considering where I had my characters riding from, so I made up a name.

And most of all… a huge thank you my dearest readers. You, your kind words, and all your support mean the world to me. *You* are the reason why I write another page even if I'm exhausted from the day job. One day I'll get to retire and just sit home and only weave more tales for you to read. Now that would be living the dream!

Until the next time, I hope you enjoyed Theobald and Ingrid's journey to finding love. Up next is Reynard's story in *Knight of Havoc*. Just wait until you learn whose father he's going to be! Take care!

With much love,
Sherry Ewing

OTHER BOOKS BY SHERRY EWING

Medieval & Time Travel Series

To Love A Scottish Laird: De Wolfe Pack Connected World
Sometimes you really can fall in love at first sight…

To Love An English Knight: De Wolfe Pack Connected World
Can a chance encounter lead to love?

If My Heart Could See You: The MacLarens, A Medieval Romance
(Book One)
When you're enemies, does love have a fighting chance?

For All of Ever: The Knights of Berwyck, A Quest Through Time
(Book One)
Sometimes to find your future, you must look to the past…

Only For You: The Knights of Berwyck, A Quest Through Time
(Book Two)
Sometimes it's hard to remember that true love conquers all, only
after the battle is over…

Hearts Across Time: The Knights of Berwyck (Books One & Two)
Sometimes all you need is to just believe… Hearts Across Time is
a special edition box set that combines Katherine and Riorden's
stories together from *For All of Ever* and *Only For You.*

A Knight To Call My Own: The MacLarens, A Medieval Romance
(Book Two)
When your heart is broken, is love still worth the risk?

To Follow My Heart: The Knights of Berwyck, A Quest Through Time (Book Three)
Love is a leap. Sometimes you need to jump…

The Piper's Lady: The MacLarens, A Medieval Romance (Book Three)
True love binds them. Deceit divides them. Will they choose love?

Love Will Find You: The Knights of Berwyck, A Quest Through Time (Book Four)
Sometimes a moment is all we have…

One Last Kiss: The Knights of Berwyck, A Quest Through Time (Book Five)
Sometimes it takes a miracle to find your heart's desire…

Promises Made At Midnight: The Knights of Berwyck, A Quest Through Time (Book Six)
Make a wish…

It Began With A Kiss: The MacLarens, A Medieval Romance (Book Four)
Sometimes you need to listen when your heart begins to sing…

Knight of Darkness: The Knights of the Anarchy (Book One)
Sometimes finding love can become our biggest weakness…

Knight of Chaos: The Knights of the anarchy (Book Two)
In the chaos of war, can one knight defy the odds to find peace with the woman warrior he loves?

Regency

A Kiss For Charity: A de Courtenay Novella (Book One)
Love heals all wounds but will their pride keep them apart?

The Earl Takes A Wife: A de Courtenay Novella (Book Two)
It began with a memory, etched in the heart.

Before I Found You: A de Courtenay Novella (Book Three)
A quest for a title. An encounter with a stranger. Will she choose love?

Nothing But Time: A Family of Worth (Book One)
They will risk everything for their forbidden love…

One Moment In Time: A Family of Worth (Book Two)
One moment in time may be enough, if it lasts forever…

Under the Mistletoe
A new suitor seeks her hand. An old flame holds her heart. Which one will she meet under the kissing bough?

A Mistletoe Kiss in the Bluestocking Belles boxset *Belles & Beaux* (2022)
All she wants for Christmas is a mistletoe kiss…

A Second Chance At Love
Can the bittersweet frost of lost love be rekindled into a burning flame?

A Countess to Remember
Sometimes love finds you when you least expect it…

To Claim A Lyon's Heart: Lyon's Den Connected World
A gambler's bet. A widow's burden. Will one game of chance change their lives?

You can find out more about Sherry's work on her website at www.SherryEwing.com and at online retailers.

Social Media for Sherry Ewing

You can learn more about Sherry Ewing at these social media links:

Amazon Author Page: amzn.to / 1TrWtoy

Bookbub: bookbub.com / authors / sherry-ewing

Dragonblade Publishing:
dragonbladepublishing.com / team / sherry-ewing

Facebook: facebook.com / SherryEwingAuthor

Goodreads:
goodreads.com / author / show / 8382315.Sherry_Ewing

Instagram: instagram.com / sherry.ewing

Pinterest: pinterest.com / SherryLEwing

TikTok: tiktok.com / @sherryewingauthor

Twitter: twitter.com / Sherry_Ewing

YouTube: youtube.com / SherryEwingauthor

Newsletter Sign Up: bit.ly / 2vGrqQM

Facebook Street Team: facebook.com / groups / 799623313455472

Facebook Official Fan page:
facebook.com / groups / 356905935241836

ABOUT SHERRY EWING

Sherry Ewing picked up her first historical romance when she was a teenager and has been hooked ever since. An award-winning and bestselling author, she writes historical and time travel romances to awaken the soul one heart at a time. When not writing, she can be found in the San Francisco Bay Area at her day job as an Information Technology Specialist.

Learn more about Sherry where a new adventure awaits you on every page:
Website: www.SherryEwing.com
Email: Sherry@SherryEwing.com